UNDER

THE

SURFACE

SONYA BLAKE

For Emily

PART ONE

CHAPTER ONE

KAIA LEFT THE highway for a winding road flanked with pines. It followed the edge of land along Maine's rugged coast, where snow dusted the trees and the dry grass on the roadside, sparkling in the silvery light of the early January evening. As she steered her ailing Corolla eastward to Quolobit Harbor, she appreciated the fact that the car had made it more than a thousand miles from Nashville, Tennessee to here. As long as it got her as far as Foley's Point and died there, she'd be happy.

As if the car could hear her thoughts, it heaved and sputtered as Kaia turned onto Main Street. She muttered a prayer as it kept chugging past the sleepy wharf, the storefronts, the steepled church. At the sight of the grandiose library, she remembered being a kid in a stroller, pointing at the big stone edifice and asking her parents if it was a castle and whether a princess lived there.

"Lots of princesses live there," her mother had told her. "And witches. And fairies. And dragons. Sirens live there, too." Kaia sighed at the memory as the library disappeared from her rearview mirror.

She turned onto the isolated gravel road that would take her to her destination. Up ahead, a line of sky fractured the ragged pines surrounding the long driveway out to Foley's Point. In the next moment, the house appeared, its cedar shakes scrubbed clean by maritime winds. A rocky finger of land surrounded the house, with the vast majesty of the ocean and the pale winter sky stretching beyond.

Kaia parked near a lopsided garage behind the house and tried to smudge away the tears, but they just kept coming. Maybe she was just exhausted from such a long ride. Maybe it was because she hadn't eaten since the rubbery fast-food breakfast sandwich that morning. Or maybe it was the fact that her band had fallen apart last summer when she had found her boyfriend-guitarist locked in a storage closet with her best-friend-fiddler between sets, leaving Kaia newly solo on stage and off, and she'd only just learned that the two of them were now expecting a baby. Maybe it was also because last week she'd been fired from her bartending job because the new management wanted to hire skinny blondes with fake boobs and faker smiles. Maybe—*probably*—she was crying because of all of that plus the looming truth: she had come all the way up to Maine to sell the old house on Foley's Point. And that meant letting go of the last piece of land her mother's feet had touched.

It was time. Kaia needed to move on with her life, and not just from working a dumb job at a bar, playing in a band that was going nowhere, or dating assholes. She needed to find *real* meaning, a purpose, a sense of who she was meant to be. Selling the house on Foley's Point was the best she could do, for now. It would provide her with enough money to go back to college and find some practical occupation. If her mother were still alive, Kaia was sure it was what she'd expect from her daughter.

Kaia got out of the car and braced herself against the wind that smacked her full in the face as she turned to the water, sending her mop of orangey-red curls flying away from her freckled cheeks. The ocean crashed against the black rocks beyond the house, sending up a wall of white spray. She hooted in surprise when the wind kicked up the wave and carried the spray right to her. The chilled saltwater tingled on her cheeks and in her nostrils as she walked toward the edge of land.

She had forgotten how good the ocean smelled. It had been too long since she'd been back to Quolobit Harbor. After her grandmother's passing, her father had opened the house on Foley's Point to summer rentals, supervised by an old friend who still lived in town. Now, imagining all the summer skies and wildflowers dancing in the breeze along the shoreline that she had missed in these long years, she felt burdened by deep regret and a healthy dose of resentment for her father, who had kept her away from such a wild and beautiful place.

A gull cried and took wing into the dimming sky as Kaia crunched through the thin layer of snow. A squall of snow blew out of the clouds, obscuring her view of the churning waves. Turning her back to the wind, she smacked her mess of curls out of her face and gazed up at the house. Though she was starving, though she was bone-tired and barely hanging on to her last thread of mental strength, she couldn't resist having a look inside the old house before heading back into town for dinner.

The dry old wood of the porch steps creaked as she climbed them. She found the key under the mat where Samuel Lowell, the property manager, had told her it would be; the door swung open easily, cold on its hinges.

Clean and sparse, the house was decorated like a cross between a Shaker farmhouse and a Japanese monastery. And it was somehow so distinctly *Maine*.

A massive fireplace, flanked by windows overlooking the water, dominated the living room. Puritanical armchairs and a groovy yellow velvet couch from the sixties surrounded the hearth. Kaia gazed down at a mess of ashes and charred wood in the grate. The house had been professionally cleaned at the end of summer, and as far as she knew, there hadn't been any renters after Labor Day—though perhaps the cleaners had forgotten to sweep out the hearth. If so, it was just as well. She'd be building a fire for herself later that evening.

Kaia's stomach rumbled as she turned back toward the hallway and went into the kitchen to find more old-school charm. A rough oak table stood in the center and everything—the fridge, the stove, the sink—was vintage. Antique, even. She opened the door to the pantry and found it empty of all sustenance except for a dusty can of clams.

"Ew. No thanks," she said aloud.

A single mug sat upside down in the dish rack on the counter beside the sink, a trace of water glimmering on the glaze. It dripped down the side of the mug when she fingered it.

"Huh."

Kaia had taken over managing the property rentals five years ago, and even though she oversaw things from afar, she always knew when there were renters scheduled. If her records were correct, no one had stayed at the house on Foley's Point since September. Yet here was a wet mug, as if someone had recently washed it. And the ashes in the hearth…

Out of curiosity, Kaia opened the fridge and found some cream. She pulled out the squat carton and glanced at the date. Still fresh, apparently. She sniffed it. Smelled good, too. In the cabinet she found a paper bag of locally-roasted coffee, fragrant enough to make her mouth water. The hairs on the back of her neck stood on end as she left the kitchen to climb up the stairs.

"Hello?" she called when she got to the top step. "Is somebody here?"

She was answered only by a gale whining around the eaves of the house.

Several small bedrooms opened off the hallway, with a narrow old bathroom to share between them. No signs of recent activity there, as far as she could tell.

The master bedroom stood at the eastern end of the hall, spanning the seaward side of the house. Kaia approached with cautious, creaking steps. She dragged her fingers on the doorframe as she entered the room and flicked on the light to see a prim, maple four-poster bed stripped of linens.

It was a relief to find the dresser drawers empty and the closet bare. In the attached bathroom, which had a claw-footed tub and a toilet with a pull chain she vaguely remembered yanking on as a child, there was no evidence of life other than a wrinkled hand towel dangling beside the sink.

Moving farther into the master bedroom, she went to an eastward-facing, glass-paned door. Attached to the bedroom, hanging out over the porch, was a sunroom. Kaia opened the door and shivered as she stepped into the colder space. She stopped short, frozen in the doorway.

A mess of paper coffee cups, crumpled paper towels, and plastic shopping bags littered the floor. A stool sat in one corner, accompanied by an artist's easel with a drop-cloth tangled in its legs, stained with splotches of deep violet, dove-gray, and aquamarine.

CHAPTER TWO

"Dammit," Sam said, and sucked on his frozen thumb, which he had just jammed against a metal crate of cod. It had been the best day of fishing he'd had in a while, and he'd only caught ten fish. Lobster had been all but gone since the end of December, and though he hated dealing with pelagic hook-and-line gear, it was what he'd have to do to survive till March or April, at least.

"Pretty pathetic, huh?" Sam said to Bobby, his sternman.

Bobby grimaced. "And it ain't gonna get any better."

Sam cast him an inquisitive look.

"With that wind farm thing they're talkin' about," Bobby explained as he knotted the rope tethering the boat to the dock. "You didn't hear about that? 'Course you didn't, living out there on your island like a goddamn hermit. I saw some kind of sign at Dunne's Hardware the other day, and there's been a town meeting or two. Wind farm. Here in Wapomeq Bay. You think fishin's bad now…"

Sam shook his head. Yes, he remembered something about a wind farm being mentioned at the last town meeting, but he'd put it out of his head as unlikely, and too far in the future to care about.

"Ya need me t'marrah?" Bobby asked.

"Nah. Storm tonight, it'll be shit out here."

"Yap," Bobby agreed. He gave Sam a salute and stuck a cigarette between his lips as he walked away.

Sam flipped the hood of his coat up against the fine, needling mist and hoisted the crate onto the stern of the *Angeline* before launching himself onto the dock. He paused, looking out to Wapomeq Bay beyond the harbor.

In the dying light, the water looked soft and gentle. It made him ache, maybe even more than it did in the summer when he could see straight through to the multicolored life thriving there. He yearned for that underwater world. Now, in the bitter cold of January, the water was gray and guarded by slabs of ice. It spoke to him of unreachable shelter and silence.

Sam huffed out a plume of breath as he carried the crate of fish up the pier steps, through the parking lot, and toward the yellow light hanging over the door to the Hook and Anchor. The pub would be empty this time on a Thursday night in the middle of winter. It was too early for dinner and too late for lunch, and besides, there weren't any tourists to fill it this time of year.

He hiked up one knee to support the crate as he freed his right hand to open the door. Harvey, the bartender, nodded as Sam ducked through the door and kicked it closed behind him.

"What you got for me?" Harvey asked.

"Cod." Sam glanced up at a halo of bright orange curls at the end of the bar. Odd to see a stranger this time of year. She turned and looked at him, curious.

"You can toss the crate on the kitchen counter," Harvey said, jerking his head toward the kitchen's swinging doors. "Matty's in there, he'll take care of it."

Sam ripped himself from the gaze of the woman at the end of the bar and ducked into the kitchen with his catch. Matty, the cook, set down a bottle of beer and greeted Sam with a smile and a pat on the back.

"What's up, Sam?" He took the crate and peered inside. "Mm, tasty. You want me to fix you up one of these bad boys?"

"Nah. I'll take a burger," Sam said, and set about washing his hands at the massive stainless steel sink.

"You're funny, you know." Matty slapped a patty of ground beef onto the grill. "Never want to eat what you catch. How can you not like fish, man?"

"I love fish," Sam reminded him. "I just don't like it cooked."

"Yeah, that's what I mean—like, what the fuck? Who doesn't like some beer-battered cod?"

"Hey, who's that out there?" Sam asked.

"The redheaded chick? Don't you know her?" Matty asked as he flipped the burger. "Harvey said she's looking for you."

Sam's stomach twisted. "Looking for *me*?"

He squeezed his eyes shut and tried to recall if he'd slept with any redheads during tourist season. Not in the past year—not that he could remember, anyway. There had been one the year before, but she had been more of a strawberry blonde, tall and lanky. Of course there was always a possibility he'd been wasted and just didn't have a coherent memory of the woman. He could've knocked her up. Shit, what would Violet say? And would he care what Violet said?

Sam had started seeing Violet in the fall, and though things were still casual between them, she was the first local he'd dated and the only woman he'd ever spent more than a handful of nights with. He wasn't a player, though he'd been called that; he just didn't like to share his time and space with anyone else, forget about his emotions. Compared to his typical run-ins with women, this thing with Violet was looking serious.

"Jesus, man," Matty said, bloodshot eyes widening with concern as he flipped the burger again. "Don't freak out. I think she's just the owner of Foley's Point. Probably wants to talk to you about the property." His grin widened, too. "She's got a killer smile and an even better ass."

A killer smile? An even better ass? Sam shook his head, forever puzzled by mankind. Sure, he had burned through lover after lover in a way he probably ought to be ashamed of, but he had done that out of pure instinct, driven by animal need. Other men objectified and belittled women with the way they talked about them and treated them. Sam knew he likely looked just as bad as the rest of them with the way he slept around, but he had always tried to be respectful and upfront with his partners about his desire to remain uncommitted.

Except for Violet. He hadn't been too clear with her.

Gritting his teeth against a twisting nervousness still grinding through his guts, Sam hung his coat up by the front door and made a feeble attempt to smooth out the front of his wrinkled flannel shirt as he walked up to the petite redhead at the end of the bar.

"Kaia Foley?" he asked.

One cheek stuffed with food, she looked up at him with round eyes. She hurried to chew and offered him a hand as she slid off her stool, revealing that she was only a hair above five feet tall. Her mass of red curls, cut to a wild bob at her jaw, somehow made her seem bigger, though. And her voice, when she spoke, was enough to fill the room.

"You bet, that's me," she said, laughing loudly, her southern twang foreign to his ears. Her blue eyes sparkled up at him and he felt them pass over his mouth, his torso, his hands, appraising him like he was some kind of prize animal at the state fair. "And you are...?"

"Sam Lowell," he answered, flustered by her frank gaze.

"Oh!" Kaia knotted her brows in puzzlement, all signs of flirtation leaving her face. "My dad told me you were his best friend growing up. I thought you'd be... older. Like, *significantly* older."

"That's *my* dad he's talking about," Sam said, chuckling despite the nervous flutter in his stomach. He couldn't place what it was about her that had him so worked up. He normally had no trouble talking to women. Pretty ones, even. "My father is, ah, Samuel Lowell, too," he said, clearing his throat of the lump that had risen in it. "I'm the one who takes care of things over at the Point lately. My dad's got a bad shoulder, bad hip... plus he moved to Florida."

"Oh, I see," Kaia said, her voice soft with concern.

She sat again and Sam took a seat too, leaving one stool between them. Harvey set a pint of Sam's favorite IPA on the bar in front of him.

"So that's... *you* I've been emailing all these years?" Kaia asked, a hint of a smile tugging at her full lips as her eyes took on that mischievous sparkle again.

"Yeah, that's me you've been emailing," Sam said.

"Hm."

As she frowned in puzzlement at her beer, Sam took a second to admire her profile, the sweet upturn of her nose, the curve of her freckled cheeks. Her skin had the texture of a peach. He looked up at the TV. He didn't give a shit about football, but he needed to get her out of his gaze for a moment, maybe just so he could look at her again.

"Well, it sure is nice to finally meet you in person," she said decisively.

"I wasn't expecting you to come up here now," he replied, still watching the television. "I think I might've left some stuff in the house."

Her laugh made him look.

"You mean like all your painting things?" Her sly smile brought a flood of heat to his cheeks.

"Shit, sorry." Sam felt his palms begin to sweat.

"What kind of stuff do you paint?" she drawled, crossing her legs toward him and leaning closer with interest.

He smelled her shampoo and laundry detergent and gripped his thighs to resist the sudden urge to touch her. He hoped his beard would hide most of his blush, and ducked his head.

"Nothin', nothin' really," he said, staring at the bubbles rising in his beer. "I just mess around."

"I wanna see," Kaia said with the eagerness of a child as she nudged him in the shoulder.

"How long you here for?" he asked.

She sat up an inch taller, pert and eager. "Does that mean you'll show me your paintings?"

He laughed, despite himself. "No. How long are you here for?"

Kaia shrugged. "I've got nothing to get back to in Nashville," she told him with a sideways glance, perhaps waiting to see if he'd ask why that was.

He didn't. It wasn't that he didn't want to know. He did. He wanted to know everything there was to know about this woman. He just didn't think he could pull it off, asking her something so personal so quickly after just meeting her without seeming like he wanted to get her into bed. And he wanted to ask her why she'd decided to sell the house on Foley's Point, too, but he thought that was simply none of his business, so he left it.

Kaia fidgeted. Pushed her plate away. He knew his quietness was making her feel awkward, as it did certain women—the intelligent kind who wouldn't fill the space with their own mindless prattle. Matty came out of the kitchen with Sam's burger and Sam ate half of it, before turning to Kaia again to find her now reading a book. She tilted it so he could see the cover, which featured a willowy woman in the arms of a bare-chested man.

"I don't always read trashy romance, I swear," she told him in her cute southern drawl. "It's something I only do when I've got too much on my mind, you know? When I need an escape from reality."

"I get it," Sam said, shrugging. His whole life was about escaping reality.

"So, what do you do the rest of the time, when you're not taking care of the house or… painting?"

Sam darted his gaze around to be sure no one had heard her talking. He kept his painting a secret these days, though he supposed that was about to change, if he was going to have that show in the gallery Violet had pushed him to try for.

"I fish," he said.

Kaia suddenly reached across the space between them and grabbed his left hand. She opened it in her own. Her tiny thumbs ran over his calloused palm; fingertips touched the bloody cuticle where he'd slammed his finger in the cooler earlier, traced a white scar across the pad of his thumb where he'd gouged himself with a fishhook years ago. He expected her to say something about his meaty mount of Venus and tell him he'd live a short and confused life.

"Looks like you do a *lot* of fishin'. Must be a hard livin'," she said, pressing her little fingers into his callouses.

"Yep."

Her own fingers felt rough, too, and Sam took hold of her hand, looking down at it.

"You've got a few callouses yourself," he observed.

"Guitar and banjo," Kaia said, smiling.

"Is that what *you* do for a living?"

She drew in a long breath and let it out in a sigh. "I used to wish it was, but now I'm not so sure. I tend bar to pay the bills. Had a band and we toured a bit"—her voice wavered and she flicked a stray curl away from her eyes—"but we broke up a while back and I just got fired from my job at the bar, so you could say I'm untethered at the moment."

It was the first moment he'd seen a break in her flirtatious bravado, and he felt something tug at his heart. "Sounds good to me," he muttered.

She blinked at him.

"I—oh, I'm sorry," Sam said. "I shouldn't've said that."

"No, no, not at all." Kaia put her hands on the bar like she was bracing herself for a blow. "You're right! It's a good thing. Or it could be, if I let it." She looked thoughtful.

Sam nodded, chewing his last bite of burger.

Harvey came up to them with a round of fresh drinks. "On me, friends," he said. "Hey, she tell you she plays guitar and sings? Look, she brought her instruments in with her."

Sam glanced into the shadows under the bar at the foot of Kaia's stool and saw two black cases side by side.

"I didn't want to leave them in the car. It's too cold out there," Kaia explained. "Bad for the wood."

"Play us something." Harvey leaned over the bar. "Come on, we're bored to tears in here and it's just us."

Kaia smiled reluctantly. Sam wanted badly to hear her sing, but he wouldn't pressure her.

"Only if you want to," he said when she cast a questioning glance at him.

Kaia's smile widened. She did have one hell of a smile.

"Beers on me rest of the night," Harvey declared in celebration.

Kaia slid off her stool and bent to open her guitar case. Matty had made a keen observation of her hindquarters, too, Sam had to admit.

"You might regret that offer, Mister Bartender Man," Kaia said to Harvey with a wink as she resurfaced with a guitar. "I sure can put 'em away."

And so Kaia Foley began to play and sing a song that sounded kind of country, kind of Celtic, about a sailor that had been gone at sea for seven long years.

"*Well met, well met, my own true love,*" she sang. "*Well met, well met, cried he. I've just returned from the salt, salt sea and it's all for the love of thee…*"

Her voice was tender and pure, and though it was smooth as a river flowing over rounded stones, it was somehow raw at the same time. Sam felt her voice stir the wildness in him, sending him somewhere he hadn't been in a long, long while. Listening to her, he felt himself surrounded by the ocean's salty embrace as he had once been. Kaia's voice rang straight into his heart and made him feel as though that part of himself he had buried years ago—the wild part, the good part—was now just at the edge of his reach.

"*Six ships, six ships, all out on the sea, seven more on dry land,*" she sang. "*One hundred and ten, all brave sailor men, will be at your command.*"

The sea shanty wrapped Sam in the memory of swimming through water like silk running over his form. It made him long for the sea so badly it hurt. He wriggled in his seat, wanting to get up and get away from her, but he was rooted in place. Grounded by gravity and his heavy, immobile limbs. Tears came into his eyes, washing over him in a wave of something he struggled to define but eventually did.

Relief. It was a relief to know that the best of him was still in there somewhere, alive within. He'd ignored it for so long, and yet here it was— his true self resurfacing.

Kaia's gaze lit on his and Sam knew she saw his tears. She kept singing anyway, a small smile on her lips. Did the woman enjoy making him cry? Hell, the tears felt so good, maybe *he* enjoyed her making him cry. He angled himself sideways at the bar so at least Harvey and Matty wouldn't see. Kaia went on and on for verse after verse, looking up at his teary face now and then, as if they were all alone. He was pretty sure she even repeated a verse or two, just to give him a chance to pull himself together. There was something so intimate about it; he felt like she knew everything there was to know about him by the time she was done with her song.

"There ya go," she said, when she was finished and Sam was dry-eyed at last. "Don't worry about the free beer," she told Harvey amid the applause of the three men now enamored with her, "I'm still working on this one and I think I'd better make it an early night. I've been on the road since before dawn."

Sam was instantly disappointed that she wouldn't be sticking around. Apparently so were Matty and Harvey, who both made *their* disappointment known. Loudly. Still, Kaia put away her guitar, finished her beer in two gulps, and got up to go.

"Nice meeting you, Sam," she said. She zipped up her coat and gave him a conspiratorial wink as if to say that that his tears would be a secret between them, and that she somehow understood. She touched his arm and gave it a soft squeeze. "Maybe you can come by and pick up your painting stuff sometime."

Sam found himself tongue-tied, as usual, and watched her walk toward the door with two instrument cases weighing her down. When she got there and couldn't easily open the door, he jumped to his feet to open it for her.

"Thanks." Her big smile hit him like a wave of warmth.

"You got it," he said, now grinning like a loon. "Let me help you out." He grabbed his jacket from the hook by the door and took one of her instrument cases.

As they walked out into the howling wind and a squall of snow, she said, "Would you be a darlin' and open my car for me, too? Keys're in this pocket here." She gestured to her right coat pocket.

"Nasty night," Sam said as he unlocked the car.

Kaia put her instruments in the back of her small, cluttered '87 Corolla. By the looks of it, it was a wonder she had made it from Nashville to Quolobit. "You sure you know your way to the Point?"

"Yep, I'm good. I was already out there, remember, Picasso?"

Sam blushed again and was glad for the darkness of the night. To his surprise, Kaia extended her arms for a hug. He was startled for a second, then bent to embrace her. She was so tiny, yet she gave him a powerful squeeze. Something he could sink into. She hugged him with her whole body, in a way that felt like they'd known each other always. He sensed that, despite their radical difference in size, they somehow fit each other perfectly. The animal in him wanted to take her mouth with his, to crawl into that tiny car with her and pull off those cute jeans of hers and—

Catching himself thinking things he should *not* be thinking, catching his body reacting to her with shocking force, Sam pulled away.

Had she felt it, too? She stood there a second, staring at him like maybe she had. Sam squinted into the icy precipitation, watching as she enclosed herself in the car and put the key into the ignition, his heart pounding.

The car gave a choking wheeze—but that was it. Kaia's face, lit by the yellowish light of the parking lot light, crumpled. She sighed visibly, then hung her head. She tried the ignition once more, with even less of a result.

"I knew this piece of junk was on its way out," she told him as she climbed out of the car again. "I'm honestly surprised I got all the way up here without some kinda catastrophe." She turned that smile on him again, her dimpled cheeks glistening. "D'you think you could give me a ride?"

Sam patted his pockets. "I, ah, left the keys to my truck at home," he said. "You don't get seasick, do you?"

CHAPTER THREE

"WE'RE HERE," SAM shouted over the wind as he dropped the anchor.

"You sure this is a good idea?" Kaia braced herself on the wheelhouse doorframe of the *Angeline*.

It had *seemed* like a good idea outside the pub, after that hug when she'd caught a brighter glimpse of the chemistry she had already sensed at the bar. But it sure as hell didn't seem like it now, as the sky spat out an unholy mix of rain, ice, and snow. The wind howled at such a speed it made her face sting, like it was being pricked with a hundred needles all at once.

Ya don't get seasick, do ya? Sam's words seemed to taunt her now. She almost laughed at the memory, but reckoned her southern drawl must sound as funny to him as his Downeaster accent sounded to her.

Kaia thought of the moment he had walked into the bar carrying a crate of fish, looking like a god of oceanic abundance, his dark hair and beard slick with rain, the scent of seawater coming off him. And then, when she had sung, Sam had cried. Quietly, discreetly. This big, silent man shedding tears no one saw but her. It was like they had shared something deeply personal, something secret. So she hadn't said yes to the boat ride *just* because she wanted to get the man into bed—she trusted him for some reason, even now as he was telling her to get into the itty-bitty rowboat he had towed with them across the harbor and north to Foley's Point.

"I'm scared," Kaia called to him, squirming as water gushed around her ankles, colder than she had expected, cold enough to make her bones hurt. She tightened her grip on the doorframe when another wave struck the *Angeline.*

"Stop," he yawped. *Stahp.* "C'mon." He waved her toward the stern.

Kaia gripped the polished wooden edge of the boat and worked her way towards Sam, gripping his hand desperately once she got there. She looked down into the little rowboat tossing in the rough water.

"Really?" she protested. "If things go south *you'll* make it, at least. You look like you were born in the sea."

He stared at her oddly a moment, then leaned over the stern of the *Angeline* to pull the rowboat closer. A breaker collided into the land, leaving churning trains of gossamer hissing in its wake, exposing black rock, jagged with barnacles and coiled weeds.

"Don't you have a life vest?" Kaia asked, grappling with her jacket to make sure her phone and wallet were still safely zipped into the pockets. She had wisely decided to leave her instruments locked in the office at the Hook and Anchor, and had stupidly—or perhaps fortuitously—forgotten her overnight bag altogether.

Sam, still hanging on to her, opened his mouth and closed it again. "I'm sorry," he said. "I don't. I should, I know, it's illegal—"

Even the best swimmer could drown in that Maine water, Kaia's father had told her, time and time again, whenever she asked how her mother had died, and why.

Kaia shook her head hard and stood taller. She was exaggerating the gravity of the situation. The waves were hardly as bad now as they had been a moment ago. The wind had died down. Sam was confident they would get from the *Angeline* to shore without incident.

She got into the rowboat and for a terrifying moment was alone in it. It bobbed as she scrambled her way to the bench, and she let out a little whoop as Sam's weight sank in a moment later. He took up the oars with broad, powerful strokes, leaping over waves that crashed into the small boat and soaked through Kaia's jeans, so cold she began to shiver. She could hardly see anything but stared at Sam's darkened face, frowning out at the horizon.

He was the last thing she saw before she was in the water, the rowboat capsized by a frothing breaker. Where there had been cold, blustering air, briny water now filled her mouth and burned her nostrils, choking her. Her muscles seized in reaction to the frigid temperature and for a moment she couldn't even move to swim to the surface.

Eventually, when she found the will to kick and got to the air, she shouted. "Sam!"

Her mouth filled with saltwater as a wave smacked into her. The powerful tide took her next breath and Kaia became helpless as a piece of driftwood, tumbling violently underwater.

When the wave didn't kill her, she swam to the surface again. She scanned for Sam, but another mammoth wave roared out of the darkness and consumed her. She was lost within it, aware only of the cold and her own weightlessness, her total lack of control.

Fully submerged, she opened her eyes. She couldn't even see the surface. Water ripped at the edges of her nostrils, needled its way into her eye-sockets and plowed into her ears and mouth. Her insides itched with the immediate need for air. Arms and legs twitched involuntarily.

Kaia opened her mouth and screamed, releasing the last of the breath she'd been holding inside. Pearls broken from their string, the bubbles left her mouth and floated away, upward.

I'm going to die.

She felt the descent of her diaphragm. The dangerous, fatal pull, the final human gesture. It was too strong to resist. Water entered her nostrils and her mouth, burning like molten metal as it filled her throat and lungs. Pain shot from the crown of her head to her groin and through her limbs. She exploded from the inside out and heard herself let out a scream that sounded as though it spread its vibration through the whole harbor. As it happened, she thought she heard another in response. An echo, perhaps, or just her brain shorting out. Then came total quiet.

Something isn't right.

The itch for air was gone. Kaia saw Sam above, face down. She arched her spine and reached her hands upward, propelling herself away from the edge of darkness with one motion of her lower half. Water seemed to course through her like air, but she didn't have time to think about that.

She found Sam limp and heavy with the weight of death. His skin shone pale and glossy; his lips were an unnatural blue. Holding him close with one arm and trying not to let him slip out of her grasp, she pulled him away from the rocks and the breaking waves.

Dragging him through the water, she entered the relative safety of a cove to the northern edge of the Point. What frightened her now was not the merciless hunger of the ocean, but the rubbery cold of Sam's neck, the mortal heaviness of his limbs, and the creeping certainty that, despite her ability to swim, something had broken inside her.

She heaved Sam's body to shore. He lay motionless and pale, his black hair plastered to his forehead and neck, his beard matted with seawater and bits of shell. She climbed onto his chest and grabbed his face as water sloshed up and over them.

"Wake up, Sam!" She peeled back his eyelids to reveal sightless eyes. "Wake up."

Kaia tried to stand so she could pull him upland and perform CPR, but she couldn't even bring herself onto her knees. She fell back alongside Sam's body.

Fearing the worst, she didn't want to look down. She was injured, she knew that much. She was probably in shock. Adrenaline must have fueled this feat of strength that would have otherwise been impossible. But then again there *was* sensation below her waist. Water coursed away from the skin of her hips. Barnacles grated. Encouraged, she gasped for air and forced herself to look down.

Her legs were gone.

At her waist, where her shirt stuck to her belly, her skin had become pearlescent and textured with scales. When she placed her fingers—now coated in veiny, diaphanous webbing—on her hips, she found the scales hard as armor and warm to the touch. The buff color gave way to tawny stripes at her thighs, growing darker and reaching a deep fox-red toward the pointed end, where a spiny fin fanned out and moved articulately.

It's not real.

She squeezed her eyes shut and breathed deeply. It couldn't be real. After a moment, she felt the sensation of water evaporating from her skin. She heard the whisper of the wind singing through the pines. The sound calmed her, reassured her that she belonged to the land.

Whatever this hallucination of a tail—a *mermaid* tail for God's sake—was, it had to have some rational or semi-rational explanation.

Illusion brought on by stress? Accidental ingestion of psychotropic substance? Manifestation of deific being latent within myself?

Sam coughed and Kaia turned to shove him onto his side, gripping his shoulders as he vomited seawater, and dinner along with it.

That's real enough.

While Sam retched, life returning in violent heaves and shudders to his body, Kaia dared to look at herself again and saw the monstrous tail still there, but changing. It was terrifying and beautiful even as it reformed into two legs, like a flower closing.

Human again, she found herself naked from the waist down. Her jeans, her sneakers, even her underwear must have blown off in the transition. She did seem to recall the sense of her expanding body ripping through the clothes, but had that actually been real? Had any of it?

Kaia wrestled Sam's soaked flannel off him and wrapped it around her waist as a makeshift kilt. Sam, senseless, shivering and curling into a ball, let out a quiet, animal groan.

"You're all right," she said, as she put her arms around him.

Sam wasn't all right; anyone could see that. And she wasn't all right either. He needed a medical team to help him cope with his hypothermia and she needed a psychiatrist. Blood poured from Sam's forehead down the side of his face as he gazed helplessly up at her.

"You just hang tight," she said. "I'm going to take care of you."

CHAPTER FOUR

SUNLIGHT SEARED THROUGH Sam's eyelids, splattering orange across the darkness. He found himself sore but whole, somewhere familiar-smelling, though it wasn't home. Someone moved beneath the covers beside him.

Sam tensed as he felt hot velvet breasts pressed against his back, a soft belly against his bare ass, the slope of thighs behind his, and the dewy starfish of a hand on his hip. She stretched her other hand up, fingers curling into his hair.

Kaia Foley, he reminded himself, the owner of the house on the Point, the woman with kind eyes and a big smile and a voice that was wild and naked, and maybe divine.

You would've met your end if it hadn't been for her saving your ass.

Sam felt her move against him and heard her let out a sleepy moan. He wanted to turn to her and take her in his arms, but a warning went off inside him.

You and your heart will always belong to the ocean, he had heard the wind say to him on days when he was out alone on his boat, beyond the the sight of land. *Always remember you belonged to her first. She is your beginning and your end.*

Sam drew in a breath and forced himself to open his eyes to the cloudy and blustering morning. Judging by the light, it had to be at least eight o'clock. He couldn't remember the last time he'd slept past dawn, and he didn't have a clue what day it was, but that didn't matter; there was work to be done. There was always work to be done.

But Kaia coiled her arm around his body and nuzzled her cool nose against his back. There was a vacant swath in Sam's memory between the instant he'd fallen out of the rowboat and the present moment.

As he moved, pushing one arm beneath the pillow to support his head, he felt a bruise-like ache deep in his chest. His head felt as though it was filled with gunpowder about to be lit. He'd almost drowned—in fact he was pretty sure he *had* drowned—and Kaia had saved his life. The blur of events was becoming clearer the longer he was awake. After she'd hauled him back to land, he'd been helpless as an infant, and Kaia had tended to him without thought for herself.

Sam decided to risk turning onto his back to get a look at her, half expecting to see something that was more than just human, something he had dreamed up in his fitful, hypothermic sleep: a woman with the body of some kind of big fish, something too real to be out of a storybook. Yet Kaia was as he remembered her from the Hook and Anchor—not much larger than a child, with the soft topography of the blanket hinting at full, womanly curves.

A pile of fiery red curls hid her face. Sam pulled on one and watched it spring back. The colors in her hair were mesmerizing: cadmium red and carmine, golden ochre, mahogany. He stuck a finger in through the mop and lifted it away from her eyes. Sunlight made her eyelids incandescent as orchid petals. She squeezed them tight and Sam dropped the lock of hair and ran the backs of his fingers over her cheek where freckles graced her fair, round face. Her full lips blossomed a pretty raspberry color—a little chapped, but beautiful.

This was a face he could spend hours looking at, figuring out if some deeper mystery hid beneath her skin. He could paint her, he thought, if he ever painted people.

Kaia stirred and grumbled something about coffee and Sam reached to touch her mouth, but stopped himself. She might not want that. She might not want him. Sure, she was naked, and when he'd woken just now she had been holding him like a lover. But they were naked simply because neither of them had had dry clothing to wear to bed, and he'd been so cold he'd frankly needed the skin-to-skin body heat to regain equilibrium. She'd risked her life for his, yes, but they hadn't touched each other in any way that was anything other than innocent or necessary. Whatever they shared—traumatic, maybe sacred—he didn't want to complicate it.

Despite a growing need to piss, he settled into the bed to watch her sleep a little longer. Almost as soon as he moved, though, her fingers sought him and she hugged him close, throwing one leg over his. Sam let himself burrow his nose into her curls. Then he felt the heat between her thighs pressed against him. His body responded.

Fuck.

This was very bad and very stupid. He could not get involved with Kaia Foley. She was just another tourist, for all intents and purposes. He'd sworn he was done with summer girls, those vacationers who were inevitably more trouble than they were worth. Kaia might've been born in Quolobit Harbor, but the way she'd talked about it the night before, she was set on selling the old house on Foley's Point, and even though she'd said she was untethered, he expected she was no different than anyone else—a slave to the status quo, or too ambivalent about life to do more than wallow in mediocrity. He was no different, he had to admit to himself, with no small degree of shame. As he saw it, she would return to her life in Tennessee as soon as possible, and he'd never see her again.

Besides, there was Violet.

Kaia wrapped her leg tighter around Sam's. His fingers itched with the urge to grab her thigh and squeeze hard. But he remained motionless and tried to breathe deeply, willing his throbbing cock to chill the fuck out before Kaia moved her knee and discovered it for herself.

He forced himself to think of Violet instead of Kaia's heat like a ripe peach smashed on his hip, her grippy little hand now lodged in his armpit.

Violet. Violet. Violet.

This thing with Violet had never been serious, but maybe it ought to be. She was a local. If he screwed it up, he'd have to deal with the fallout maybe for the rest of his life.

He should take Violet out to dinner some time. Or better yet—breakfast. Maybe that would make the difference to her. Maybe then she'd see him as more than a blue-collar lobsterman with pipe-dreams of being a painter. Maybe, but probably not.

As Sam lay there, miserably pondering just how deep that relationship could ever get and trying to ignore the sensation of Kaia against his bare skin, it occurred to him that today was Friday and there was something important he had to do.

Renew the boat registration? No. *Someone's birthday?* Not that, either.

It had to do with Violet, he remembered that much. And paintings. Yes, that was it. Friday at noon, he had an appointment to meet Violet's sister Emory at the gallery to show her his paintings. Recalling the dread and anxiety he'd been carrying around in relation to this meeting and coming out of the closet as a painter, Sam found himself settled enough to move.

Getting up, he went to the bathroom in the hall instead of the one attached to the master bedroom, hoping he could shower and get off Foley's Point before anyone—especially Violet—noticed the *Angeline* had been moored there overnight.

CHAPTER FIVE

KAIA BLINKED AND it hurt. Sam was gone. The bed linens lay rumpled in his place, the quilt and blanket thrown to the middle of the bed. She let her head fall back onto the pillow and shut her eyes to the headache pounding in her skull. Reverberations of the surge of energy that had ripped through her body and enabled her to save the fisherman's life still pulsed through her now, aching in her back, tingling in her feet. The body remembered what the mind would not—like that finned tail where her legs should have been.

Kaia opened her eyes again, just a millimeter. The room was empty save for a battered Shaker-style dresser and the maple four-poster bed. It didn't *feel* empty, though. Outside the sky yawned, and white-feathered flashes flew back and forth in the stormy gray sky.

She lifted the covers and found herself to be fully human, and without a stitch of clothing. Even though her body radiated a deep heat, an inner blossoming like she'd just had three good orgasms in a row, she'd spent half the night keeping that man alive. No orgasms for her—though she reckoned Sam Lowell would make one heck of a lover. And it had been that particular notion that had led her to such peril...

Kaia sat up and pushed her curls away from her face as a swell of nausea overtook her. "Oh, sweet Lord," she moaned as a flash of hot and cold passed over her skin. She ran her hands down her thighs, just to remind herself they were there, to survey the damage. Her knees and the heels of her hands were scraped to ground meat from barnacles, but other than a bruise on her bottom and general aching and queasiness, she felt physically whole.

Mentally whole: not so sure.

Someone began to hum a tuneless and meandering melody just on the other side of the wall behind the bed. The faucet squealed. Water pattered into the tub. Wrapping herself in a soft cotton throw blanket, Kaia made her way downstairs.

She peered into the dryer in the kitchen. Pulling out her shirt, she recalled dismally that the rest of her clothes were long gone, lost during her *metamorphosis*—or whatever the hell had happened out there. Out of options for bottom-coverage, she put on Sam's boxer shorts and rolled them up at her hips.

The faucet squeaked again from upstairs and the house made a clanking, lurching sound as the flow of water stopped. Sam would be out in a matter of moments dressed in nothing but a towel, and they'd have to exchange an awfully strange good-morning. She quickly gathered up his jeans and threw them at the bathroom door upstairs before retreating back down.

Hearing floorboards protest as Sam moved around upstairs, Kaia pulled on her coat. It was still somewhat warm from the dryer, but her phone, which even now was still zipped into the pocket, was well and truly dead. Leaving the kitchen, she stepped into a pair of galoshes by the door as she snuck out onto the porch. Beyond the snow-blown grass and the shivering thorny briars that buffered the land from the rocks, the ocean glowed. It was now calm as a stone, marbled with reflections of the morning sky.

Sam's boat, the *Angeline,* moored off the southern side of the Point, looked spitefully fresh and cheery. Kaia stepped out into biting wind to look at the exterior of the house. Grayed cedar shake siding in various stages of weathering covered a no-fuss frame built to withstand any blow; window boxes where she recalled her mom planting petunias; a laundry line out back where her grandmother used to hang sheets that had been in use since Kaia's dad had been a boy. She felt a rush of longing to remain at the house on Foley's Point but instantly quashed it, reminding herself that she was here to sell the place, plain and simple.

As Kaia turned to go in, a breeze shot up from the water and goosed her, as if the ocean demanded her attention. Her nose caught its delicious and disturbing tang in the air and her mouth watered in response.

Oh no, please, not again.

Fearing she would have another hallucination—or worse, an actual metamorphosis—Kaia hurried inside and shut the door behind her, leaning against it with her eyes closed, letting the quiet strength of the house hold her safe.

It felt so real, that tail. I can still feel it now.

Kaia was thinking of phantom limb syndrome and gripping the chilled skin of her thighs when the steps creaked. She opened her eyes to see a barefoot man in nothing but jeans coming down the stairs. Woad-blue animals intertwined in a Nordic design up his right arm and sprawled over his shoulder and the top of his pectoral muscle. His damp black hair was brushed clean away from his finely-formed face. The man was at least six-foot-three and had to weigh nearly two hundred pounds.

How? How could I have saved him?

"Do I still have a shirt?" he asked, lifting his brows as their eyes met, both silently acknowledging what serious trouble they had miraculously scraped their way out of, and the foolish attraction that had led them to it.

Kaia felt heat rise to her cheeks. "Oh, um, yeah," she stammered. "It's still in the dryer."

She followed him into the kitchen, where he pulled on his T-shirt and the flannel over that, then draped his coat over the back of a chair.

"Coffee?" he asked, running a hand over his damp, dark hair. The man was even more good-looking than she remembered.

"I don't know if I'm there yet," she confessed, rubbing her head, pained at the very sight of him. Or of anything, for that matter. "You got any aspirin?"

Sam snorted a laugh as he dug a bottle out of the cabinet. "Might be expired," he said.

"I don't care," she said. "Hand it over."

After taking three tablets and a guzzle of water out of the tap, Kaia sat down at the table while Sam began to make coffee. He had the economy of motion of a man accustomed to working in small, cluttered spaces, and seemed to know where everything was, from the coffee can to the teaspoon. To her relief, there seemed to be no need for small talk or awkward embarrassment with Sam. He didn't smile or frown, but maintained the stoical expression that she figured to be his default.

"You seem like you're feeling okay." Meanwhile, she not only felt maybe about to die of nausea or spontaneous cranial explosion, but also embarrassment for how flirtatious she had been last night. She palpated her temples and listed sideways onto her uninjured left butt-cheek.

Sam stooped to pull a dishrag out of the third drawer beside the sink and turned to look straight at her. "Why do you need to sell this place?"

Taken aback at his stark question, she drew in a deep breath. "I... want to go back to college," she answered hesitantly. "Maybe become a school teacher." It wasn't at all what she had pictured for herself in the past, but it would be a solid, responsible way of living. "Did you go to college?" she asked.

And instantly regretted it. He was a fisherman, and that was really all that mattered. Plenty of blue-collar workers would take offense to that kind of question, her father among them.

"I went to art school in New York," Sam told her. "Studied painting."

"Damn," she said.

He stood straighter and returned Kaia's gaze. He was so tall. Massive, really. But not so bulky that he couldn't move around gracefully. He was built like a man who could've been a football player but who'd chosen ballet instead. Regardless, there was no way she could've pulled that man to shore in the weak, trembling form she currently inhabited. Sam continued looking directly at Kaia for longer than was comfortable. She fidgeted.

Did he see? Does he know?

"So you really are a painter," she said at last.

Sam snorted and dried his hands, then went about the business of pouring coffee beans into a hand-crank grinder.

"You sure you're set on selling?" he asked, returning to the subject Kaia would rather avoid. Clearly he didn't want to talk of his creative pursuits. She'd have to respect that, for now.

"Yes, I'm sure."

"You're sure," he repeated with a hint of sarcasm, like he didn't believe her. "How long's it been since you've been back?"

"I was five when we moved," she said, swallowing hard. Her dad had decided he needed to get away—away from the ocean, away from the memories of her mother. "We came back only once, for my grandmother's funeral. That was ten years ago. My father could barely stand to be here a minute longer than necessary."

"That's why you left Maine?"

"The memories, yeah," Kaia answered.

Maybe it actually *had something to do with what happened to me last night.*

The idea made the nausea swell through her again. Kaia gulped. "Once this place is on the market, it'll go pretty quick. Won't it?" she asked, her words coming out too fast and nervous.

"I have no idea," Sam said. "I don't pay attention to real estate."

"Where do *you* live?" she asked, out of a desire to change the subject to something less stress-inducing.

"Come see." Sam motioned for her to follow him out of the kitchen and into the hall.

He walked through the living room and went to the window beside the hearth, pointing into the bay. Nearly lost in the rain and fog, a small island sat like a gem on top of the water. Coniferous trees towered over its rocky back, where a single cottage was nestled.

"Thursday Island," Sam said, as he looked out the window. "That's home."

"I don't see any other houses." Kaia leaned against the window frame as she gazed at the island, aware of Sam's body heat close to hers. "You have a whole island to yourself?!"

"Yep."

"But don't you get lonely?" She gazed up at his dark eyes.

Sam shook his head. "I'm not much of a people person."

The scent of coffee drifted in from the kitchen, and Kaia lifted her nose toward it. Sam grabbed her hand.

"Hey. I'm—I'm shit with words, but I'm sorry, and—and thank you."

His eyes grew glossy and his voice frayed as he spoke. "You saved my life, and I shouldn't've brought you out there in that storm."

Moved by his sudden tenderness, Kaia threw her arms around Sam's torso and hugged him, pressing her cheek to his chest. He stiffened at first, then put his arms around her slowly. His body was warm and firm, but at the same time giving to hers as he held her close. She could collapse into his strength, if she let herself. She could let go of the absolute terror she held inside—the terror that she was either utterly insane, or something not altogether human.

"We made it," she said instead, trying to sound cheerful.

"Yep, we made it." Sam pulled away and gave her a small, shaky smile. So he had been scared shitless, too.

"Coffee?" she said.

Back in the kitchen, she caught Sam throwing a glance at her tush in his boxer shorts, but he didn't say anything about her thievery as he poured their coffee. She was thankful for that. How would she explain? *Oh, sorry, lost my pants when I turned into a sea monster.* Hell no.

"Hey, Sam, can I ask you something?"

He lifted his brows in wary permission.

"When I sang at the bar last night, you… you cried." She feared that asking this meant treading on very personal ground. Maybe even trespassing. Still, she couldn't help herself. Besides, he had no problem grilling her. "Why?" she asked, taking a sip of coffee.

Sam drew in a long breath as he sat at the table with his mug cradled in his hands. "You reminded me of… of something I'd forgotten."

"And what was that?"

Sam's lips curved into a smile and he shook his head. The man clearly had his secrets. She sensed there were plenty of them hiding behind that calm facade.

Several moments passed, and her question disappeared into the sound of the rain pattering on the tin roof of the kitchen. Sam finished his coffee quickly, but Kaia barely sipped hers. Sweat poured off her. She felt like she might be sick at any moment and wondered if saltwater could cause a hangover.

Sam stood and went to the window over the sink. "Looks like the dingy washed up."

Kaia stood up too fast, then sat down again as her stomach flipped.

"I'll have your car towed to the shop near the wharf," he said, and took his coat off the back of the chair.

Wharf. That was a word she'd prefer not to hear spoken aloud. Her guts recoiled. Oh, she knew this feeling, but typically only after a tequila-whiskey-vodka-gin-Chinese-pizza-burgers kind of night did she wake up feeling the fiesta. And even on the worst of those nights, she'd never envisioned turning into a mythical creature.

"I'll bring your bags and stuff later today, and I'll pick up something for you to eat, okay? Build you a fire out in the furnace first, so we can get some heat goin' in here," Sam muttered as he zipped up his jacket and flipped the hood over his shoulder-length black hair. His eyes caught hers, dark and deep as the ocean itself. "I keep wood stacked out by the shed for when I come to paint sunrises in your bedroom," he admitted with a shrug.

Kaia swallowed and chewed on her tongue. She prayed her belly wouldn't take the notion to toss up its contents at this very moment.

"Sam, wait," she said as he went to the door. "Did you see... did you see what happened to me last night?"

Sam shook his head and frowned. He looked directly into her eyes for a second longer than was comfortable.

"Nope," he said, and went out the door.

CHAPTER SIX

THE ART GALLERY on Main Street had been stripped bare except for several muted watercolors of Monhegan Island, painted by an artist emulating the legendary Andrew Wyeth, that capturer of Maine life who had become the touchstone for all who followed. An indefinable sculpture stood in the center of the room, still wrapped in packaging, but other than that the Water's Edge Gallery was quiet and empty. It was January, after all. Sam would be surprised if they had a single customer between here and June.

He hated the way his heart pounded. Why did he care what anyone thought of his paintings? He painted for himself, for his own peace of mind, and that was it. If they told him he couldn't have a show, it wouldn't change a thing. It wasn't as if anybody would see his stuff in the gallery during winter, anyway.

"Hello?" he called.

The main door opened behind him and Violet Wilde came in, smiling. Her glossy dark hair hung straight and heavy to her narrow waist, and her makeup was, as always, meticulously applied. She was wearing her typical winter gear—an oversized cashmere sweater, leggings, and a pair of shearling boots. Even though she was dressed casually, she still somehow looked elegant. Wealthy. She was one of those people who dripped money, from the top of her well-groomed head to the tips of her manicured toenails. It was like a smell that hung around her.

He kind of despised all this about her, but despite that Sam felt a pang of guilt for waking in Kaia's bed. In her arms. Naked. *Nothing happened*, he reminded himself, and he tried to return Violet's happy smile.

"I thought I was meeting your sister," he said.

"Emory told me she'd be a few minutes late and asked me to meet you here." Violet frowned up at him. "What happened to your head?"

Sam touched just above his left eye where he had acquired a little nick the night before, a reminder that he'd nearly lost his life.

"Nothing. Got a bit rough on the water last night."

"You were out there?" Violet's green eyes narrowed. "That was quite a storm, Sam. Next time you're caught on the mainland, let me know. You can stay with me."

Violet had never asked him to stay the night at her house before. She reached up to adjust the collar of his shirt, running her thumbs along the bare skin of his neck and sending a shivering bolt of sensation straight to his crotch.

"Ah—" Sam wiggled away from Violet as her smile spread.

"Maybe when we're done here you should come over to the apothecary and let me fix you up. I've got a calendula-rose solution for wound care. New batch." She sidled closer and rested her hands on his hips, pressing her body to his.

Sam took a step back. Although he recognized that this opportunity to show his paintings at the gallery was essentially Violet pitying him and convincing her sister to give him the least desirable spot on the calendar, he wanted to appear professional. If Emory came in to see him making out with her sister—him, a local lobsterman for Christ's sake—well, it wouldn't look good. He pulled away from Violet and glanced around the place.

"Where I can set up?" he asked.

Violet drew him into the back room, where floor-to-ceiling windows overlooked the wintry harbor. "Emory uses the table in here for consultations." A broad plank table stood in the center of the oblong room. She put her hands on her hips as she smiled at him. "You know, you look really sexy in a shirt and tie."

Sam set his portfolio on the table. "What'd you think I'd wear? Jeans and a flannel?"

Violet stroked his tie and let her fingers drift to where his shirt was tucked in, gripping the waist of his pants and yanking him closer. "Yes, or maybe your orange coveralls."

Just as Violet's lips were about to touch Sam's, he heard a noise from the front and stepped aside. Emory Wilde sailed in—a tall, Scandinavian blonde, the carbon-copy of her twin sister in every aspect besides hair color.

"Sorry I'm late," Emory said breezily. "Oh, Violet! You bad girl! Is this your hipster-fisherman?"

Sam grimaced. *Hipster-fisherman?*

Emory kissed Violet's cheek, then offered Sam her hand. "Sam Lowell, please don't look at me like that, Violet has had only the *very best* things to say about you," she cooed, with a not-so-subtle glance at his crotch. "I don't think we've met before, but I've seen you down at the wharf."

Hauling lobster out of the Angeline, *probably,* Sam thought with a mixture of pride and embarrassment. Emory sized him up as they shook hands. He knew she felt the roughness of his palm and judged him for it.

Yes, I'm a man who works with my hands. I labor to earn my living. I bet that's something you and your kind have never known.

Moving out of her scrutinizing gaze, he unzipped the portfolio and drew out the three square-framed canvases he had brought. He set the paintings on the table in a row, putting the dark storm first, the white breaker in the middle, and then the one he called 'Purple Sky', for lack of anything better. He thought with sudden panic that he might have to name his work.

"So violent," Emory observed, half-whispered, to her twin.

Sam stood back from the Wilde sisters to let them look on their own. Violet said something inaudible, and Emory glanced over at Sam and smiled. He'd never seen the fair-haired Wilde twin up so close before. It was creepy how alike Emory and Violet looked. Their similarities went deeper than just looks and mannerisms, though, Sam thought. Though they wore different clothing and seemed to have unique personalities— Emory breezy where Violet was brooding and intense—their voices were the same, the way they looked at him was the same, the way they were leaning over the table just now and eyeing his work… it was uncanny.

He crossed his arms and hoped this would be over quickly. He'd like to grab a coffee at The Better Bean, get on the *Angeline,* and retreat to Thursday Island. The mainland made him nervous, no matter how briefly he was there, no matter that the water was still in sight. He felt sweat prickle in his pits as he gazed out at the harbor with its scattered buoys, the pines stretching to the edge of Foley's Point, and Kaia's house out there, all on its own. He hoped she was doing better than she had looked when he left her.

Emory turned to him. "I'd like more of the…"

"Storms. Mm, yes," Violet murmured, nodding, while Emory smiled.

"We like your storms, Sam," Emory cooed. "A half-dozen maybe, in addition to these you already have. How does that sound?"

"Ah, yeah, I mean—when?" Sam stammered. "When are we doing this?"

"How about you get them to me by the last week of January, and we have the show February first?" Emory suggested.

It was a lot, but he could do it. "I'm in," he said, and smiled.

"Wonderful. Oh! Look at those dimples," said Emory. "Gosh, you're easy. Wish all the artists I dealt with were so un-psycho. Hey, maybe we could even have live music for your show, what do you think? It'll be mostly locals who come, I'd imagine. We should make a party of it!"

"I know a musician. She'd be perfect," Sam said quickly, thinking of Kaia's voice and the way it would complement the mood of his work.

"Oh?" Emory said lightly, and he felt Violet's questioning glance. "That sounds great." She reached her long, slender arm to pick her purse up off the table. "Oh, I need you to come up with a title for the show. Okay?"

"Ah… okay," Sam replied, dazed.

Something was missing: a negotiation about prices and percentages, perhaps. He didn't know what the protocol was, and before he could formulate a thought and turn it into something verbal, Emory tossed off a comment about needing to get to dinner in Portland and strode out the door.

"So, that's it? I have a show?" Sam turned to Violet, who stood with her hands on the table, looking at his paintings.

"Congratulations." She smiled slowly, one hand toying with the old-fashioned skeleton key she always wore on a long cord around her neck.

"I had no idea you were so talented, Sam. These are beautiful, really. They belong in a museum."

A sinking feeling anchored itself in his belly. "Do I *have* to name the show?"

Violet laughed. "Oh, stop. That's no big deal. Come on, let's celebrate." She pushed him up against the table and began unbuckling his belt.

"Wait—what if your sister comes back?" Sam protested, pressing his hand over hers.

"She won't."

"Yeah, but—" He glanced around in panic at the wide, un-curtained windows overlooking the harbor. "Maybe we should go on a date, or something," he blurted out.

Violet's eyes widened. "We've been fucking for six months and you're asking me to go on a date *now?*"

He nodded. "Dinner?"

"Okay, Sam. Tomorrow," Violet stated, and continued yanking his belt out of its buckle. "But I need you. Now."

She purred in approval as she stroked him. He shut his eyes and sent himself back to his first waking moments that morning. Violet climbed astride his hips, and as she lowered herself onto him, he envisioned his own boxer shorts wedged into Kaia's butt and throbbed in response.

"Sam, look at me."

But he couldn't. He didn't want to lose hold of the feeling he'd had waking up beside Kaia, spending the morning with her. He tried to imagine her face once more, but instead he only saw the immensity of the sea and himself helpless within its cold embrace. Then, as the automatic and almost painful rush of pleasure shot through every nerve in his body, he saw a flash of a gleaming tail like that of a fish, only much larger and more terrifying.

Chapter Seven

Kaia slept for a good three hours after Sam left. When she woke in the afternoon, she made another pot of coffee and looked out the window over the sink at the spot where she'd dragged Sam to land. The memory of his body floating lifeless made her feel sick. The memory of what she had seen happen to her own body made her feel even worse. Leaning over the sink, she lifted the window, needing fresh air. It creaked on chain pulleys as a gust of wind pushed the curtains back. She salivated at the tangy brine of the ocean.

Go back in the water. See what happens.

No, no. The best thing was to move on, to quit her nonsensical woolgathering and do what needed to be done so she could get back to Nashville and pull her life together.

The breeze blew in again and Kaia lifted her nose to it.

Go on. Find out if you're crazy or not. Get in.

The rocks were jagged as broken ice under her bare feet. Kaia tossed her T-shirt and Sam's boxer shorts onto a bush, along with the cotton blanket she'd had wrapped around her shoulders.

"I am *not* a fucking mermaid," she said between her teeth as she tottered into the ice-cold waves. "What I am is crazy. I'd p-put my money on that." She shivered uncontrollably as she babbled to herself. "I just hope I don't d-d-die."

The frigid water stung her knees and thighs. Her bones ached so intensely there was a moment when she thought she might fall over. She stopped before the water reached her hips. She could no longer feel her feet.

"Not a mermaid," Kaia muttered again as she squirmed away from a wave cresting up to her belly. Then, deciding it was now or never, she plunged in.

The cold knocked the breath right out of her. She remained under as long as she could, but nothing happened except maybe the cold seemed less and less terrible. When she couldn't wait any longer to breathe, she stood up. She felt refreshed and newly centered—if a little frozen—but still completely human.

Determined, Kaia tried submerging herself again. Still, no metamorphosis. Proof she had imagined everything, that her altered perception the night before had been stress-induced. She squeezed her eyes shut and remembered the feeling of being consumed by the water as she sank away from Sam's boat. Terror did a little dance in her chest, spreading like a hatching of arachnids disturbed from their hidden corner.

What are you really afraid of? Give yourself to the ocean; see what you get in return.

The water here was shallow enough for her to get out at any time. All she had to do was stand. This thought settled her enough to push off the rocks and drift a little farther from the shore break.

Breathe.

It went against all instinct. The very thought of it made her heart race. *Breathe. You want this.*

When her body began its involuntary protest, arms and legs flailing, she opened her eyes. Her mouth released a stream of silver bubbles up past her face, toward the light of the surface.

Maybe you've got to let this body die if you want to be reborn as another.

The gentle movement of the tide nudged her closer to land as her feet scrabbled to push off the rocks on the bottom, resisting the current and her intentions. She shook her head back and forth, desperate for breath.

Do not fear pain. Do not fear yourself.

Empty and wanting air, wanting water—at this moment she wasn't even sure which she wanted more—she pushed herself out farther and swam down into the dark green shadows between the weed-covered rocks. Her head felt about ready to burst. She lay on the bottom, where a frightened hermit crab skittered into a plume of bladderwrack. Madly resisting her desire for air, Kaia grabbed hold of the seaweed roots and squeezed her eyes closed as her body thrashed. The underwater sounds surged around her. Kaia felt her own heartbeat disappear within the water's constant swell and she opened her eyes and her mouth.

Now, she told herself, but found herself resisting, her human instincts still in charge. She was about to let go and let herself float upward, when some other, darker part of herself that had kept silent finally spoke.

What do you have to live for? the voice asked.

Dad. He needs me, she thought in reply.

The other inner voice laughed sadly. *He's been checked out since your mother died and he'll drink himself to death before you're thirty-five. Be honest with yourself. You know that the steady job, the happy family, the picket fence, those things will never be yours. And even if they could be, would you want them? You think there's more, and there is.*

Kaia screamed, using air she hadn't known she'd been saving inside her lungs. She inhaled, and the water burned like a snort of wasabi. Then came the rush of energy, bolting through every atom of her being. In that moment she ceased to exist at all and became nothing but the sea herself, blue and endless. Yet at the same time she was so very small, no more than a tiny drop in the great big ocean. She was nothing.

Then, just as suddenly as that sacred nothingness had gripped her in its embrace, she became conscious of herself again. The ocean floor appeared before her: shadows darker, bright spots brighter, the colors of seaweed and rock more vibrant. Far in the bay, sunlight struck a school of fish and turned them to silver.

Something brushed past Kaia's shoulder and she spun around. She realized it had been one of her own fins, and laughed. Powerful and articulate muscles lined her body from the waist down, freeing her to coil and dart, ready to fight. Feeling around her neck and ears, she located two new openings just beneath her jaw, and as she dropped her diaphragm she felt the water being sucked into these tiny apertures. She ran her hands down the sides of the thick, long tail. It had to be at least three feet longer than her legs, and double the mass. Stripes of buff and foxy red marked the scales. She'd never felt more strong, or more beautiful.

In a moment of pure joy, Kaia flipped and spun and swam away from land, celebrating her new body. She only had to spread the wide fin, which she found she could control with just a thought, and as she gently undulated her tail, she found herself moving at a speed that sent her hair flying away from her face and forced her eyelids open.

Out of nowhere, a booming sound hit her whole body with its vibration. Every muscle contracted as she heard the churning sound of a boat engine approaching from the north, heading into Quolobit Harbor. The mid-sized vessel came into view, a ferry perhaps.

"Shit," she said. It came out like a burp.

Kaia turned toward the safety of the cove, where belts of kelp and mossy beds of laver waved among grass-like chains of bladderwrack. Waiting for the boat to pass, she busied herself observing the varied and delicate plant life, making sure her tail did not crest the surface. Small fish and crabs moved in and out of shadows; bright anemone opened questing fingers into the tide.

When the coast was clear, Kaia climbed onto the flat rock in the cove on the northern side of Foley's Point. She lay there in the stinging breeze, gasping, and felt a moment of terror that she wouldn't be able to return to her human form. She'd been betrayed by her body before. Two small surgical scars on her lower belly served as permanent reminders of her mortality.

She rested her hands over the marks and inwardly spoke the mantra that had gotten her through the painful weeks following the surgery that had scarred her.

I am whole. I am safe in this body.

Thankfully, the transition back to her two-legged form was far less traumatic and took only a few moments of breathing dry, frigid air, but she was nevertheless nervous that someone might observe her there on the rocks. As she stood unsteadily and stepped into the galoshes she had worn down to the water, she scanned the ragged edges of the rose bushes for her clothes and the blanket, but didn't see them anywhere. The wind hit her wet, bare skin. She shouldn't be able to cope with this. She should be unable to move, succumbing to hypothermia or worse, and yet she only felt cold—cold enough to hurt, but nothing more. There had to be something supernatural about it. She squinted back toward the tree line, thinking her things might have blown that way.

A dusky shadow moved between the pines and hemlocks.

Kaia felt the electric current of a gaze upon her naked skin. Whatever pervy jokester had thought it would be fun to steal her clothes and watch her would get the fire-crotch he'd come for, she decided, and started up toward the house. Heart pounding in a rush of panic and adrenaline utterly unrelated to the metaphysical transformation her body had just endured, she gave the general area of the woods the middle finger as she began to crunch through the thin crust of snow.

She had half expected to hear a catcall of some kind, but when there was nothing she turned and looked over her shoulder. Between the trunks of two trees, a corner of the blanket flapped then moved out of sight.

Kaia screamed at the top of her lungs. "Hey, asshole! I want that blanket back!"

Then she waited, teeth chattering. He'd want another look, she was sure of that. Who knew how much he had seen? He very well could have seen her in half-fish form down there.

A face appeared between the feathery pine branches. Shadows obscured the details, but the face was oval-shaped, its owner tall, raw-boned, and very pale, with long white hair and strangely colorless eyes. Kaia's heart leaped into her chest. If the person hadn't stolen the blanket and clothes, she would have thought him a ghost.

Now that she believed she was a mermaid, she'd have to believe in ghosts, she thought. She'd have to believe in everything.

"Screw it," she muttered, and started off toward the woods, crunching through the thin layer of snow.

At her advance, the person began to move. Kaia's heart pounded as she entered the forest, somehow keeping her warm from within even as the wintry air burned her naked skin. There *had* to be something about her newfound physiognomy that protected her from cold. Tree branches scraped at her as she chased after the white, fluttering blanket. It went in and out of sight as she trampled north along the coast, the galoshes slapping against the backs of her calves. Kaia came upon the blanket at last, hanging haphazardly from a broken tree branch.

"What the hell?!" she shouted, spinning around and searching for the prankster who had made off with her shirt and Sam's boxers.

Fully flustered, Kaia wrapped herself in the blanket as she started back toward the house. She was within twenty yards of the shed when she noticed the rusted blue pickup parked in the drive.

"Shit," she said, and stopped short as someone dressed in a suit and tie got out of the truck.

It took Kaia a second, but she realized it was Sam Lowell, staring slack-jawed at her. His arms were full of brown paper bags whipping in the wintry wind. In an instant he dropped the groceries into the snow and ran toward her at full bore. Kaia stumbled backward.

"What the hell happened to you?" he asked, his hands on her shoulders, in her icy hair. "Why're you out here like this?"

His eyes scanned her bare legs beneath the blanket and Kaia wrapped it tighter around herself.

"I... I..." She was shivering now. The frailty of her human form had finally caught up with her, it seemed.

"Come on." Sam bent and scooped her into his arms and started off toward the house. "You need to get inside."

Her teeth were chattering so hard now she couldn't bring herself to protest as he trundled her in through the kitchen and up the stairs, where he deposited her in the bathroom. As he bent to fill the tub, Kaia slumped onto the lid of the toilet and watched numbly.

I am a merm—no, I am a siren, she thought, remembering how her mother used to correct her whenever she used the fairytale term.

"But why do you call them sirens, Mommy?" Kaia had asked.

Fiona had answered, "Because they don't like the word *mermaid*."

Kaia had taken that as gospel, never questioned it, and never used the word again. Now, though, she was wondering if her mother had known something about her, something she was only just discovering about herself.

I am a siren. With a tail, fins, gills—everything.

She rubbed behind one ear, finding only smooth skin now.

Sam turned to her, straightening his tie. He looked like a fashion model in that suit, Kaia thought distantly. He tested the temperature of the water with his fingertips. "You get in there and warm yourself up," he said. "I'll leave your duffel bag in the bedroom and fix you something to eat."

✵

After a long soak, Kaia made her way downstairs dressed in a pair of leggings and a baggy sweatshirt. Smells of garlic and tomato filled the house. In the kitchen, Sam had removed his jacket and tie, untucked his shirt, and tied on an apron. He handed her a fresh cup of coffee and, though she'd been fully prepared for it, didn't ask what was wrong with her and why the hell she'd been out swimming in January.

"Feeling better?" His dark eyes were filled with something she couldn't define. Laughter or suspicion, or maybe something else. His gaze lingered in a way that made her squirm.

"Yep." She took a sip of coffee and felt the warmth of it spreading through her. "Smells amazing. What're you cooking?"

"Spaghetti marinara." Sam opened the oven door and Kaia peered inside to see a glass baking dish full of sizzling tomato sauce.

"You make it in the oven?" she exclaimed.

Sam nodded. "Squish up some whole tomatoes, garlic, and anchovy, throw in half a stick of butter and let 'er roast. It's, um, cream and one spoon of sugar, right?" He gestured to the mug in her hands.

"Oh." Kaia sipped the coffee again. It was absolutely perfect. "Yes."

A man who could carry her up a flight of stairs without so much as a grunt. A man who could cook, and remember just how she took her coffee. He couldn't be real. Sam's eyes held hers as he sipped his coffee from a battered blue and white marbled enamelware mug. Kaia let herself gaze directly back, waiting for him to ask why she'd been naked and wet in the woods, challenging him to do so. Instead, he turned and lifted the lid off a pot of boiling water on the stove.

"You must think I'm nuts," she said as Sam sank a generous fistful of pasta into the pot.

He shrugged, his back still to her. It wasn't that he didn't care, Kaia realized with a flash of clarity. It was that he didn't want her asking him questions about himself in return. His secrets were his own and he wanted to keep it that way.

"There was someone watching me," Kaia told him. "Someone creeping around in the woods."

Sam turned around now, his eyes dark as a storm cloud.

"They grabbed my clothes and the blanket and ran off with them. Probably just some perv playing a prank on me while I was..." Kaia paused. Should she say it? "While I was... swimming."

Anybody in their right mind would question the intelligence of swimming in the remorseless North Atlantic in the middle of January, but Sam just swallowed what she had said impassively and gave the pasta pot a stir.

"I left the blanket and my clothes on the rocks and when I came back in they were gone. I saw someone up in the woods with my stuff and ran after them," she said. "But they disappeared."

"Did you get a good look at him?" Sam asked.

Kaia frowned. "Not really. I saw white hair, a pale face. This sounds weird, but... do you know any albinos?"

Sam shook his head.

"I think you coming up the drive must've scared them off," Kaia said, and sipped her coffee.

✍

Sam sure as hell didn't like the idea of someone creeping around Foley's Point and spying on Kaia. A few times he'd been out here to check on things after renters had left and seen evidence of kids messing around on the rocks in the cove, leaving behind beer cans and cigarette butts, but nothing more. Something about what Kaia described made his hair stand on end, his heart beat a little faster.

"I'm guessing you lost your phone last night," he muttered.

"It was in my coat pocket, so I've still got it, but..." Her pretty blue eyes gazed up at him. "It's dead as a doornail. Still got my wallet though. I sure am lucky that's all I lost."

She looked tired. Haunted. Scared. He wished he could put his arms around her and carry her up to that big bed upstairs and—

Quit while you're ahead, buddy, he cautioned himself.

"There's a landline here if you need it," he said, indicating the old pull-cord phone on the wall beside the refrigerator. "I'll leave my number for you."

"Are you leaving?" she asked with a tone of sudden panic.

"Not till I've eaten."

He watched Kaia settle back into her chair, cross one leg over the other, and stare blankly ahead. It all made sense to him now: the fact that she'd been capable of saving him from drowning, the creature he kept seeing in his mind when he closed his eyes, the reason she'd been out swimming— in *January,* for Christ's sake.

She was, like him, more than human.

"You okay?" he asked.

Kaia nodded, her damp curls bouncing. "Fine, yes," she said, clasping her hands around her coffee mug.

She was a bad liar. He liked that about her, too.

"You, um, you have some lipstick on your shirt," she said, wiggling a finger toward her own neck.

Sam looked down and saw a smudge of Violet's nude-toned lipstick on his chest. He snatched up a dishtowel and dampened it to scrub at the stain.

"Girlfriend?" Kaia asked.

Sam shrugged, then turned to the oven to give the sauce a stir. It was almost finished and turning jammy. When his eyes met Kaia's as he was transporting the pasta pot to the sink for draining, she wore an expectant expression.

"I don't know," he blurted out as he dumped the pasta into the colander, the hot steam billowing up around his forearms. "It's not a real relationship," he found himself adding as he tossed the pasta in the colander then dumped it back into the pot.

He brought the pot of pasta back to the oven and caught Kaia shaking her head disapprovingly, rolling her eyes at him. Great. Now she thought he was one of *those guys.* Well, he was one of *those guys,* wasn't he?

Sam clenched his jaw and bent to pull the sauce out of the oven, tossing it into the pasta over low heat. When the sauce and pasta were good and blended, he mixed in parmesan cheese and a handful of chopped parsley.

"This looks amazing," Kaia said as he set a bowl down in front of her. "Thanks for cooking for me."

"You got it," he muttered as he tucked into his own bowl, his belly growling enthusiastically.

They ate in silence for several minutes and Sam was thankful for it. He didn't feel the need to entertain Kaia or explain himself to her. She seemed to be lost in her own thoughts, for that matter, and as hungry as he was.

"This is really good," she muttered eventually, with her mouth full. "Like, restaurant good. Or even better. I mean, it's the *best* spaghetti I've ever had."

Sam smiled. "I usually only cook for myself," he told her, "but it's nice to hear a compliment."

Kaia lifted her brows in appreciation and shoveled another twisted forkful into her mouth.

"Could also be it tastes so good 'cause I'm starvin'," she said, giving him a wink, her sweet little drawl coming out as she teased him.

He shrugged.

"Nah, I'm just pullin' your chain!" she told him, reaching across the table to grab hold of his wrist. Her hand was warm on his skin. "It really is the best spaghetti I've ever had."

Her hand slid away from his but her gaze lingered, questioning, before she went on eating.

Did you see? Did you see what happened to me last night? Her question from that morning came back to him.

He opened his mouth and tried to form his own question. "So, last night, what... what do *you* think happened to you out there?"

Kaia let her fork rest on the edge of the bowl and chewed, eyes large and mournful as the ocean in winter. She swallowed, then wiped her mouth on the back of her hand.

"I was trying to figure that out," she said, licking a spot of tomato sauce off the corner of her lips, "when you showed up here."

"And did you? Figure it out?"

Kaia lifted her shoulders. She blinked at him. "I think so."

"Well, that's good, isn't it?" he asked.

She swallowed again, nervously this time. Shook her head. "I dunno. Maybe not." Her cheeks and nose grew red, her eyes shining like diamonds. "No, it's *not* good." She stifled a sob and clapped a hand to her mouth as tears dropped from her lashes. "I think I'm nuts, Sam. I mean, I think I really lost it."

He shook his head and reached across the table to take both her hands in his. "I doubt that," he said. "Tell me."

Never tell anyone what you are, Sam, his father had warned him. *To do so will lead only to trouble.* How could he ask this of Kaia if he wasn't willing to give her the same?

"It's okay. I'm like you," he said, even though it made his heart pound in terror. Sam drew in a long breath. Was he really about to tell *her*— this woman he had just met not even twenty-four hours ago? "I'm... I'm a selkie."

Kaia said nothing for a moment. Didn't even move. Sam considered running out the door. Then she pressed her lips together thoughtfully.

"A *selkie?*" she murmured. "Does that mean you can turn into a... a seal?"

Sam shrugged. "It's more complicated than that for me, but yes. And, unless I'm wrong, you're a siren."

Kaia's face went pale. She pulled her hands away from his as she stood and knocked the chair over behind her, running out into the hallway bathroom. He heard her puking. Something told him not to go offer to hold back her hair.

Kaia appeared in the kitchen door some minutes later, pale, wiping her face with a dampened hand towel. "I swear, that was still the best spaghetti I ever ate," she murmured.

Her eyes were red-rimmed and filled with tears, but her lips twitched with a smile. He found himself standing and walking around the table. He stopped short before taking her in his arms, afraid of making any assumptions.

"It's gonna be okay," he told her, weakly, wishing he could do more for her.

"Well, shit," Kaia said, laughing and crying at the same time. She threw her arms around his middle and buried her face in his chest.

"I remember the day I found out." He held her closer, cradling her to him. "Worst day of my life."

After a moment, Kaia drew away, looking up at him with her big, brilliant eyes. "Will you tell me about it? All of it?" she asked.

Sam nodded. "What do you say we get a fire going first?"

⁓

"I thought I was going to die out there last night," Kaia said. "When you and I fell in, the water was *so* cold. So cold I could barely move."

Sam grunted in agreement as he stuffed a ball of crumpled newspaper between pieces of kindling in the living room hearth.

"And this one big wave came and pulled me under," Kaia went on haltingly, "and I didn't know which way was up. Eventually, you know, after so long, I had to breathe. And that's when it happened."

Sam looked over his shoulder at her. She was pulling on one curl and staring out the window at the horizon.

"It hurt worse than anything," she murmured, "and then it was over, and I could swim." Her eyes met his. "And I swam to you. I didn't even know what had happened to me, didn't care. It wasn't till I got you on land that I looked at myself and"—she licked her lips and swallowed—"and I saw what I was."

Sam struck a match and turned to watch the flame take. Bending to blow on the flame to give it encouragement, he watched the fire burst into life.

"And today?" he said. "What the hell were you doing out there?"

"Had to see if I was crazy or not," she whispered, eyes big as an owl's.

Sam stifled a smile as he sat on one of the big leather armchairs facing the couch. "And, crazy or not, you're a siren?" he offered.

"Guess so." Kaia laughed and shook her head, drawing her knees up to her chest, wrapping her arms around her shins. She went quiet for a moment, then asked, "What's *your* story? I mean, I think I kinda know, but what *is* a selkie?"

Sam let out a breath. He hadn't talked openly of his nature in so long, it felt foreign to him now. But he remembered the story he'd read about the origin of selkies, and figured it wouldn't hurt him to tell Kaia.

"Well, they're—*we're* rare, for one thing," he said. "More rare even than sirens. They say that the first selkies came from Scotland and Ireland, where people live in a close relationship with the sea. Legend goes that a lonely widow was walking the beach not long after she'd heard of her husband's death, drowning at sea. She came upon a seal. And that seal seemed to know her, to want to speak with her. She believed it to be the spirit of her dead husband in a new form."

Kaia nodded, the firelight catching in her hair and turning it to burning embers. Sam steadied himself and went on.

"The woman fell in love with this seal, and the seal with her. And they had a child. Don't ask me exactly how that happened, a seal and a human. It just did. But instead of being born a human baby, it was a seal pup and he lived with his father. For a while.

"Eventually, the seal-child began to change, to get restless and curious about land. And one day, unable to resist his curiosity any longer, he went to shore and shed his sealskin to find that he was a human. The young man hid his sealskin in a cave and walked until he came to some people in a little village, who gave him clothes and food and taught him how to live.

"But he was never content. That feeling of restlessness, of curiosity, could never be satisfied. So he took his sealskin and moved on. Went to a bigger island, a bigger village. He watched the people there from the sea for a long time, debating whether or not to try his luck among them.

"He was about to move on, when he heard something more beautiful than anything he'd ever heard before. He followed the sound, swimming around the island until he came to a cove, where there was a young woman collecting sea dulse and singing. The seal was drawn in by the sound of her voice and he came closer, wanting to see her face.

"The young woman saw him and walked to the edge of land, singing the whole time. The seal swam to shore, wanting to be near her. They stayed on a rock for hours, just looking at each other.

"He returned the next day, and the next. And eventually, he pulled off his sealskin and revealed himself to the woman he had fallen in love with. The two decided to be married, and the seal gave her his sealskin for safekeeping.

"They were happy for a while, of course, but eventually his old restlessness kicked in. It wasn't that he didn't love his wife, or that he hated being a fisherman—he was good at it and made more money than anybody else on the island—but there was this primal urge, pulling him always back to the sea. At least, that's how I imagine he felt," Sam added.

"Then what happened?" Kaia asked.

"Well, he began looking for his sealskin. His wife told him she'd hidden it away, somewhere he'd never find it because she knew, deep down, that once he did, he'd be gone."

"Let me guess—he found it?"

Sam nodded. "She'd hidden it under the roof thatch. And, one night, he pulled it out and went back to the sea."

Kaia's eyes went wide. "And that's it? That's the end of the story?"

Sam chuckled. "Yeah, as I know it. That's it."

Kaia was quiet, her eyes drifting to the fire. Then she asked, "How'd you end up here?"

"I was born as a seal," he began, pausing for a deep breath. "Then, one day, I became a human."

CHAPTER EIGHT

COLD. BRIGHT. THE rocks had never felt so hard before. The seal felt too weak to fight. He would be safer in the water. He lifted his head and tried to heave himself into motion so he could slide into the water, but his body was too rigid and frail. Coagulated slime coated his eyes, blinding him.

A shadow appeared, a long upright figure moving over the stones. The seal tried harder to move, to get away, to save himself, but he was helpless. He couldn't drag his body anywhere.

As the tall creature approached, the seal turned and nipped at the heavy thing weighing him down. He found it to be his own brindled pelt. The pelt was attached to him still, but sloughing off, sliding over his skinless body. The seal screamed, but the approaching creature wasn't intimidated. It cooed as it teetered toward him.

Needing to clear his vision, the seal struggled to clear the slime from his eyes by rubbing his face on a rock, and succeeded in part, though the barnacles scraped his now-furless skin. He tried to bark as the creature came closer, extending its strange slender limbs. Sunlight caught an object in the creature's hand, and flashed.

The seal smelled the scent of the roses that grew riotous and wild along the coastline, only the scent was stronger than ever before. He thought he'd been wrong about the long creatures: they weren't animals but plants—and this one was a rose. The rose moved closer and uttered meaningless noises. The seal knew his body was destroyed already, so he lowered his head and shut his eyes, hoping his flesh would at least keep this strange rose living for a long time yet.

Then a bolt of pain stabbed his back, slicing along his spine, ripping skin from muscle. He cried out and didn't recognize the sound of his own voice.

The rose ran off with his pelt, hopping nimbly on the boulders between the sea strand and the forest.

The metallic reek of his own blood penetrated his nostrils as the laceration oozed on his back. Knowing he'd go to scavengers and be re-embraced by the infinite, the seal shut his eyes and prepared to go home.

But he woke again when another one of the long, upright creatures pounced on him. This one growled in a low voice and smelled of seawater and fish, quite like a seal itself. The seal lifted his head and cried at this creature, who lifted him fully into the air and then sloshed into the waves. The seal, at first devastated to still be alive within his ruined body, then felt a surge of gratitude for this creature bringing him back to the water, where he might at least die in dignity and return the borrowed form of his body to the sea where it belonged.

Unlike the rose, this creature did not make much noise. It transported the seal into the water, and then, just when it seemed that liquid sanctuary was close, it put the seal into a small boat and brought him to a larger boat that stank of fish blood and gasoline.

Light brown hair covered the head and face of this creature, and its eyes were the color of the sky on a clear summer day. It wrapped the seal in a warm, furless pelt and wiped the seal's face, pulling pebbles and bits of weed from his eyes and mouth. Then it held out a container of water.

The creature advanced and shoved the container into the seal's mouth, forcing him to drink. It wasn't normal water. The seal choked on the saltless substance, but it went down easily and tasted good.

When the seal finished drinking, the creature stepped back from him and bent down to a bucket to pull out a small fish. The seal barked eagerly, and the creature took out a utensil and used it to peel away bits of fish meat.

The seal lay on the floor of the boat and ate the fish as the creature returned to its work, turning the great big wheel this way and that as they rode over the waves, instead of under them. Eventually, they came to a halt and the creature once again approached the seal; only this time it did not lift him into its arms, but tried instead to bring him to an upright stance the same as its own. The creature hauled him on end and dragged him onto an island and into a cabin.

There the creature took care of the seal, gave him more water and fresh fish, and then tended to the wound on his back. It made few noises—quiet, angry growls—and kept silent most of the time.

When night fell, the seal waited until he thought the creature slept. He had made it halfway into the water at the edge of the island when the creature came running out of its dwelling, screaming. It dragged the seal away from the water and pulled him back into the cabin, then did a terrible thing. It tied the seal up, tethering him near the fire, which frightened the seal. He had never seen flame so close up before. But more frightening than the flame was that the line of rope holding him was tied around the ends of two thin, foreign limbs sprouting from his own body, ending in the same splaying digits that the long creature had. He screamed until his throat was raw and he could no longer see straight, and then he fell asleep, blanketed by the warmth of the fire.

CHAPTER NINE

KAIA LOOKED AT Sam leaning with his elbows on his thighs, folding his hands over and over within each other as he stared into the fire. He had told his story without bitterness or resentment, without much emotion at all.

"And that man?" she asked.

Sam drew in a long breath and met her gaze. "That's my dad," he said. "He took me in, taught me how to be a human—or tried to, anyway. I think I'm a slow learner on the subject."

"And what happened to the sealskin?"

"I don't know who has it now, but I think maybe it was a woman who took it," he said with a pensive look as he brushed his fingers over his dark mustache and beard. "It's a curse, you know. Whoever has it can use it to hurt me, if they want to. Stab it and I'll bleed. Touch a match to it and I'll burn."

The room grew cool as the sun began to set. Seeing that the fire was getting low, Kaia got up to add more wood to it. Sam joined her on the hearth rug, kneeling to poke at the smoldering embers.

"I've never told anyone the whole story before," Sam said as an afterthought.

Kaia was aware of his knee touching hers as she watched his thick, strong hands nudging the fire back to life. She put a hand on his shoulder.

"Thank you," she said. "It does make me feel better knowing there are… others."

He dipped his head shyly and nodded. "Before this, you really had no clue you were a siren?"

"No."

She had already racked her brain and had only come up with that time her mother had told her to use the word *siren* instead of *mermaid*. She'd been too young at the time to take much notice of the circumstances surrounding those memories.

Sam added one more log to the fire, then returned to his chair. Kaia missed his closeness. In all honesty, after everything she'd been through, she badly wanted to be held. She sat looking at him for a moment, thinking how good it'd feel to climb into his lap and curl herself into his arms. She thought maybe he was looking at her like he wanted that too, but she couldn't be sure.

He turned and glanced out the window over his shoulder, where white snowflakes danced in the gray. "Damn, these days are short," he said. "I should go before it gets dark."

Kaia sat back on her heels. Her heart picked up its pace. She was scared, she had to admit—scared to be on her own. But she wouldn't ask him to stay. She didn't need a man to make her feel safe, she told herself.

"All right," she said, making her voice light as she stood and dusted the wood shavings off her knees, pulling the stretched-out collar of her sweatshirt tighter around her throat.

"The truck's for you," Sam said as he stood and stretched his long, lean body. "I thought you could use it until yours is out of the shop."

"Oh," Kaia said, surprised.

"You can drop me off down the wharf and keep it till whenever," he said.

✒

Along the way to the wharf, Sam pointed out the real-estate agency where she could list the house, Penfeld's Market, the post office, the gas station, and his favorite coffee shop, The Better Bean. Kaia left him at the parking lot outside the Hook and Anchor and was going to make her way to Penfeld's to buy some groceries before heading home, but she wasn't exactly eager to get back to Foley's Point just yet. It gave her a chill just thinking that she'd be alone in the house all night, twitching at every creak, wondering if the white-haired voyeur would return.

As she scanned for ways to kill time, an old-style apothecary on Main Street caught her eye. She parked Sam's pickup along the street and crossed to the apothecary just as a woman was pushing out a baby stroller. Kaia held the door open for her and smiled down at the tiny bundle in the stroller as the herbaceous scent from inside the apothecary wafted around her.

"Hi there," said a soft, smoky voice when Kaia entered, her eyes still trailing the mother and her tiny baby.

A slender young woman was rearranging a jar of flowers on the counter. She tucked a strand of shiny black hair behind one ear as she smiled at Kaia.

"You still open?" Kaia asked.

"For you, sure." She smiled broadly, her lips perfectly glossed in a petal-soft nude color. "Want to try my lavender and meadowsweet hand salve? I've got a sample going right here."

"Sure," Kaia said, and paused to dip her fingers in the little glass pot the women held out to her. "Smells great," she volunteered.

The woman smiled again as she asked, "How long will you be visiting Quolobit?"

Kaia laughed. "Guess you can tell I'm not from around here."

"Small town." The woman shrugged. "We don't get many strangers in winter."

"I see," Kaia said. There was something she didn't particularly like about the way the woman called her a *stranger*. "I'm staying a few days, maybe a week." She remembered her defunct car and felt her shoulders sink. "Could be longer."

The woman's green eyes narrowed, evaluating Kaia's face. Kaia's skin flashed hot and cold with panic as she suddenly worried that the woman could see through her, *into* her. She was afraid the woman knew that under the image of a normal human there was something else. She was about to turn and begin walking—or running—away, when the woman leaned across the counter and took one of her hands.

"Would you be interested in modeling for me, if you're in town long enough? I've got a line of beauty products and I want to put images on my website." She touched Kaia's hair. "You've got just the look I've been searching for. I've had the worst time finding the right lady." Her smile took on a soft sweetness to it that was almost childlike. Kaia felt guilty for her suspicions. "I'd pay you, of course," the woman added.

Kaia laughed and felt color rising to her cheeks. She had never been singled out for her looks before other than to be teased for her mop of red hair, her plague of freckles. "You want *me* to model for you?"

"Yes. You're perfect as a wildflower. Here, take my card and check out my website. See what you think."

Kaia slipped the card into her back pocket.

"And here, take this lip tint as a gift. It's a new formula I created, colored with beet and alkanet root in a coconut oil base. Good for lips, and cheeks, too."

"Thanks, that's very kind of you," Kaia said, taking the small tin. "And I appreciate the offer to model, but I really don't know if I'll be around. It kind of depends on this real-estate agency. They were closed when I drove by before."

The woman gave a glance out the door to Sam's truck parked across the street, and she clasped a hand around an antique-looking skeleton key hanging from a cord around her neck.

"Do you know what's going on?" Kaia asked.

The woman continued staring out the window, not answering.

"With the realtor?" Kaia clarified.

"Winter in Maine." The woman shrugged. She began taping up a small cardboard box for shipment. "Maybe try calling them."

"Oh! Speaking of calls, do you know where I might be able to buy a cell phone?"

"Without going inland, your choices are slim," the woman replied. "Maybe try Dunne's Hardware on Milk Street."

Kaia nodded. Sam had pointed out Milk Street when he'd shown her where the market was.

"What house are you trying to sell?" the woman asked, furrowing her alabaster brow.

"It's the one out there on the Point," Kaia said. "Foley's Point. I'm Kaia Foley, by the way," she said, and offered her hand.

"Violet Wilde." Her handshake was cool, but firm. Her green eyes leveled with Kaia's and her lips spread in a perfect smile. "It's nice to meet you, Kaia."

Kaia left the apothecary with her free gift of lip stain, feeling a little squirmy. There was something about Violet she didn't like, but she couldn't put her finger on it. As Kaia climbed into Sam's truck to make her way to the market, she glanced back at Wilde's apothecary and saw Violet looking out the window, lifting her hand to wave. The woman was harmless, obviously. It was Kaia who was paranoid and whacked out of her mind.

After stopping at the market for yogurt and fruit and a bottle of locally-made kombucha, among other things, Kaia decided to skip the search for a cellphone at the hardware store and head back to the Point. She wanted to get there before all the light was gone from the sky, and she was cutting it close.

Before heading into the house, she braved the wind and flying snow and went to the shed to add more wood to the furnace. The fireplace in the house would only get her so far, Sam had told her before they left the Point. He had made sure the furnace was running hot before leaving, and Kaia dumped a half dozen logs inside before banking it for the night, like he'd shown her.

After heating up some leftover spaghetti, Kaia made tea and sat by the fire in the living room as the night came. The darker it got, the more vividly she could visualize the person in the forest—the white and stark face with gaping eyes and mouth, long limbs moving at ungainly angles.

❧

Only firelight lit the living room when Kaia woke at the sound of a noise. She was so tired she could barely bring herself to open her eyes, but something had dragged her out of her slumber. Forgoing the big lonely bed upstairs, she had let herself fall asleep on the yellow velvet couch in front of the fire, wrapped in a fluffy gray blanket, her head propped on a down-filled pillow.

She wasn't used to the quiet or the darkness here. Her apartment in downtown Nashville had been bathed by yellow street lamps all night long, the sounds of cars and late-night revelers passing under her window till the early hours of the morning. It wasn't exactly silent out here, though, she noted. The sound of the ocean crashing was constant, soothing in one way, disturbing in another. But that wasn't what had woken her.

She sat up and felt her skin prickle. In the dimness of the living room stood a lanky, swaying figure. Long white hair hung over her bare breasts. Her long, lean arms hung slack, hands not bothering to cover her nakedness. Kaia screamed as she met the woman's large, staring eyes.

The naked woman turned and ran upstairs. Kaia's belly twisted in fear and sweat prickled her hands as she made herself perfectly still, straining to listen over the pounding of her heart. The boards overhead creaked with the weight of the woman running down the hall.

When there was a moment of eerie quiet, Kaia got up and dashed for the phone in the kitchen. Something told her the cops wouldn't be helpful in this situation, so she dialed the number Sam had left scrawled on the fridge.

He answered quickly, but sounded like he'd been asleep. "Yeah?"

"Sam, it's me, Kaia," she said into the phone, her hands trembling. "I need you here."

She told him about the intruder. After hanging up the phone, she went out into the cold and locked herself into the truck, waiting for the lights of Sam's boat to cross the dark expanse of the water. Eventually he appeared over the edge of land, dressed in a parka and jeans tucked into tall rubber boots. Kaia slid out of the truck as he strode toward the house.

"What're you doing?" she demanded.

"Going in there," he told her, not slowing down as he took the porch steps, his voice swept away by the wind.

The cold bit Kaia's cheeks and fingertips, her stockinged feet, as she scampered after him. If he was going inside, then so was she. Sam went straight in and headed upstairs, flicking on the light in the master bedroom.

The woman stood in the middle of the room, glancing back and forth between Kaia and Sam with cagey, dark eyes. Her long, sinewy legs were covered in moony down. Her hair, a faintly greenish white, went to her hips. She picked up a fire poker from the hearth with thin fingers, revealing pointed, claw-like nails, and bared her teeth.

"Sam, be careful." Kaia gripped the sleeve of his jacket.

Sam took one step closer and the woman opened her mouth and let loose a high-pitched, inhuman scream. Kaia felt it through her eye sockets. She choked on it. The woman screamed again.

"I think she feels cornered," Kaia said, and stepped aside to the wall of the hallway, pulling on the back of Sam's jacket.

Letting the poker clatter to the floor, the woman ran past them in a white blur. Sam gave Kaia a wide-eyed glance, then followed the intruder down the stairs and out through the kitchen door. They stood on the back porch and watched her run over the rocks, fall—hard—then get back up and splash her way into the water. She threw herself into the waves and disappeared into the foam.

When several minutes had passed and the white head did not surface for air, Kaia turned to Sam.

"She's like me... isn't she?" she murmured.

"Seems so."

"Under any other circumstance, I'd say we need to inform the police that somebody escaped the loony bin and is now putting herself and others in danger," she said, "but in this case I'm afraid that if we do call the cops, I'll be the one who ends up in psychiatric evaluation."

Kaia felt the earth spin beneath her feet as Sam put an arm around her. He led her inside, closed the back door and locked it.

"I can stay a while," he said, "if you want."

Kaia nodded. "Thanks. I'd feel better having you here."

This time she didn't resist her need to be held. She went to him and wrapped her arms around his middle, pressed her cheek into his chest as he folded her into his embrace. She let the tears come, let herself tremble and sob, and all the while he held her, murmuring that it would be okay. She had soaked through the flannel of his shirt when she became aware of the soft warmth of his breath in her hair, the bristle of his beard and the pressing of his lips against her forehead.

"I only met you yesterday," she said into his chest when she could speak again, "but I feel like you're the only person on Earth who really knows me."

Sam chuckled, a low, pleasant rumble under her cheek. His big hands cradled her closer and she felt herself wanting more of him, wanting less clothing between them. "Yeah, well, I've gotta say, my life has gotten a whole lot more interesting since you came to town."

"I'm sorry," she said, pulling back and wiping her nose on the tattered cuff of her sweatshirt.

"Don't." Sam cradled her face in his hands. "Don't apologize."

His gaze dipped for a moment to her lips and Kaia felt it there, almost as good as kiss. She felt the deep, humming warmth of desire fill her body like she was melting from the inside out. If he wasn't so damn tall, she would've kissed him herself by now.

She took a step closer and felt her breasts brush his body, felt his heat radiate through his clothing. Sam dipped his head to hers and shut his eyes as he brushed her lips with his. His lips were cold, dry, chapped. He pulled away an inch and licked them, bit them till they were warm and soft, then leaned in again. He touched his lips softly, questioning, to one side of her mouth and just stayed there, very still, as though he was waiting to see what she might do.

Kaia breathed him in. He smelled like the fresh salt air and hand-made soap scented with sandalwood, patchouli, and lavender. His beard was rich and thick under her hands as she touched his face. He pressed her hard against him with a hand to the small of her back and all the fear melted out of her, replaced by desire for him, an ache she was suddenly desperate to soothe.

She stood on her toes, arching her back as she kissed him in return. A low moan escaped his lips, his breath rushing past her own lips as she sucked in a deep lungful.

"Kaia—"

She wasn't sure if he was saying her name in protest, if he'd tell her they'd only just met and that this was crazy, but she didn't care. It seemed he didn't either, as he pulled on her lower lip, asking her to open more for him. His tongue slid slowly, achingly slowly, against hers and she felt her knees tremble beneath her. Just that gesture had her burning straight to her core.

He came willingly with her when she pulled him toward the kitchen table. She sat on top of it and wrapped her legs around him. Gripping the firm muscles of his bottom through the denim of his jeans, she pressed him closer as he leaned over her and kissed her deeper, his mouth soft but demanding.

∽

"Hang on a second." Sam drew away from her. It took every ounce of his willpower to do so. He was pulsing and throbbing for her from his head to his toes. He could easily yank down those leggings of hers right then and there, bury himself in her until he forgot his own name.

Kaia lifted her brows and bit on her lower lip. "The girlfriend?" she asked.

Sam drew away, gripping his cock and adjusting himself through his jeans to ease the strain and his raging need. He couldn't think straight in this state.

"No," he said. "Not really." He swallowed, hard. His pulse battered his temples and balls. His stomach ached for Kaia.

"*Not really?*" Kaia pushed her legs together and slid off the top of the table.

This wasn't going the way he would have wanted. He could feel the situation spinning out of control. Himself, spinning out of control.

"I don't *love* her," he said, too loud. Kaia's eyes went wide as she sank into a chair. He might as well say the rest of it, he thought. "Not like I think... I could love you."

Her eyes lifted to his; her soft lips opened. She blinked. "Oh," she said, quietly. Her plump, cute little hands folded on each other over the rough table-top.

Shocked by what he'd just said aloud, Sam went to the sink and poured himself a glass of water. He drank it down before turning back to her. His heart was still pounding, though now it was with something other than desire.

"You terrify me," he confessed.

Kaia gaped at him. "*Me?*"

Sam braced himself on the back of a chair at the end of the table. "I don't know if this is the best way to explain it, but ever since I came to live on land, I've wanted nothing else other than to go back to the water," he said. "I told myself I'd get there someday, and that until I did I wouldn't let myself become too rooted here."

She pressed her lips together in a line and nodded slowly.

"I'm afraid you're gonna take this to mean I don't want to invest in a relationship," he said. "And a day ago, that would've been true."

Her ruddy brows drew closer over the bridge of her freckled nose.

"But now, I'm thinking everything could change," he said, his hands sweating as he gripped the chair. "And that's probably a lot for you to take in, just meeting me."

She shook her head. "No, Sam, I get it. I showed up here yesterday and threw your life into a tizzy. My own, too. You've got something goin' on with someone else and you need to sort that out."

"But it's not just that," he said, eager to make himself clear. "I think that this—me and you—this is something… different." He shook his head, frustrated with his lack of words.

Don't be a cornball and say it's special.

"Something *better*," he tried. "Better than anything else. Maybe even better than—" Could he really say it, say that what he had felt kissing her just now was better than being a seal in the water? Could he admit that she held more power over him than the entire ocean?

"Sam, you don't have to explain."

Kaia came to him and took hold of his shirt collar in a way that made him ache to kiss her again, to feel that velvet-soft mouth—

He contented himself with putting his hands into the warm wool of her wild red curls. She sighed, frowning.

"I got my heart blown to pieces six months ago," she confessed. "I'm in no rush, really." Her eyes narrowed. "Especially if you're involved with someone else."

"Okay." Sam contented himself with rubbing his hands through her hair, feeling the contours of the back of her head, the warmth of the nape of her neck. "No rush," he whispered.

Her fingers gripped the fabric of his shirt as she shut her eyes again, bending her head back at his touch like a cat. A wicked little smile came over her lips.

"But, dammit! I want you, Sam," she said, and stood on her toes to kiss him again.

She sucked and nibbled on his lips and pulled him by the shirt into the living room, where they fell onto the couch. He gathered her on top of him, letting his hands take in the shape of her full thighs under the soft fabric of her leggings, the roundness of hips and ass, the gentle give of her waist.

He was so hard for her it hurt. Tumbling closer, the shadowed curls of her sea-scented hair curtaining their faces, she kissed him, grinding into him until he thought he'd burst.

Fuck it. I can't wait. Can't be patient. Not about this.

He was about to reach between their bodies to unbuckle his belt when she pulled away and retreated to perch at the far end of the couch, biting her lips and pressing her fingers to her cheeks as she stared at him. She shook her head, laughing wryly.

"No, no, no," she said, maybe to herself. "Despite what it feels like, I only just met you yesterday."

"Yes. You did." Sam sat up and straightened his clothes, pulling his flannel discreetly over his lap. One of them had to be rational, and apparently it was her turn.

"You've got… someone," Kaia added.

Sam nodded, reluctant. "Sort of."

"Yeah… that's weird. And I don't really know you."

"You know my deepest secret," he told her, like that would justify his wanting to take her to the big bed upstairs and rock her till they both fell asleep, lost in each other.

"And you know *my* deepest secret," she said, letting out an adorable series of short, exasperated pants. "But I only just learned it myself. It's all new. A lot to take in."

Sam nodded, tried to deepen his breath and slow his racing heart. "No, it's better if we... don't."

Kaia's gaze drifted to the dying embers in the grate and a pensive silence settled between them. Sam got up and told her he was going outside to make sure there was no one hanging around, and to add more wood to the furnace.

Once he was out in the bracing cold he felt his head clearing like the sky overhead, brushed clean by the wind. The stars shone like hard little diamonds stuck into black velvet. Gazing up at the Milky Way, tears came into his eyes. He told himself it was just the cold wind, but that wasn't all it was. He was happy and terrified and felt more alive than he had in the fifteen years he'd spent in this flawed human body.

When he was good and done with his tears and had the furnace cranking, he came back inside to find Kaia curled up on the couch, a blanket drawn around her.

"Go up to bed," he told her with a touch to her shoulder. "Get some rest."

Kaia sat up, bleary-eyed. She reached for his hand. "Will you come?" she asked. "Just to sleep, I swear."

Sam shook his head, laughing. "Don't tell me you actually think that'll be possible," he replied, knowing himself well enough. "I'll stay down here, keep a lookout."

Kaia stood and stumbled into his arms, lifting her head with a sleepy smile. He gave her one chaste kiss on the forehead, inhaling the delicious scent of her hair, before gently pushing her toward the hallway.

CHAPTER TEN

"Any more naked ladies running through the house in the night?" Kaia asked when she came into the kitchen the next morning.

Sam stood leaning against the counter with a cup of coffee in hand, his jeans and white undershirt wrinkled. Kaia could tell from his body language and the fact that he hadn't so much as put a piece of bread in the toaster that he was planning on leaving the house early.

The heated closeness that had been between them last night was gone, replaced by an awkward sense that they were little more than strangers who had shared one or two weird experiences together.

"You want breakfast?" she asked. "I've got yogurt, oatmeal—"

Sam shook his head and set down his mug in the sink. "I've gotta take care of some things today," he said, his face guarded.

Kaia felt her heart sink. Maybe they'd just gotten carried away last night, caught up in the chaos. Maybe he was regretting the things he'd said to her. *I don't love her. Not the way I could love you.*

She hovered at the opposite end of the kitchen table, afraid to get any closer to him, afraid he'd see how her emotions were boiling up inside her. She dipped her head and looked down at her stockinged toes. Her feet were cold, even through the thick wool.

"Okay, well, I'll see you around," she said, trying to be casual as Sam went to retrieve his jacket by the door. "I'll let you know as soon as my car's ready so you can have your truck back."

Sam came to her and put his wide, warm hands on either side of her face. A smile spread on his lips, his dark eyes sparkling beneath the sweep of his brows. "I'd like to come back here later and check on you, if that's okay," he said.

A tingle of pleasure radiated through her at his closeness and she felt it morphing dangerously into that tidal pull she'd felt for him the night before. "Oh, sure," she said, breathless. Then, chancing it, "Maybe... I'll make dinner?"

Sam smiled wider. "That sounds great." He rumbled with a low, satisfied chuckle that was really more like a purr and pulled away, cheeks dimpled.

Kaia was all but squirming. She gripped the edge of the table as he made his way to the door. What a fine man he was, so tall and lean, his hair thick and dark, eyes always holding some hidden light. And, maybe, just maybe, he'd be *her* man. The mere thought was enough to make her want to squeal with glee.

"See you later," she said, just managing to contain herself as she waved him off.

Once he was out the door she ran to the windows in the living room and watched him make his way down the wooden steps to the raised dock on the southern side of the point, making certain he didn't go overboard in the short journey between there and where the *Angeline* was moored.

CHAPTER ELEVEN

VIOLET WILDE STOOD at her kitchen window with a cup of tea going cold in her hands as she gazed at the icy harbor. The *Angeline* was there, moving away from Foley's Point, where she'd been moored at dawn when Violet had gotten up to practice yoga.

Kaia Foley.

Kaia Foley.

Kaia Foley.

The name rang in her head like a tolling bell. Violet knew that in addition to Sam taking care of the house and property on Foley's Point during the summers when it was rented to vacationing families, he occasionally went there to paint in the mornings.

Best view of the sunrise in the whole country, he'd say.

Was that what he'd been doing at Foley's Point this morning? Working on something new for his show? Maybe. But that wouldn't explain why she'd seen *Angeline* moored at the Point yesterday morning, too. Or why Kaia Foley was driving Sam's truck around Quolobit Harbor.

"Don't jump to conclusions."

Emory's voice gave Violet a start. Her tall, blonde twin sauntered up to the coffee machine and began making her morning latte. Violet let her gaze drift back to Sam's boat, coursing toward Thursday Island. She felt him slipping away from her.

CHAPTER TWELVE

WHEN SAM WAS safely on his way back to Thursday Island, Kaia turned and set her hands on her hips. There was plenty yet to be explored in the house, plenty that needed a little TLC, and she had the time. As she started straightening the living room, patting the striped pillows on the couch and folding the fluffy knitted blanket, it hit her with a pang—she hadn't realized just how hard it would be to sell the place.

Foley's Point was more beautiful than she had remembered. On top of that, she now felt that the ocean might become an integral part of her future. And, she had to admit to herself, meeting Sam had also made her want to change her plans.

She released a long sigh as she crouched to sweep ash and wood particles from the granite hearth. She'd be crazy if she let a man she'd only met two days ago have that kind of power over her. Maybe it was good that he had left early this morning. She needed time to cool off, to think. Maybe when she saw him again later she wouldn't be so taken with him. There had to be something about him that would turn her off—a nasty habit, a personality dysfunction of one kind of another (hey, everyone had them). Or maybe it would be something else. Like she'd realize she didn't like his smell. She would realize how silly she'd been to think of herself as falling for the fisherman whose life she had saved.

It was understandable that they might think they had some kind of connection, considering their near-death experience, along with the fact that they had shared a strange truth with each other. They had let themselves get caught up in it. Understandable, yes. Reasonable, no.

She moved on to the second story. A mess of vines covered the windows in one of the spare bedrooms overlooking the northern edge of the property. Peering through the tangle of leafless, thorny vegetation that looked to be roses, she took in the breathtaking view of rugged rock and the wall of towering pines buffering the land from the ocean's wild winds. The gray-blue waves came in choppy, sweeping shapes fringed with lacy white, hitting the rocks with a never-ending show of froth.

Kaia's skin tingled at the sight. Her mouth watered. She pressed her fingers to the cold, frost-rimed glass. She wanted to go out there again.

Was she nuts? It couldn't be more than twenty degrees outside. Yet there it was, the undeniable urge to get out there and swim.

Maybe later, she told herself, not wanting to risk another encounter with her white-haired friend.

After making up the bed in the master bedroom, she took a bath—perfect with a pile of bubbles filling the big old claw-footed tub and an orange-blossom-scented candle from Wilde's apothecary—then made a list of things to get in town.

Kaia gazed in the mirror of the thrift store as she held up a big Irish cable-knit sweater. Her clothes weren't meant for Maine winters, and she was frankly tired of feeling cold. Staring now at her mass of red curls, her freckled cheeks, her wide blue eyes, she told herself, *I am a siren.*

In some way she felt her body had kept a secret from her, a kind of betrayal. Tears of anger stung her eyes. The tiny, twin scars on her lower belly tingled suddenly, reminding her that she'd been angry at her body before.

I am whole, she reminded herself.

Angry or not, she had to take care of her body and keep it warm. She bought the big sweater and a pair of flannel-lined boots the lady behind the counter called 'Bean Boots', along with an oversized green wool hat and a pair of mittens to match.

After donning her new acquisitions awkwardly in the parking lot beside

Sam's rusty truck, she drove to the hardware store feeling a sense of self-satisfaction that at least now she looked like a proper Mainer. One sentence out of her Southern mouth and anybody'd know otherwise, of course.

Brushing past a drooping Christmas wreath, she walked into the hardware store, and a handmade sign taped to the side of the front counter caught her attention. Purple marker depicted a wind turbine in the ocean; the word *PROTEST* was scrawled in giant letters at the top. Scratchy ballpoint pen at the bottom of the page gave details for some kind of meeting. Though the poster looked like it had been drawn by a kid, the words seemed serious.

Save Our Water, it read. *Don't let big corporations take Wapomeq Bay away from us.*

"Good morning," the woman behind the counter said. Her rich, dark skin gleamed beneath intricately braided hair piled high on the top of her head like a crown. "Looking for something particular?"

"What's this about?" Kaia asked, tapping the handmade poster.

The woman sighed. "My daughters made that. There's some big corporation saying they're going to build a wind farm out there in Wapomeq Bay," she explained. "Claudette and Tessa want to fight it."

"And you?"

"Me?" The woman let out a short hoot of a laugh. "I'm fighting to get their laundry done, their bellies fed, and trying to keep this store up and running. I haven't put a thought to it. Doesn't seem serious yet, anyway. Town hasn't voted yet."

"Oh." Kaia frowned at the drawing of the wind turbine with several bloodied birds hacked to pieces strewn around it. "When's the vote happening?"

"End of the month, I think," the woman said.

Kaia turned to look at the store's quaint, cluttered interior. The space was narrow with ancient wooden floorboards, every inch packed with goods ranging from building tools to good-luck charms. A fat white cat appeared from an aisle. It rubbed its face on Kaia's ankle and then tumbled to the floor at her feet, trying to seduce her into petting it.

"Do you have cellphones?" Kaia asked.

The proprietress shook her head and sighed. "No, sorry. You'd have to drive to Rockport or Camden. You need to call someone? You want to use my phone, honey?"

"Oh, no. That's all right." Kaia knelt to rub the cat behind its head. "What a sweet kitty you've got."

The woman's amber eyes held Kaia's for a long moment. She seemed to be considering something that had nothing whatsoever to do with cell-phones. Or friendly felines.

"Well… how about house paint?" Kaia asked as the woman continued staring. "I've got some floor moldings that are pretty scuffed up."

She blinked, then pointed a finger adorned with a gigantic garnet ring. "First aisle to the left, halfway down, middle shelf. Under the romance novels and next to the rabbit feet."

The cat mewed in protest as Kaia stood. She skirted a container of float-ing noodle toys, went past an array of incense and burners, and found the paint supplies exactly where the woman had said they'd be, next to a bin of rabbit feet. She picked up two small cans of paint, a brush, and some tape.

"I see you," the woman said, lifting one arched brow as Kaia set her items on the counter.

Kaia turned to look behind her at the cat, slinking around a container of live bait fish.

"No, no. I see *you*." The woman pointed her finger at Kaia. "*Siren*."

"What…?"

"Siren. Descendant of the ancient deity Atargatis, I think, by the looks of you." She eyed Kaia. "The siren clan out there in Wapomeq Bay will want to know why you're up here walking around on land."

"Excuse me?" Kaia took a step back from the counter.

A clan of sirens… that would explain my stalker.

"Oh, come on now. Don't look at me like I'm off my rocker, because we both know you're not straight-up human." She cast a discriminating eye at the screen of her register. "That'll be fourteen dollars and seventy-two cents, sweet pea."

Kaia fumbled with the zipper of her jacket pocket, digging to find the cash while her mouth chewed on a number of responses. Just then, a tall willow-branch of a girl with swinging braids appeared from a side door and leaned against the counter, dressed in fashionably ripped-up jeans and a soft, gray, cropped sweater that showed just an inch of tawny skin. The girl gave Kaia a longer-than-polite look before addressing the woman at the counter.

"Mama, can I go get hot cocoa with Justin now, puh-*lease?*" she whined dramatically. "I washed the dishes, I put Tessa's peepee sheets in the machine, *and* I'm done studying for my chem test."

"I'm grilling you tomorrow," her mother responded sternly. "Be back by three o'clock this afternoon or you're not doing doodly-squat next weekend. You understand, Miss Claudette?"

"Yes, Mama." The girl grabbed a jacket from behind the stairwell door and exploded out of the store.

"Goodness me. I'm thirty-four and that girl has me feeling like forty-eight." She took the money Kaia offered and put it in the register. "You got kids?"

"Ah, no," Kaia said, and glanced at the beautiful girl running down the sidewalk, away from the store.

"Name's Felicia Dunne, by the way."

Kaia uncertainly shook Felicia Dunne's offered hand. "I'm… Kaia Foley."

"Foley, of Foley's Point, I assume." Felicia walked around the counter, examining Kaia over the rims of cat-eye tortoise-shell glasses. "Your people haven't been up this way since at least the mid-nineties, as the local lip-flappers tell it. Oh, now, don't look at me like that. It's just that that old house on Foley's Point is a landmark. People always ask about it. So, don't you know yourself, siren?"

Kaia could only open her mouth and close it again.

Felicia shrugged. "It's all right; you don't know what to say. You're scared, but you don't need to be afraid of me, and there's no one else in here to hear what we're talking about. I'm able to see things other people don't, or won't. Seeing the other side is in my blood."

"So, when you say you *see* me, you mean…"

"I mean I *feel* you, I get a sense about you," Felicia explained. She lifted a shoulder. "Like gaydar."

"Oh." Kaia felt light-headed.

Felicia frowned and put a hand on Kaia's shoulder. She clucked gently.

"As a siren, you're an *elemental*. You're precious and rare, like Mami Wata—the water spirit—and dangerous, some say." Felicia grinned, and shrugged again. "Dangerous to men, at least."

Siren. Kaia felt the world collapsing in on her as tears gathered in her eyes. *I am a siren.* It somehow felt more real now that she and Sam weren't the only two people who knew.

"I, um, I only just found out," she murmured to Felicia, gripping the edge of the polished wood counter. "It's been a long time since I've been to the ocean."

Felicia nodded, her dark, sculpted face shining with sympathy. "It's been with you all this time, though, hasn't it?"

When she had been little, and when she had been a teenager, and actually, always—Kaia had dreamed of the ocean. Felicia Dunne was right. The ocean and this siren thing had been waiting under her skin, asleep inside her all along.

You're just homesick, her father had whispered when she'd woken in the night as a kid, talking about the waves. He'd tell her maybe they'd take a trip to the Carolinas someday, when he got the money. Maybe Florida. They'd take a swim in the deep blue sea. They'd snorkel and scuba and find a sunken ship full of treasure. He'd tell her a story of his own childhood in Maine until she fell asleep again, and went back to dreaming about weightlessness in the blue…

They never did go to the ocean. Even when her dad had had the time off, they'd go set up camp somewhere out in the country and fish their way up a river. Kaia had always loved the water then, but not like she did now.

"Yes, I guess you're right," she said. "This, um, thing… about me… it *has* been with me all this time."

"You come by any time you need to." Felicia gave a gentle smile as she rubbed Kaia's arm. "I'm always here. Me and my girls live upstairs. You come by anytime you need anything—I mean it."

Shaken by being called out and reminded of her new self-discovery, Kaia thanked Felicia in a daze and walked out of the store, wondering if her father had known about her all along and, if he had, why he'd kept her away from the ocean all this time.

Chapter Thirteen

It was ten minutes after five when Sam walked into the apothecary to find Violet dressed in a navy blue sweater dress with leather knee-high boots that looked like they had been hand-polished by a team of seventh-generation Italian leatherworkers. She was vigorously wiping down the glass countertop with a white cloth, her hair and silver bangle earrings swinging.

"Oh, hey," she said, off-handedly, like she had forgotten he was coming.

"You said five." Sam stopped at the edge of the mat at the door, not wanting to track the floor with the salty slush encrusting his galoshes.

Violet scowled down at his footwear. "Did I?"

"I'm a few minutes late," he admitted, shoving his hands into his coat pockets. Sometimes he'd take his coat off and hang it on the rack and she'd flip the sign on the front door to *Closed* and they'd lock themselves in the back room for half an hour. Today he kept it zipped and buttoned, the cold still lingering around his shoulders like a heavy cloak.

"I, ah, need to talk to you, Violet."

Her bright green eyes shot to his. She stopped wiping the counter.

Sam had been prepared to feel anxious entering this conversation, but for some reason he didn't feel nervous now. Maybe it was the fact that he knew he'd be eating dinner in Kaia Foley's kitchen tonight, and the deep sense of peace and simple happiness that gave him was more valuable than any quick thrill he'd ever had with Violet.

"I can't do our date today," he said.

"Okay, whatever." She moved like a dancer as she went to wipe down a table in the center of the shop. "Why don't you kick off those boots," she said, without looking at him.

"No, I gotta head out." He stepped in and took hold of her shoulder.

She scoffed at his feet leaving scummy tracks across the newly cleaned wood floor.

"Sam, come on!" she scolded.

He stepped back onto the mat, mumbling an apology. He wanted to say: *It's over between us and I wanted to tell you, officially, even though it was never that serious.* But he couldn't. It wasn't the right time. Or the right place. He hadn't really thought it through.

"So are you going to move to Tennessee with her once she's sold the house on Foley's Point?" Violet asked, not pausing in her work, tidying a jar of bath bombs. "Think you can live in a landlocked state, Sam Lowell?"

He gaped at her, unnerved by the triumphant smugness on her face. She crossed her arms over her chest and shook her long, dark hair over her shoulders.

"Where are you getting all of this?" he asked.

The sound of her laughter made him cringe. "Quolobit Harbor is a small town, Sam. There's a jalopy with Tennessee plates parked at Murphy's shop, the *Angeline* was moored at Foley's Point this morning and yesterday morning, and if that wasn't enough, a perky little redhead bumbled in here yesterday after pulling up in *your* truck." Violet lifted her brows victoriously. "I'm guessing she doesn't know about me."

Sam flinched. "I don't know what you're talking about," he said. Deferring to absolute denial was his first course of defense, though probably not the smartest in the long run. "She's a friend," he said. That was a lie, sort of. Friends didn't kiss and leave each other panting like he and Kaia had.

"You and I *did* start things out very casually." Violet shrugged as she walked closer. "Treated it like it wasn't serious. At least half of that was my own fault, wasn't it?" All of her glib acceptance evaporated. Her lips trembled, eyes brimming. "Please give me a chance?"

Sam rested his hands on her shoulders. "Violet." He wanted to tell her it was too late, that he'd already let someone else into his heart, but he couldn't speak the words. He didn't want to give her that knowledge. Not yet, anyway.

"I used to think I wanted to get out of this town, you know," she went on, at the edge of tears. "I wanted something bigger, better for myself. I never imagined that I could have this business and that it would do so well here and online, or that I'd actually come to love Quolobit as much as I do, or... meet someone like you."

Sam sighed, a small part of his resolve deflating inside his chest.

"I mean, not that I just *met* you," she said, brushing away a stray tear. They had known each other since they were teenagers, albeit circumspectly. She sniffled. "And now that you've got this show coming up and you asked me to go on a date, like a real date, it made me think you wanted this to be more serious." Her large eyes widened as she looked up. Her low, smoky voice was quiet and hypnotic. "Can you *please* not cancel our date? Can you give me the chance I deserve?"

Chapter Fourteen

Kaia drove back to Foley's Point after picking up everything she'd need to make sushi at Penfeld's Market, which she had found to be surprisingly well-stocked. She called her father as soon as she walked inside, palms itching with sweat as she sat at the kitchen table, bouncing her knees in anticipation. The phone rang. And rang. And rang.

"H-hello." Not a cheery greeting.

Kaia could tell from that one word that Hank Foley was well into his daily six-pack, and possibly on to the whiskey that often followed. In the background was the sound of a football game on TV.

"Who's there?" Hank blustered. "If this is one of you idiots from the—"

Kaia hung up. She couldn't talk to her father about her being a siren when he was in this state. She was half tempted to call him again and give him a piece of her mind for getting trashed all by himself, but no. She'd been there too many times and was wise enough to know there was no point in wasting her energy.

Instead, she walked a pathless mile over snow-crusted rocks and through dense trees, hoping to distract herself until Sam arrived for dinner. The property of Foley's Point neighbored state land, and from where Kaia stood there was not a single house to be seen. That total privacy would be a selling point, she thought, and made note of it as something to mention it to the realtor, once she finally called their office.

She stood on a rock at the edge of the water, on the northern-most border of the property where a river emptied into the tide. God, she wanted to get into that water. No—she needed to. Her ears began to ring. Her eyes watered. Her skin burned.

Don't deny your truth. It'll make you sick.

She clambered over the rocks toward the water, removed her clothes, and got in. The transition hurt less this time, and seemed to happen faster than previously. Maybe she was getting good at this. As she swam out toward the beckoning darkness, the water became deeper and, oddly, warmer against her skin. Far beyond where she could see, she heard the chatter of porpoises.

If she ran into the other siren, maybe this would be an opportunity to introduce herself properly, and have a little chat about boundaries. Could she even speak in this state? Curious, Kaia drew in as much water as she could and opened her mouth to let out a *Hey!*

A long, high-pitched squeal came out instead.

Shocked and somewhat embarrassed, though there was no one to hear, Kaia tried to vocalize again. She only managed a series of unintelligible chirps. Wondering if she could control her pitch, Kaia opened her mouth and began to sing the lilting melody of an Irish ballad, and found, to her relief, that singing came a hell of a lot easier than speaking. She still couldn't quite get words out, but melody and rhythm were no problem.

So she sang and swam, flipping and turning, shooting in and out of the shadows, twisting to look at the splendor of her tail. It was nothing like any artist's interpretation she'd ever seen. She reminded herself more of a dragon than a fish. A sea dragon. The idea made her laugh, and she let out a strange, musical sound.

Suddenly, a flash in the water caught her eye. Kaia remained motionless. She hadn't even thought about predators until this moment, she realized as she watched the darkness beyond, waiting for whatever was out there to reappear. If she wanted to swim like this she ought to at least have something to defend herself with. The ocean was a wilderness, after all.

Just as she turned for land, something slammed into her back and cracked into her right shoulder blade. Before she could move in reaction, she found herself pinned face-down into the rocks with her own blood and something white and soft floating around her. Hair. Long, pale, and silken.

The albino siren proved to be strong enough to hold Kaia down, but when Kaia grabbed a rock and shoved it backwards overhead, connecting with what felt like a shoulder, her assailant recoiled. Kaia twisted and took in the sinewy siren's white tail, gleaming and iridescent, larger and more developed than her own. The siren was bleeding from her shoulder. She put her webbed fingers up to touch the wound.

Seizing this chance, Kaia began to swim toward shore as fast as she could, keeping her arms close to her sides and letting the muscled tail do all the work. She got past the shelf and made it into the tidal zone, but found she had drifted north of where she had entered the water. Depending on the terrain, getting out of the water might be impossible here.

As Kaia scrabbled for a grip on a seaweed-covered boulder to get a better look at the land, the white siren advanced toward her with smooth, silent speed and seized her by the neck. Bucking against her as they sank together back into the water, Kaia took a handful of the colorless hair and yanked hard to one side, feeling the grip of the other siren's strange, webbed fingers release her. She managed to jab an elbow into the white siren's ribs, but the siren lashed out in retaliation and scratched the side of Kaia's face with long, sharpened nails.

Kaia's eyes shut involuntarily as her skin stung. She tasted the metallic tang of her own blood giving itself to the salty ocean. It would be fatal to try to fight this animal off. And that was what she was, clearly—an animal. Escape was the only option.

Wrestling free, she managed to swim a few strokes toward land. But before she could make it to the shore-break, the siren clutched her around the waist once more. They tumbled in the rolling waves. At last, the ribbed curve of a large bay scallop shell caught Kaia's eye. A weapon. She barely managed to grab it. The shell sliced deeper than she expected into the soft, almost-human flesh of her attacker's belly. The siren let out a strangled, wailing cry and fell back from Kaia as blood unfurled from her body.

Oh shit. That was one sharp shell.

Kaia had never hurt anyone intentionally before. She felt instant remorse, but had to check her instinct to try to give aid to the creature who had been trying to kill her moments ago.

She'll kill you if she has the chance. Get out while you can.

Kaia swam away, but gave one more glance at the siren, whose huge, luminous eyes looked much more human now that she was injured. Moving as quickly as she could, Kaia hauled herself onto the rocks and dragged her body away from the water. She watched the white foam of the waves as she breathed and waited for her human form to return.

Exposed in the dying afternoon light, Kaia stared down at her tail. Ten feet long, striped fox-red like her hair, ending in dark, rich auburn fins streaked with deep maroon. Anyone passing by on a boat would see her in all her oceanic, metaphysical glory.

She wished the transition would happen faster. It seemed air brought on the change, for the more quickly she breathed, the more deeply she filled her lungs, the more rapidly the tail shrank and reformed into legs. So she breathed with all her might, watching her tail shrink and go dull and split.

As soon as she was able, she scrambled up to the sheltering trees and ran the short way back through pines and hemlocks, through damp sphagnum moss thick as a pile of pillows, all the way to where she'd left her clothes. She trembled, pulling the clothes onto her wet body, not bothering to dry off as she tried to figure out why the other siren had attacked her.

Is it territorial? Is it simple animal instinct? Are there others? If the siren has the ability to come onto land and transition into a human, why hasn't she followed me?

After dressing, Kaia lingered behind a sticky, resin-scented pine, watching the water and waiting for a sign of the siren, but she never reappeared. After several minutes, wet and cold and trickling blood from her cheek, Kaia gave up and began the hike back to the house.

Sam steered the *Angeline* toward Foley's Point, leaving the quiet sanctuary of Thursday Island behind him in the dying blue of twilight. It had taken a good-sized dram of Laphroaig to help him gather the balls he needed to go tell Kaia he'd have to cancel the dinner they'd planned, and that he was a general ass.

"Hope you like sushi," Kaia said, bustling past him quickly once she'd let him in through the main door.

She was dressed in an un-dyed Irish sweater that came nearly to her knees over a pair of leggings, with thick wool socks pulled up over the tops of a pair of classic Beaners. Adorable.

"You're looking like a real Mainer," he told her, unable to stop himself from grinning.

She laughed, a deep, womanly laugh unlike her soprano speaking voice. Sam felt a tug at his heart and dropped his gaze to the floor.

Of course, he could have just called, but Foley's Point was on his way to Violet's and it only seemed right that he should say it to Kaia in person—they couldn't have a relationship. Not at this moment, anyway. Not when he ought to give Violet a chance. A real chance. And he thought Kaia deserved to hear that from him directly.

And then, of course, there had also been the plain fact that he wanted to see Kaia for his own selfish reasons. He had to admit that to himself now as he looked up at her face.

There was something wrong with it. She was injured.

"What the hell happened to you?" He stepped forward and pushed her hair away from her cheeks. There were scratches on her right cheek, and redness around her temple and cheekbone that looked like it could develop into a shiner.

She drew away, frowning. "I… got into a fight," she said. "In the water. With the siren. It's like she's just out there all the time, waiting for me."

"What the fuck." Sam rested his hands on Kaia's jaw to tilt her face upward, examining the lesions on her cheekbone. He felt the whoosh of her breath on his mouth and nearly dipped his head two inches closer, but stopped himself. "Are you hurt anywhere else?"

She shook her head. He felt her fingers touch his beard, saw the fringe of her eyelashes drop as she gazed at his lips. His own breath quickened, but he pulled away from her.

"Where're you going?" Kaia protested.

"I'm going to make sure she's not out there now," he said, "and if she is, I'm going to find out what the hell she wants from you."

"Sam, no." Kaia pulled on his arm, drawing him into the warm light of the kitchen. "She's not coming back for a while."

Sam stopped short at the edge of the kitchen table as he caught sight of the spread Kaia had laid out: rows of salmon nigiri glowing like pink gems, California maki, a bowl of pickled ginger and another of wasabi, and a platter of steamed dumplings. His mouth watered at the scent of fresh fish, which wasn't a scent a human nose could detect, but a delicate and sweet perfume he knew by heart.

"You made all of this?" he asked.

"Uh-huh. Sushi's my favorite food."

"Me too," Sam told her, smiling. "Must be the animal in us, wanting to eat raw fish."

Kaia's bubbling laughter cascaded over him. "Well, don't dilly-dally— I'm starved," she said. "Pull up a seat."

Sam stuffed his hands into his jacket pockets. "I, ah... dammit." He was a fucking idiot. And an asshole. "I forgot I told, ah, the woman I'm seeing that we'd get dinner. I'm sorry."

"Oh." Kaia tucked a curl behind her neat little ear and gazed morosely down at the spread on the table.

Sam wanted to bang his head against the wall. He hated seeing her so disappointed, hated knowing it was because of him. Every cell in his body was screaming for him to stay, to eat this food—which was making his mouth water—and be with this woman.

"You—you said you hurt her? The other siren?" he asked, wanting to stall his departure.

Kaia's brows gathered over her stormy blue eyes. "I feel terrible. She was bleeding all over the place. Screaming." Kaia's gaze went to the window over the sink, where the cove was visible.

"You think she'll try to come back?"

Kaia lifted her shoulders. That was all Sam needed. He began unzipping his coat.

"Wait, what're you doing?" she asked. "Don't you have dinner with— what did you say her name was?"

"I'm not going anywhere," Sam told her. "Not when the thing that did that to you is probably coming back."

"She's not a *thing*," Kaia said.

"Sorry."

"And Sam—I'll be fine. Really." Kaia crossed her arms. There was a closed look to her face now, something he hadn't seen before. "The last thing I want is to destroy someone's relationship by being the other woman."

Sam hated the cold, unreachable feeling he was now getting from her. Somehow the idea of losing Kaia's simple friendship was worse to him than the idea of losing his whole relationship with Violet.

"It was me who messed up," he admitted. "I got carried away last night. I said things and did things... things I should've thought about for a while before saying and doing."

"Me too, Sam." Kaia groaned and hung her head, shaking her ruddy curls. "You said you had a—a someone and I should've respected that by stopping you from saying what you did, and the rest... well, the rest... I don't think I had the willpower to stop that." Her large blue eyes landed on his, bare and honest. "Which is why I think you should probably leave."

"Nope," he said, yanking down his jacket zipper all the way and shrugging off his coat. "Not leaving you here alone."

"But, Sam—"

"I'm staying for the food, not you," he said, and sank his weight into a chair at the table. He pulled out his cellphone and texted Violet.

At Foley's Point with Kaia. She's been having trouble with an intruder at the house and was attacked today. I want to make sure the place is secure. Sorry.

There was no point in hiding it. Violet would see the *Angeline* there if she looked out the windows of her house. Violet began texting back and Sam watched the three dots avidly, awaiting her response. The three dots disappeared.

"Want a beer?" Kaia asked. "I got this Smuttynose Shoals Pale Ale in the fridge."

Sam lifted his brows, impressed. "That's a damn good beer," he said. "Penfeld's must've started stocking it, like, yesterday."

He looked back at the screen of his phone as Kaia opened two bottles of beer. Violet had responded.

It's okay. I get it. Hope she's okay. And I trust you, Sam. I'm sorry for acting like I didn't before. I was being stupid and jealous.

Violet, jealous? It was something Sam couldn't quite imagine. He was pretty sure jealousy was something Violet Wilde had never felt in her whole life. Not her, the woman with parents who had given her everything as a kid, who had seen her dream of a successful business come to life, who had been born with a model's looks and the brains of a mad scientist.

"Everything okay?" Kaia asked as she sat across from him.

"Yeah," he answered, putting his phone—and thoughts of Violet—away.

They ate without much conversation for a while, nothing more than *pass the soy sauce* or non-verbal noises of appreciation. Sam was grateful that Kaia didn't talk much while eating. Eventually, though, he had to ask.

"So what do you think the other siren wants?"

Kaia had just popped a dumpling into her mouth and was chewing. She took a sip of beer before answering. "I'm not sure, but I think Felicia Dunne might know," she said.

Kaia explained how she'd met the woman who owned the hardware store on Milk Street—how she'd called Kaia out on being a siren and indicated that she knew there was a whole clan of sirens living in Wapomeq Bay.

"I'll admit, she kinda took me off guard," Kaia said.

"Felicia will do that." Sam nodded. "She caught on to me pretty quick, too. Back when I'd run in there for boat parts and lamp oil for my dad and could barely speak English. She was the one who taught me about the selkie curse. Had some kind of book on it."

"I guess I could just go out there into the bay and try to find out what the clan wants from me," Kaia said with a doubtful shrug.

Sam stopped chewing and swallowed the last lump of salmon nigiri whole. "That sounds like suicide."

Kaia grimaced. "It's either that or wait around for them to attack me again."

"Talk to Felicia," he said. "See what she knows."

After finishing dinner, they went into the living room, where Sam knelt at the hearth to stoke the fire. He noticed Kaia gazing at her guitar case.

"Will you play something?" he asked.

She lit up with a smile. As he twisted newspaper and broke kindling twigs she began picking, the strings vibrating with life as she pulled a melody out of them. Soon she started to sing a country tune about falling in love with the wrong kind of man.

"*I'll take a wrong turn, take a wrong turn, darlin', if it means I'll end up in the right place,*" went the hook of the chorus.

"That's a damn good song," he said, when she was finished and he was sitting beside her on the couch.

"Thank you. I think it was my best one," she said, quietly. "Just sold it to an up-and-coming country singer trying to make it big. Made myself a few thousand. Not much really, but it paid my last month's rent at my apartment and the security deposit I lost for breaking the lease."

"Is it about… him?" he asked. "Your ex?"

Kaia nodded, clutching her guitar to her body. "He was the guitarist in my band," she said. "Found him with my best friend, our fiddle player. No more boyfriend. No more best friend. No more band."

It was no wonder she didn't want to be the other woman. Sam felt a pang of guilt for putting her in that position.

"Then I got fired from my job, so…" Kaia trailed off and shrugged. She diddled out a riff on the guitar and then kept talking. "I moved my shit into my dad's garage and here I am. Thought I'd sell this place and make some money to start fresh, go back to college, maybe buy a little place of my own down in Tennessee and become a schoolteacher… but then I got here and this place is so beautiful, and I met you, and I found out… found out I'm not even the same species I always thought I was. And it's only been two days!"

She attempted a roguish smile, but Sam saw through it.

"You don't have to put this place on the market till you're ready," he said. "Won't sell in winter, anyhow. You've got time."

"I feel like this is where I need to be." She sighed, her big eyes resting soft on his. "I obviously have some things I've gotta figure out about myself."

CHAPTER FIFTEEN

VIOLET WAS USED to spending her Saturday nights alone, but somehow this one felt worse. She was annoyed at herself for getting attached to the idea of a date with Sam. As for being jealous of Kaia Foley—well, she wasn't.

Even from their momentary acquaintance in the apothecary, Violet was able to pin Kaia as the sort of fool who always trusted the universe to provide for her and to blame herself when it didn't, then pull herself up by her bootstraps and keep going. She was the kind who took her life passively, unlike Violet, who had painstakingly carved out every micron of her existence because she knew from her hundreds of lifetimes that handouts were few and far between, and most people would trample and take advantage where they could.

Her Mercedes gave a cheery beep when she locked it and walked through the garage door and into the mudroom of her house. Kicking off her snow boots, she padded into the spacious, open-concept kitchen of the showy waterfront Victorian her parents had originally kept for summering away from Boston. She threw her purse onto the labradorite countertop and went to the fridge for some veggie juice left over from the morning.

No. Better to keep an empty stomach. The work she was about to do would require total focus and purity of intent. While being hungry wasn't comfortable, it was common witch's wisdom that a certain degree of hunger sharpened one's wits and lent itself to more potent spellcraft.

Violet climbed the sweeping staircase in the center hall, ascended to the third floor, then took the narrow stairwell to the cupola room at the peak of the house's impressive tower. The maple and oak floor was designed in a starburst pattern radiating from an eight-pointed star in the center, widening to the octagonal walls with their cushioned window seats below mullioned windows. She lit three white pillar candles on a simple, undressed table in the center of the room, then went to a large trunk against one wall. It was made of the heaviest oak and inlaid with iridescent shell. The latch gave a smooth click when she unlocked it with the key she kept always around her neck.

The winter wind careened around the cupola, carrying with it the crash of the ocean against the rocky edge of land to the north of the harbor, where the water was rough and wild. It must be a constant sound in the house on Foley's Point, Violet thought. Sam must be hearing the ocean crashing right this very moment, and he must love that. She squeezed her eyes tight, trying to choke off the suddenly-materializing image of him leaning in to kiss Kaia, his big, strong hands on her coiled thighs.

Bitterness twisted and tore through her stomach as she lowered her hands into the trunk. Her fingertips found the thick, smooth fur within. She felt her knotted innards loosen. Gathering the heavy pelt, she lifted it out of the trunk and into the candlelight. Laying it out on the table, she ran her hands over the lush, spotted fur, admiring the way it caught the light like a dark gray pearl.

Chapter Sixteen

Sam told himself he'd bank the fire in the furnace in the shed on Foley's Point and then head home to the island. But when he stood out there in the frigid dark, smelling the tang of the ocean and the warm sweetness of woodsmoke, listening to the distant sound of Kaia singing as she did dishes inside, he wanted to stay. Badly. He looked up at the light from the kitchen window and wanted nothing more than to go into that warmth and remain there till morning, with her.

They'd already said goodbye—a platonic hug and an awkward smile. It would be stupid for him to go back inside now. There was no reason to. They had behaved themselves and given each other nothing to regret. It'd be smart not to mess that up.

Yet, even as he started moving one foot in front of the other in hopes that his path would take him down to the cove where the dinghy waited to transport him to the *Angeline*, he found himself heading back toward the kitchen door. Kaia's voice beckoned to him, lilting and floating in effortless, unaffected beauty. The light broke upon him as he swung the door open.

Kaia looked up from the sink, up to her elbows in suds. Her full, gorgeous lips parted in surprise. Her ginger brows lifted over her wide eyes, blue as wild irises.

"Forget something?" she asked, utterly innocent.

That innocence about her, that honest openness—it turned him on to the point of distraction. He loved it like the nip of a freshly squeezed lemon, or the zap of heat from a dash of good hot sauce on his tongue. He craved her.

Sam crossed the floor in two strides and cupped her face in his hands, finding the warm softness of her lips with his. She tasted of the ocean and good beer, and she released a small, satisfied moan as she let her body lean into his. God, he wanted to hear more of that. He wanted to hear her growl with pleasure, and he wanted to be the one to make her do it.

As she began to unzip his jacket, he sank his head to her shoulder and kissed the velvet softness of her neck, where she smelled of shampoo and soap, and the wooly scent of her sweater. Her hands slid his coat off his shoulders as her lips took his again.

If it were up to him, he'd set her round rump right on top of the kitchen table and take her then and there, but she was leading him into the living room, entering the warm circle of firelight beside the hearth, pulling her sweater overhead. He ached at the sight of uninterrupted, creamy skin above her yoga pants, her breasts each the perfect size of half a grapefruit and already peaked with excitement. He didn't want to let her out of his sight, but even more than that he wanted the sensation of her skin on his, and so he forfeited looking at her for the moment in order to get out of his own shirt.

Now with the heat of the fire on his bare torso, Sam dropped to his knees on the hearth rug, running his hands up the curve of Kaia's hips, pressing his fingertips into her waistband. He looked up at her as he began dragging her pants down over the slope of her ass, grabbing her panties as he went. Her mouth fell open, her eyelids half-closing over her eyes.

The skin of her belly was warm and soft as he rubbed his nose against it, relishing the feel of her fingers gripping his hair. Sitting back on his heels, he pressed his lips to the cleft between her legs and dipped his tongue into her.

CHAPTER SEVENTEEN

KAIA HAD NEVER wanted anybody like this. Never wanted anybody so bad it hurt. She was throbbing for him, and what he was doing was, at the moment, only making the ache more intense. Throwing her head back, she released a shameless groan.

"This okay?" Sam asked, pausing as he looked up at her.

"Don't stop," she replied, stroking her thumbs along his high cheekbones. Even though she wanted him to stop. Because she wanted more than this. She wanted everything.

He kissed the top of her hip, trailing gentle kisses back toward the apex of her thighs, and she ran her hands over his hair and his dark beard, taking in the span of his strong shoulders. The wild tattoo covering his arm seemed to writhe in the firelight, flickering with the movement of his muscles as he touched her, so softly. Nothing more than a whisper of pressure, but it made her tremble and groan. Gently, he pressed two fingers against her, sliding in and pulling out with a steady, even stroke, eyes watching her all the while. His tongue was slick and firm, laving and sucking until her knees went absolutely shaky and she had no choice but to hold on to his shoulders for support. Then he closed his eyes and moaned into her, growling until she felt the vibration shoot straight into her belly.

Kaia cried out at the explosion of pleasure, feeling energy rocket through her entire body, bringing her to her knees. She clutched Sam's chest. She could easily have collapsed onto the carpet in a pile of satisfied, humming pleasure, but his hand stayed with her, his fingers gently stroking as he began to unbuckle his belt with his free hand.

"I want you," he whispered, his eyes searching hers as he pushed his jeans and boxers down around his hips.

"I can see that," Kaia said, biting down on her lower lip as she lifted her head to get a look at him. Everything about the man was impressive, it seemed. "I want you too. I don't think I can wait another minute."

"Me neither." One side of his lips curved in a smile as he looked down to roll on a condom slipped out of his wallet. "At least we've got that figured out, huh?" he said, now leaning over her, clutching his sheathed cock with one hand and gripping her waist with the other.

He began to enter her gently, eyes glued to hers. She took hold of his hips, wanting to fill herself with him, wanting to know what it was like to have all of him. But he smiled as he pulled away and leaned down to lick her again, boldly, like he was a dying man and she was his oasis. She arched against him, hands scrabbling for purchase on the rug as he pressed his fingers inside, gliding over the spot where pleasure was still buzzing deeply within her.

"Oh my God," she cried, slamming her fists into the floor when he made her come again, almost instantly.

He chuckled as he kissed her hipbones, her navel, up to her ribs. She squirmed delightedly at the tickling of his beard brushing her skin as he took one nipple between his lips, tonguing it and rolling it gently between his teeth until she was writhing.

"Now, Sam," she begged, desperate to feel him inside her, gripping the back of his neck and sealing his lips with her own. "I need you now."

He tasted of brine and sweetness, smelled of woodsmoke and the cold ocean outside. "All right," he said, softly.

Her jaw dropped as he edged in for real this time, all the way.

She'd never known fullness like this. It felt as though a column of molten gold had been drawn tight through the center of her body. He pressed until his body was flush with hers, his face slack with languor, then coming to life as he drew in a satisfied breath and smiled shyly.

"Does that feel... okay?" he asked, moving with caution. "Because I know I'm..."

"Kinda huge?" Kaia offered. "You feel amazing."

She threw back her head and laughed with pure ecstasy.

CHAPTER EIGHTEEN

HE BURROWED HIS head in her wild red curls as he began to thrust steadily, pressing her hips open now that he knew she could handle him doing so. She was so tight and hot he felt like he'd inserted himself into a burning Chinese thumb trap, in a good way. A really good way. He wanted it to go on forever, but her slickness and the sound of her moaning was driving him to the brink.

He gathered her hips into his hands and lifted them from the floor as he let loose and pounded into her. At the sight of her breasts bouncing, Kaia throwing her head to the side and shutting her eyes, the feeling of her inner muscles contracting against him as she came for the third time, he gritted his teeth and cursed, striving to contain himself.

He wanted to turn her over. Her ass. He wanted to see her ass. He wanted to grip her by the tight little waist and hoist up her hips and pound against her round, full—but it was too late.

"Fuck!" Sam gasped as he came, throbbing hard inside her. She came again—was that four now?—gripping him tight with her strong thighs as she gasped and moaned.

He fell into the soft tumble of her hair, his heart thudding against the wall of his chest, sweat cooling between his shoulder blades and on the backs of his knees. After a few moments, when the spasm of pleasure had left and his body felt like unformed clay, he dragged himself off her.

She was grinning, but covered her mouth bashfully with one hand.

"What?" he asked as he knelt back onto his heels and peeled the condom away.

"Nothin'. Just happy," she said.

It had to be the best thing he'd heard in a while. Maybe ever. Sam sighed, deeply satisfied himself. He rubbed a hand on her thigh, gazing at her languid, sprawled body.

CHAPTER NINETEEN

VIOLET COULD NOT see what he saw, or hear what he heard, or even feel what he felt, but she knew Sam was with Kaia Foley at that very moment, betraying her. Hot, bitter tears streamed down her cheeks as she hugged the seal pelt to her chest, breathing in its familiar smell.

She'd found him on the rocks north of Marlan's Cove, where she'd been collecting wild roses for a perfume she wanted to make. Her first perfume.

Emory—sporty and smiley—had made friends easily with the privileged girls at their private school in Boston. But not Violet. She lived for their summers in Maine and eventually convinced her parents—through terrible behavior that led to her expulsion from said private school—to let her remain in Quolobit with a full-time tutor, where she could walk across the street to the Quolobit Harbor Public Library whenever she felt like it, or take a bagged lunch and set out solo on the northward track that led out of town through mile after mile of undeveloped coastal forest. She'd been walking that way when she'd come across Sam.

He hadn't been Sam then, though. He had still been a nameless creature. Wounded, wailing, he had frightened her at first. She watched him from the cover of the trees until she saw that he was not an animal from the sea, but a boy. A skinny but strong boy, naked and smeared in blood and seaweed, partially covered by a dark, slick thing that looked from a distance a little like a black trash bag.

Only it wasn't a trash bag. And he wasn't alone.

Out in the water at a short distance, the sun caught the wet, rounded head of a seal. Its black eyes were focused on land. The seal barked, and the boy barked back as he tried ineffectively to move towards the water. Violet edged her way to the open rocks, her hands sticky with pinesap, red and pricked by rose thorns.

This was no normal boy. Violet had read of such legendary creatures—selkies—ones who came from the sea to live as humans for a time. The pelt, still partially attached to his back, could bring her great luck and power, and give her complete control over him.

The rocks rumbled under her sandals as she stalked closer, foraging knife in hand. At the sight of her the seal dove into the water, its sleek body disappearing. Helpless on the rocks, the selkie boy looked up at Violet with wide, dark eyes, seemingly unaware of his nakedness as he screamed at her.

"You're still mine," Violet said now as she ran a hand over the cool fur of Sam's sealskin. One of the candles guttered on her table. She pressed her lips to the ear of the seal pelt. "Go home, Sam. Leave Foley's Point and go home."

CHAPTER TWENTY

SAM CAME BACK from the hall bathroom and began dressing immediately, a quiet, closed look on his face. As she pulled on her panties and the tee she'd been wearing under her sweater, Kaia asked, "Everything okay?"

Sam shot a look at her like he hadn't realized she was in the room. He stared at her a moment, seemingly forgetting what they'd just shared. "I, ah… " He rubbed his head, squeezing his eyes shut, then opening them again. "I've gotta go home."

"What?" Kaia said, confused.

He grabbed her hands then, his eyes searching hers. "But I want you to come with me," he told her, with a hushed tone in his voice that almost sounded like fear. His eyes darted away from her, into the shadows of the room.

Kaia let out a nervous laugh. "Sam? What the heck's going on?"

"I don't know." He shook his head hard, rubbing his eyes with the heels of his palms. "I feel like there's something I have to do… I just know I have to go home right now."

"Okay," Kaia said, gathering her leggings and sweater. "But is everything all right?"

Sam finished buttoning up his flannel. "Everything's fine, yeah," he said, his tone coming back to normal, sort of. "I need to work on some paintings for my show, and I want to do it first thing tomorrow morning." The faraway look dissipated somewhat from his eyes, though he still seemed distracted as he tilted his head and gazed at her. "Maybe you'd let me paint you?"

Kaia chalked his odd behavior up to his artist's temperament, and nodded. "I'd love that," she told him, brightening. "I'd love to see your house—your island. And did you just say you have a *show*?"

As Sam spread out the embers in the hearth to make sure they didn't reignite while no one was home, he told her about his upcoming show at the Water's Edge Gallery on Main Street.

"That's amazing, Sam! Congratulations," Kaia said as she zipped up her coat and stomped into her Bean Boots.

Sam's smile was part proud, part terrified. Kaia sensed there was something he wasn't telling her. "You'll do great," she assured him, knowing what it was to be jittery about an upcoming engagement.

"I think it'd be amazing if you played at the show," Sam told her, "if you're still in town, that is."

He held the door open to the howling night wind.

✒

They arrived at Thursday Island just as the moon began to rise from the ocean, massive and golden amongst a smattering of tiny silver stars. Kaia followed Sam up the windswept walkway to the cottage and, following his example, grabbed an armful of wood before trailing him inside. They dumped the wood beside a hulking black shadow she took for a wood stove in the center of the living area. A slender tabby gave a chirp as it jumped down from the kitchen counter while Sam held a match to the wick of an oil lantern at the kitchen table.

"Well, hello," Kaia said to the cat, bending to pet its silky head. It mewed loudly in approval. "What's your name?"

"That's Joni Mitchell," Sam said. "She likes to sing. As best as she can, anyway. Which is nowhere near as good as you."

Kaia blushed as he turned to give her a slow, burning kiss, leaving off just before she could take him in like she wanted to.

Pleasantly ruffled, she set down the small overnight bag she'd packed with a change of clothes and rudimentary toiletries as he bent to light another lantern. "No electricity, huh?"

"Not for lights, no," Sam said. "I've got a generator going for the refrigerator and the water pump, but that's it."

The lantern light revealed the cottage's knotty pine walls and wide plank floors, the small, tidy kitchen, and the contrastingly chaotic living area over the counter. Kaia gravitated toward paintings propped on a table against the far wall.

"Storms at sea, misty mainland mornings, the moving lights I see on the insides of my eyelids when I close them on a dark night," Sam explained.

"Holy smokes, you're good."

The pleasant post-orgasmic heaviness still lingering in her body made her instinctively sink into the couch in the center of the room as she continued admiring Sam's work. His current work in progress stood on an easel, a world of black and deep sea-green, smattered with scarlet and turquoise, glowing with the faint, faraway moon as seen through water.

"That's, ah, that one's the night I almost drowned. The night you saved me," he explained as he knelt to pile wood in the cast iron stove. "There's still something missing from it. I want it to be a little less Pollock, a little more Monet."

Kaia snorted. "Well I think it's damn perfect just like it is."

Sam smiled at her. His weird mood seemed to have lifted, but the strange suddenness of it hadn't quite left her. Still, she didn't want to prod him about whatever had made him change tack so abruptly back at the point. She was just glad to be with him, to see where he lived and worked. She pointed to a whitish painting with a gray smudge of land and the lines of a familiar house emerging from the fog.

"That's my favorite," she said.

"You should have it. It'll be your little piece of Foley's Point after the house sells," he said.

Kaia sat up straighter, feeling like she'd just been smacked in the face. "Whew! I've gotta admit, I sure don't like the sound of that—selling the house. Makes my heart flop around somethin' crazy."

Sam smiled as he closed the woodstove door and left it open a crack for the fire to take. "I know what you mean. I don't know what I'd do if I had to leave this place."

"But doesn't it get lonely?" Kaia asked, taking in the impenetrable quiet surrounding the cottage.

"I like to be alone," Sam said, "though I guess sometimes I wish there was someone to talk to, to eat with, you know. Someone to blame for the dishes. Someone to bring me toilet paper when I run out and I'm stuck on the shitter."

Shittah.

Kaia laughed. "Someone—like a woman? I don't imagine you'd have too much of a hard time getting yourself one of those, Sam Lowell, if you tried."

Maybe she shouldn't have said that. *Jesus. Way to sound pushy,* she thought.

"I mean, this woman you've been seeing, what's up with that?" she added, trying for a casual, fraternal tone.

Stop while you're ahead!

Sam lifted a shoulder. "It's nothin' serious," he said. "I have a hard time trusting people, I guess," he went on, pensively. "A hard time getting close."

Kaia nodded. "I know what you mean," she said.

He sat on the couch beside her, at arm's length. "Do you? You seem like you make friends easily. Like you'd… find a lover easily." His eyes lingered on hers.

Kaia gave a little laugh, wishing he was closer to her, wishing they were still by her fire, tangled in each other's arms. "Growing up without my mom was tough," she explained. She gave a half-hearted shrug. "I think it made me strong in some ways, weak in others. I'm not as outgoing as you seem to think I am."

"What was the hardest part, growing up without her?" he asked.

Kaia felt like she'd just been punched in the guts, and let out a breath. "Damn," she said. "You want to get right to the meat of things, don't you? First the selling of my house, now my dead mother…"

Sam shook his head and leaned back. "I'm sorry," he said. "I'm really sorry. I can be so fucking stupid sometimes—"

"No. Stop that," Kaia said, and touched his arm.

He fussed under her touch in a moment of childlike frustration, then leaned closer and pressed his forehead against hers. He shut his eyes. His beard was thick and soft under her fingertips. He kissed her softly, but pulled back immediately, like he was uncertain of what her reaction might be.

"Sam… I'm glad you asked about her," Kaia told him, meeting his doubtful gaze, wishing he hadn't drawn away again.

Sam chewed on his lower lip and knitted his brows.

"Most people are afraid to look right at another person and see them for everything they are," she said, "you know, their flaws and their hurts. Most people see whatever they *want* to see, and they don't care too much if that's the truth, or not." Kaia drew in a long breath. "You asked what the hardest part was, growing up with out my mom, and the hardest part was and *still is* how my grief is kind of like a flower—just when I think I know what it is, it goes and opens itself up more to me. It takes on a new shape, a new perfume, and it affects me in a new way. Like, now that I'm here in Maine, I'm thinking of that house as some relic of my mother's spirit, and it's going to be hard as hell to let it go. I don't remember much about my mom, so whatever I can hang onto ends up meaning a lot more to me than it should. Like, if I were to find even a scrap of paper with her handwriting on it, I'd have to keep it. Isn't that crazy?"

"Not crazy," Sam said solemnly.

In his eyes, Kaia saw sadness, humor, the ocean. A good man. She leaned back onto the cushions and reached for his hand.

"I'm really glad you asked me to come here, and I'm glad you asked about my mom," she assured him. "I need to talk more about her, about her death. Pretending she didn't exist, pretending it didn't happen—that's not good for me."

"It was a sailing accident, right?" Sam asked quietly. "My dad told me about it."

Kaia nodded. "She tripped on rigging, fell over the side, hit her head." She found her throat constricting, her eyes filling with tears. "They were traveling fast, and by the time my dad got back to her, well… He thought she'd be able to swim on her own. Save herself. But she'd hit too hard. He thinks she might've broken her neck in the fall. He blames himself to this day. And that's what I was thinking of when I jumped into the water to save you."

Sam leaned his head back against the couch and stared up at the ceiling contemplatively, his hand warm but loose in hers.

"I feel like I can tell you anything," she said, testing the ground, wondering why he was acting so distant.

"You can." His eyes rested on hers.

Kaia smiled, curling her fingers around his. "Will you tell me about how you started painting?"

CHAPTER TWENTY-ONE

AT FIRST, IT was hard for Samuel Lowell, a sixth-generation Maine fisherman, to tell if the boy he'd found on the shore was a selkie or not. He had heard of the legendary creatures plenty while he was growing up in Quolobit Harbor—back when it was a rugged fishing community, before all the tourists got wind of it. But he had never believed in those legends.

He thought at first that the kid could have some kind of neurological condition—that would explain the lack of speech, the atypical behavior. Or, the boy could've been out on a boat for a family tour when he fell into the water and got banged up. Only that scenario didn't make much sense, given that it was November—long past tourist season—and Samuel would've heard about an incident like that over the radio.

No, Samuel thought the boy was indeed likelier to be something from the whispered tales passed from generation to generation, tales of another kind of people who lived in the ocean.

"Now don't do that." Samuel snatched a fish out of the boy's hands. They were out on the boat, bringing in the day's catch to the wharf. "You can't eat it raw. Not anymore. The bones'll hurt you."

The boy looked confused and disappointed, but not angry. His large, beautiful eyes drifted once more to the bucket of fish, but he tucked his hands between his thick wool sweater and the bib of the orange coveralls Samuel had given him. The boy sighed, resigned, his cheeks flushed from the cold.

"I know you're hungry," Samuel said as he steered the boat to the pier.

"You've been a good sternman. You're stronger than you look, you know. Skinny now, but I 'spect you'll fill out good. We'll boil up a couple bugs soon as we get home, have 'em with some taters."

"Home," the boy said, trying the word. He pointed out to Thursday Island. "Home?"

"Home," Samuel repeated, and laughed for joy. The boy laughed, too.

It had been four weeks since Samuel had pulled his bloody body off the shore, and this was the kid's first word. The boy pointed questioningly to the bucket of bait fish.

"Fish," Samuel told him.

"Vish. Vish."

"Fffish," Samuel said, pointing to the way his upper teeth rested on his lower lip when he formed the word.

"Fish," the boy said.

They weighed in their catch at the pier and on the way home they covered *boat, water, sky, man, you, me, lobster, trap, rope, net*, and *bird*. When they approached Thursday Island, the sleek, rounded head of a harbor seal came into view in the turquoise break of the surf, finishing its fishing for the evening. The boy nearly dove into the water, but Samuel grabbed him by the back of the coveralls, fighting with all his strength to keep his lanky but strong charge from going overboard. The two of them ended up slipping on the wet decking and nearly colliding with the dock.

Samuel managed to get the boat tethered up while still hanging on to the kid, then dragged him over to the side of the boat.

"Seal." Samuel pointed to the animal in the waves and then pointed to himself. "Man."

"Seal! Seal!" the boy shouted hoarsely, his voice cracking as he struggled against Samuel's grip with tears streaming down his wind-burned cheeks. Pounding his fists into his own chest, he cried over and over again, "Seal! Seal!"

"Not anymore you aren't! Man!" Samuel stabbed a finger into the kid's chest, his suspicions about the boy's nature confirmed. "You're a man now." Samuel prodded him again. "Seal." He pointed out to the water, looking to see if the kid understood. "You are *not* a seal. You are a *man*."

The boy cried for hours after that.

If he came to accept the permanence of his circumstances, he was not at any point enthusiastic about learning words, not like he had been that first time. He seemed to view understanding human conventions as a dull but necessary means to survival.

"Man. Thirsty," the boy said one evening in January beside the woodstove after eating a bowl of mussels.

Samuel looked up from his own bowl. "Get a drink. You know where the water is."

"No water." The boy pointed to Samuel's beer bottle.

"Beer?"

"I want beer, man."

Samuel shook his head. "Samuel. My name is Samuel. And you can't have beer. Not for a few years yet." Samuel didn't think the boy could be more than fourteen at most.

The boy's brows shot up and his mouth bowed downward. He learned human expressions fast enough, that was for sure. "Why?" he asked, wailing frightfully. "Why, man?"

"Samuel!" Samuel raised his voice and smacked a hand to his own chest. "I am *Samuel.*"

The boy began to cry. He looked down into the empty bowl in his lap and shook his head back and forth, another gesture he had picked up recently—one that seemed to suit his stubborn, reticent personality all too well.

"My name is Samuel," Samuel said, more softly.

"*Name?*" The boy looked up at him with bleary eyes.

"Stop crying. You want a beer that bad? Go ahead, but only one. You won't like it—bet you a hundred bucks." Samuel took a slug of his own beer and then pointed the bottle toward the kitchen.

"I want name." The boy wiped his face with the cuff of the flannel shirt Samuel had given him. "I want beer. I want name."

Samuel set his beer down on the small table beside the chair. He was touched by the boy wanting a name, and felt suddenly guilty for not already seeing to that human rite of passage.

"I'm sorry," Samuel said.

"Sorry?" the boy parroted, his lips swollen from his tears. "No Samuel?"

"No. Jesus!" Samuel stood and shook his head.

"*Jesus?*"

"Stop it, will you?!" Samuel nearly shouted.

The boy cowered against the couch cushions, spilling his bowl of shells and brine.

"Goddammit." Samuel snatched up the bowl from the boy's feet. "You're going to stink up the whole house now. Come on."

The boy began to cry harder, though his sobs were silent. Samuel put the bowl on top of the side table and sat beside the boy, resting his hand on his shoulder. He was not a nurturing, gentle man by nature, but he would have to try harder for the child. "You want a name?" he asked.

The boy's large, black eyes met Samuel's. He nodded.

"I'll call you Samuel, like me." He was not a creative individual, and it was the first thing he could think of. Samuel ran a hand roughly over the boy's thick hair. "Samuel."

"Samuel?" The boy repeated it slowly. "*Your* name Samuel."

"It's your name now, too," Samuel said, and the unfamiliar threat of tears stung his eyes. "I'll call you Sam for short."

"Sam," the boy said, warily. "Why Sam? Why not seal?"

"Never were a *seal*," Samuel said between his teeth, uncertain about what he was getting himself into. "You are a selkie. Means you're both seal and man. And you can't be in the water anymore because someone stole your sealskin the day you came to land."

"Who?" young Sam asked.

"I don't know."

"Why?"

Samuel heaved a sigh, sorry not to have answers for the kid. "I don't know."

The drawing began not long after the boy learned to string words together, when Samuel was trying to explain something or other to him. The exchange of money for labor, maybe. Samuel drew pictures of himself and the boy fishing, working all day, then giving their findings to another man in return for money, which they could then take to the store and give to the people there in exchange for goods.

The boy loved drawing and was inclined to draw more than talk when it came to telling Samuel anything, so much so that at a certain point Samuel had to take away the paper and the pencil to get him to use his mouth to speak. He never became much of a talker, and for that Samuel was frankly grateful, though he did learn to speak in a normal enough way. Eventually Samuel let him have his paper and pencils back, and then the kid drew all the time.

Young Sam drew seals, mostly, and even drew images of himself being cut out of his sealskin. These drawings were dark and disturbing, and Samuel eventually told the boy he had to stop making them. "You need to forget about that now, Sam," Samuel said. "Forget about the sealskin."

"Who has my sealskin?" the boy asked, as if Samuel had all the answers. "Where is it?"

"I really don't know, but you need to move on."

When Samuel got him a set of paints for Christmas he began to paint the ocean: not from above and outside the water but from inside, from within. The paintings were obscure and vacant to Samuel's eyes. He told the boy as much.

"I can't tell what's going on in the damn painting," he admitted. Samuel had no great knowledge of art, and it was difficult for him to offer an objective critique. "It's all just black and green, Sam. It's, ah, it's empty."

"Yes!" Sam agreed, and nodded emphatically.

"That what you're going for, then?"

"Yes. *Empty!*"

"Okay, buddy." Samuel ruffled his hair. "I don't get it, but that's fine."

Sam seemed disconcerted. "Why don't you get it, Dad?" he asked.

Samuel had instructed the boy to call him his father if anyone asked about their relationship, but he hadn't anticipated Sam thinking of him that way. It still caught him off guard when Sam called him Dad, but he liked it, too. It made him feel like, for once, he belonged to someone.

"I—I—maybe because I never lived in the ocean, the way you have," Samuel said, trying for a better response to the boy's painting. "Maybe we see with different eyes. Maybe when you paint... Oh, Christ, I don't fuckin' know... maybe you need to be more, ah, explicit—"

"*Mebbie.* What's *mebbie*?"

"*Maybe,*" Samuel clarified. "Forget about it. It's a stupid word. Not worth using, ever."

"Okay. What is *ex—explicit*?"

Samuel was getting himself in too deep now, he thought. "Detail," he said to Sam. "Here." Samuel grabbed the pencil and paper from the table where they left it for moments like these and drew a sloppy circle, then a neat and accurate one beside it. Then he wrote the words *ambiguous* and *explicit* under each, respectively. He added *unclear* and *clear* to the page, *inaccurate* and *accurate, specific* and *vague*, and, for good measure, *wrong* and *right.*

"You get it?" Samuel asked.

Sam nodded. "Explicit," he said. "Accurate. Sp—spe-ci-fic. I need to show *your* eyes what *my* eyes see."

Young Sam's astuteness impressed Samuel. After that, the boy made paintings that still remained abstract to Samuel's eye, but which used more varied nuance and gave him a distinct—if unnameable—feeling when he looked at them.

"I understand now. Painting is a language," the boy said to Samuel, several weeks later. "Like the alphabet. Symbol. Symbol for thing, idea, place. Makes my idea your idea."

"Hm. Kind of," Samuel replied.

"Not same, not same." The boy waved his hands wildly. "Your idea. Different than my idea. I give it to you. Then it's yours. Like language."

"No, it's not exactly like language," Samuel said. "It's more like… music."

"Music?"

Samuel realized he had not yet introduced the boy to music. Though he didn't have a regular radio or television, he did have a record player and records stowed in the back of his closet. They were a painful reminder of the only woman he had ever really loved, who had left Quolobit Harbor and him many long and sad years ago.

"Show me music," Sam commanded.

Samuel looked down at the kid, his messy mop of black hair, sunburn across his nose and cheeks, his huge, curious eyes. His eagerness was hard to resist.

"Please, Dad," Sam said. "Show me music."

Samuel could have chosen any record of the two dozen or so he had, but most were flash-in-the-pan folk or rock bands, and it struck him as important to give Samuel the best education he could before sending him out into the real world and putting him in school. So he chose an album of Vivaldi's *The Four Seasons* and plugged a headset into the record player so the boy could get an undiluted experience of it.

At first the kid went wide-eyed, twitching his head this way and that as he listened to the music, but then he grinned, gasped, and laughed. Samuel sat across the room and watched him all the while, seeing how the child did not disguise what he felt while listening. Tears fell from his eyes at a certain point, and Samuel came over to put a hand on his shoulder.

"The ocean," the boy explained, holding his fingers to the headset as he looked up at Samuel through his tears. "Music is the ocean."

Samuel showed him the back of the album case and pointed to the title of the work. "*The Four Seasons*," Samuel said. He realized he had put the record B-side up, and the boy was probably on the second track or so. "You're listening to *Autumn*."

"What?" Sam pushed the headset off his head.

"I said, this music is called *The Four Seasons*. That's what the composer—the artist—named it. And the part you are listening to now is called *Autumn*. The season, autumn. You remember the seasons, don't you?"

"Spring, summer, autumn, winter, yes," said the boy. "I remember. But I thought this was *music*."

"It is. Your painting is of the ocean." Samuel said. "This music is about autumn." It was a limited explanation, but it was the best Samuel could come up with.

"Ocean... " Samuel's gaze drifted off as his mind worked. "But I heard the ocean."

"Sure. That's how all art works. Music, too. The artist doesn't have that much control over other people, what they will see, or hear, or feel. That's the point of art, I think. To make people see or feel something for themselves. That's when it's good."

Sam nodded. "Good." He replaced the headset on his head and lay back on the cushions of the sofa beneath the window, gazing up at the sky as he listened to the rest of the record.

CHAPTER TWENTY-TWO

"I JUST REMEMBER *constantly* thinking this body was so… strange," Sam told Kaia. "Every inch of it was weird and unfamiliar to me. I'd stare at other humans, trying to figure them out, or at myself in the mirror, or just, like, at my body, at my hand, or my foot, or whatever." He shrugged. "And going to school, ugh, forget it. What a nightmare. Before I really grew into myself and became bigger than most of the other guys, those first few years were really rough."

"Did you get beat up?" Kaia asked, wincing.

He snorted and nodded, folding his arms across his chest. He felt a sense of relief to be telling someone about himself. These were secrets he'd kept for so long that the truth behind them had almost faded into utter oblivion. It was important that he didn't forget his truth, and he'd felt it slipping further and further from him in recent months, like it was being leeched away somehow.

Kaia dipped her head and stared at the glow in the glass window of the woodstove door. He knew she'd sensed something was up with him, but she was choosing not to push the issue. He was glad for that, because he didn't know what he'd tell her. It was just as he'd said—he had suddenly felt that he needed to get home, for no particular reason. It was as strong an urge as the one he'd felt to turn back to her when he was going to leave Foley's Point after dinner, only that had felt *right*, and this—this sudden compulsion to sail back to Thursday Island—had felt strange and oily, like a thought that wasn't his own.

Kaia yawned and stood. "Where's your bathroom?"

"Take one of the lamps with you," Sam told her. "Just be careful not to drop it, or you'll burn the place down." He pointed her toward the kitchen and into his darkened bedroom.

CHAPTER TWENTY-THREE

Not wanting the pressure of destroying Sam's home, Kaia opted to bring a long taper candle in a pewter-handled candlestick instead of a lantern. She trailed into the bedroom, which smelled of cedar and linen. She found the bathroom and shut the wrought-iron door latch as she set the candle down on the edge of the sink.

A massive, porcelain claw-footed tub took up most of the long, narrow space, which was lined with raw wood on the walls and ceiling. The floor was covered in a colorful woven rag rug, and a set of fresh, fluffy white towels hung on the rack. Sam's toothbrush and a scattering of beard trimmings decorated the sink, but the tub was sparkling clean, and beckoning to her.

After peeing, she turned the faucet on the tub and wiggled her fingers under the stream until she got the right temperature. As the tub filled, she dumped in some Epsom salts found in a jar on the shelf and sniffed at Sam's collection of handmade soaps from Wilde's Apothecary. One was labeled *Winter Forest*: sandalwood, smoke, and vetiver. It smelled manly and dark. The other was labeled *Moon*: lavender, palo santo, and patchouli, which smelled earthy and celestial at the same time, and was perfect for her mood tonight. She ran the bar under the stream and let the water take up its intoxicating scent.

Once the tub was filled and she had sunk herself into it, there came a knock at the door.

"Come in," she called, sinking deeper into the cloudy water, slightly self-conscious now that they were no longer in the heat of the moment.

Sam ducked in, significantly taller than the bathroom door. A smile brightened his face. "Great tub, isn't it?" he said.

Kaia lifted a brow. "I think there's room for two."

Sam bit his lips and looked down at her with heavy-lidded eyes. His movements were slow and deliberate—perhaps a vestige of his unfamiliarity with his own form—and steam swirled around him as he pulled his shirt overhead and began unbuckling his belt. Kaia let herself greedily take in his body, lean but muscled, with hands and arms that were thick from his work. The elaborate tattoo was striking against his fair skin. Kaia felt her heart quicken as she watched him push down his jeans and boxers. He reached for his toothbrush, utterly un-self-conscious as he began brushing his teeth.

His back to her, she now observed the long, thick scar along his spine where his sealskin had been cut from him and stolen away. The scar was the length of her forearm and thick as her thumb, raised and pink. Other than that, his back was lean and muscled too, and marked with the occasional freckle. His butt-cheeks were firm and downy, giving way to the dusky hair of his thighs. Brushing vigorously, he turned to face her again, giving her a full view of everything else.

"Where'd you learn to make sushi?" he asked, his words garbled by his brushing.

Kaia laughed, impressed by his nonchalance. But of course he had no shame. He'd never learned it. "Took a class," she answered. "It was a Christmas present from my dad when I was in high school. He got sick of me begging for sushi takeout. Said it was too expensive. I sucked at it at first, but, as with all things, practice and Youtube make perfect."

Chuckling in agreement, Sam spat and rinsed, then came to step into the tub. To make room for him, Kaia had to sit up a bit, revealing the tops of her breasts, her nipples bobbing at the top of the milky, clouded water. Sam didn't seem to be interested in ogling her, though. He groaned with satisfaction and closed his eyes as he sank into the bath.

Eyes still shut, he lifted his arms out of the water and extended his hands to her. "Come," he said, beckoning her close.

Kaia drifted through the tub's deep water, sliding in beside him, tucking herself into his body as he wrapped his arms around her. She clasped one of his legs between her thighs, deciding that they were far more comfortable and familiar together—after after only a few days of knowing each other—than she'd been with anybody else, ever.

Chapter Twenty-Four

Sam wrapped a towel around Kaia's shoulders as she stood from the tub. She smiled up at him with soft, sleepy eyes as she scrunched a hand towel against the ends of her curls, which had turned a dark fawn color with the water. He had never felt anything like this before—this urge to take care of another person, to protect them, to shelter them.

"Let me get a look at that gash on your cheek," he said.

"Oh, it's not a *gash*." Kaia laughed, but consented to let him examine the wound and put some antibiotic ointment on it.

"Your bed looks like a cloud," she said, when they left the bathroom and he rested the candle on the table beside the bed. The rumpled goose-down coverlet, in a soft gray linen duvet cover, glowed silver as the moon crested the square skylight window directly above. Kaia looked up at it and grinned. "Wow."

"That's why I put the skylight in," Sam explained. "So I could lie here in bed and look up to see the moon and the stars, like I used to from the water."

Sam sensed that Kaia was feeling shy now, possibly sleepy, maybe even sore from their earlier encounter. He didn't want to her to feel like he expected anything of her at this moment, other than to sleep in his arms. "I'll go grab your bag," he said, making for the door.

But she stopped him with a touch. He let her draw him to the foot of the bed, his pulse quickening as she ran her fingertips over his shoulders and chest. A shiver went through him as she touched his sides, making his muscles flex involuntarily. His skin felt more alive than ever, conscious of every millimeter where hers connected with it. The scent of her shampoo, reactivated by the humidity in the bath, wafted around him like a cloud of hothouse flowers.

"I don't need anything but this," she whispered, gently pulling at the back of his neck, bringing him closer as she stood on her toes to kiss him.

She sucked on his lower lip, her warm little tongue darting to meet his with a dancing stroke. His body reacted quickly, heart racing, temperature rising. Soon she was pressing a hand against where he was hard and straining against his tightly-wrapped towel.

He sank onto the bed as she knelt on the floor and tugged at the towel around his hips. When she took his cock in her hand he shut his eyes for a moment to revel in the reality of her touch. But when he felt the heat of her mouth close over him, he had to look at her. Her full, gorgeous lips surrounded his cock as she locked her gaze with his, as she slid her hand up and down, as she squeezed till he thought he'd burst, as she took more and more of him. He wanted to throw his head back and howl, to come like a rocket, but he grabbed the comforter in his fists and trembled, sinking into the pleasure and hanging onto his restraint like a lifeline.

Seeing his state, she drew her mouth away and smirked. She let her towel fall to the floor. He groaned, out of his skull with desire at the sight of her. Cupping her face, he kissed her as he stood and brought her to her feet, his body brushing hers.

"I don't think I could ever get enough of you." He wrapped one arm around her back and the other under her knees, lifting her into the air, swinging her around and bringing her to the side of the bed.

Letting her down gently, he crawled beside her, guiding her onto her belly. Kaia bit her lip and brushed her curls away from her face. She watched him with wide eyes as he knelt beside her and admired the perfect creamy softness of her skin, running a hand down the curve of her spine, and lower.

"I want to look at you," he said, tracing her curves with his fingertips. "Is that okay?"

"Mmhm," she hummed, a smile on her lips. She turned her face bashfully to the pillow and kicked up one foot. He caught it, bringing his lips to the tender inside of her arch. He kissed her there, her toes curling against his fingers.

Ducking under her shin, he maneuvered himself between her legs, kneeling with wide knees to nudge her thighs apart. He lifted her hips toward him a fraction and gazed admiringly down at her ass like a split peach in front of him. Seeming to know what he wanted, she lifted and arched her back against his touch, opening herself more as he squeezed her cheeks apart with both hands, gazing down.

Kaia groaned, perhaps in pleasure, perhaps in frustration.

"Tell me," he said roughly.

She moaned into the pillows. "I want you so bad, it actually hurts."

He could practically see the ache in her glistening flesh. "Me too," he whispered, not trusting his voice. His cock felt like it might explode.

"Just feeling you *looking* at me," Kaia said, "it's... it's driving me insane. Don't stop."

"You're so beautiful," he told her. The most beautiful human body he'd ever seen. The only one he'd ever seen quite like this.

Kaia was so full of trust, so willing to let him explore; he wanted more and more, but was afraid of pressing boundaries too quickly. Still, he couldn't resist touching her and gorging himself on the sight of her, pink as a wild rose. Somehow, with one hand and only a very small percentage of his brain, he got the condom on.

"We're going to have to take this one real slow for my sake," he told her as he drew her hips to him and pressed inside, feeling her quiver again. "Does it hurt?"

"Only a little," she peeped, "but in a good way."

"If it's too much, you just tell me." He squeezed his eyes shut, praying for the self-control he needed not to pound the living daylights out of her and blow his load in a matter of heartbeats.

CHAPTER TWENTY-FIVE

His cock burned into her, somehow bigger, harder, better than she remembered. She felt tears sting her eyes as he took her, inch by inch. Finally he filled her. He stayed that way without moving, hands on her waist. Adjusting, she could breathe, at last.

"Okay?" he asked.

His concern was touching; it made tears come hot and fast. She groaned and flexed her spine, rocking her hips in reply to him.

Sam had exposed her like no one ever had, touched her and made her open herself to him in a way that might have made her feel embarrassed and ashamed—yet she didn't, not with him. She felt beautiful, wild, and strangely at peace.

As he picked up the pace, he struck her core, again and again, and she felt her body coiling, heating toward a massive release. When it happened, she felt like she was suddenly in an earthquake, at its very center, and was only distantly aware of him squeezing her waist with his strong hands and bending over her back, crying out as he came with her.

Kaia collapsed onto the bed, Sam still inside her and partially covering her body with his. He thrust slowly, lazily, hips grinding against her ass as they sank into the mattress together, panting.

"Holy fuck," he said.

"Holy fuck," she agreed.

They lay for a long time in silence, bodies cooling together. At last, he rolled toward her and slid one hand over her belly.

"There's more I need to tell you… about me being a selkie."

She looked at him across the pillow in the pale moonlight and touched his cheek, glided the backs of her fingers over the thick, glossy brush of his beard.

Sam's dark eyes rested long on hers before he spoke. "If I ever get my sealskin back, I'll go back to the water and swim away from here."

The way he said it, there was no negotiating the fact. Kaia felt it sink into her like an anchor falling to the sea floor.

"Because… that's what you would *want* to do?" she asked.

"I used to think I wanted nothing more than to go back to the water," Sam admitted after a thoughtful pause. "But no. That's not how it is for me, now. I don't want to leave land forever. I've lived half my life here. I have friends here. My dad lives here. Anyway, that's not how the curse works. If someone takes a selkie's skin he's enslaved to them. And if he gets it back, he'll be *compelled* to leave land, forever."

Kaia felt some part of her heart that had been dancing go still. He was trying to tell her he'd leave *her*. He called it a curse, yet he spoke with such frankness, as if he'd already accepted his fate.

"You must feel like it's a time bomb ticking, waiting to go off the minute you get your sealskin back," she said.

"It makes me cautious," he said, "about getting too settled here on land."

She could easily read between the lines on that one.

"Now don't—don't think like that," Sam said, moving closer, cradling her face. "You're changing everything for me, Kaia. Changing my whole world."

"But you're not sure what that means yet."

"My world has changed once already," Sam said, "and it was traumatic, I'm not gonna lie."

She felt his chest fill with air, then deflate as he sighed. Part of her wanted to comfort him, to tell him no more harm would come to him, but she couldn't make him a promise like that any more than he could tell her he'd never leave her. For the moment she had no choice but to resign herself to being suspended between the deep satisfaction she felt with Sam and the certainty she knew he couldn't give her.

"Let's take it one day at a time, then," she suggested, running a hand through his hair.

He smiled and kissed her cheek as he sank into the pillows, arms coiling around her. She turned to her side and he burrowed his nose into the curve of her neck, and though she was bone-tired, she lay awake listening to the sound of his breathing deepening until she knew he was asleep. It took her what felt like hours to fall to sleep herself, her mind keeping her awake with thoughts of Sam as a seal, herself as a siren, and the whole ocean wanting to claim them both.

PART TWO

Chapter Twenty-Six

Violet lay on the floor of the cupola room, wrapped in the sealskin as the sky lightened with the first hint of dawn. There had been hundreds of thousands of dawns between this and her first, and she was cursed to remember each one. Well, most of them, anyway.

She sat up, stretching sore muscles and a stiff neck. This body was one of the better ones she'd walked in—especially since she had been able to split her consciousness into the dual form of twin sisters—but it was already growing flawed, even at the young age of twenty-seven. She could feel it in the mornings when the feet and ankles were tight for the first few steps she took out of bed, or when she woke with a headache after drinking too much wine. She had seen a silver hair in the lush black mane a week ago, and plucked the bastard out.

The one thing that had been making her feel content within this particular body was the lover she'd found to please it with. Sam Lowell, with his strong shoulders, his burning eyes—his big cock—was a lover for the ages, but he wasn't only that. Violet could have had any number of handsome, skillful partners. And she had, over the centuries. But Sam was different than all the others.

He was a selkie, an enchanted being. Her first. Finding him, stealing his sealskin, hunting him, toying with him—it made her feel alive again. Well, not alive. Because she'd been that for over a thousand years. He made her feel real again, that was what it was. He made her feel like she had something to fight for, like she wasn't just waiting out her days in yet another dull lifetime.

She'd found him when she'd been in this *particular* body—or set of bodies, if you wanted to include her twin, Emory—for about sixteen years, when she had been occupied with feasting herself on the latest in literature, music, fashion, and technology most of all. She hadn't needed the selkie boy then. She'd kept his sealskin, knowing what it was and how she might use it, knowing that someday, once she could feel the darkness of decline begin to steal over her borrowed form, she'd need an outlet. A reason to live. A way to stay occupied until it was time to find the next vessel and transition again.

The human life was tragically short. Certainly, bodies could live well past seven, eight, or even nine decades, but how much of that time was actually pleasurable? In her experience, after three decades the body was wasted. Finished. At first, she had lived out the days and let those bodies reach their natural end, but in recent lifetimes she rarely wanted to stay past the prime, much less the decline.

Sam had been making her feel otherwise, though. All those years ago, she couldn't have known what a man the selkie boy would grow into, or that he'd make her feel that she might just be willing to stay for a while longer, to possibly experience a real lifetime—with him. It had been hundreds upon hundreds of lifetimes since she'd wanted that. She hadn't truly felt this much for a man since her very first, the one who had destroyed her heart and cursed her to remain in the cycle of consciousness for eternity without real love. Sam Lowell, she thought, just might be the one to break the spell that had long ago been cast upon her wounded soul. And perhaps, if he truly was the one, this life might be her blessed last.

She could only hope so.

Violet pressed her nose to the soft, thick fur of the sealskin and inhaled. Was it love she felt for Sam? It was desire, she could say that for sure. He had awakened a need in her she hadn't felt in so long—a need that made her feel twisted and weak inside, but still she loved it. Though she saw now that she had been foolish to believe she could have kept him for herself without using the sealskin.

She ought to have known better. Men were wont to wander. And she, in her complacency, her ambivalence, hadn't thought to take precautions with Sam to make him hers and hers alone. Was it too late?

"Ahh." Violet let out a sigh as she stood and stretched again.

It wasn't too late. She had a tool to help her keep Sam as long as she wanted him. She had proven that to herself last night when she had commanded Sam to return home and moments later the *Angeline* had left Foley's Point and crossed the harbor, bound for Thursday Island. Yes, he had brought that stupid little whore with him and fucked her brains out in his bed, the bed Violet had yet never seen. But still—he had obeyed her command.

The jealousy she felt was cutting, enveloping, delicious. She reveled in the pain, eager for the reminder of life it gave her. Her heart was not dead.

Picking up the sealskin, she cradled its weight in her arms as she walked over to the chest where she kept it stowed. Pressing her lips to the sealskin's ear, she whispered. "Come to me, Sam."

Chapter Twenty-Seven

White winter sunlight poured into the window behind the headboard and the skylight above, warming Sam's bed, where Kaia lay. She turned over and found the mattress empty. She listened for the sound of the shower, the clinking of dishes, but heard nothing other than the endless crashing of the ocean.

"Sam?" She sat up and squinted in the shaft of light descending upon her. Her hair fell around her cheeks, loosened from the bun she'd put it in before sleeping. She noticed her hair tie on the nightstand and dimly recalled Sam gently tugging her curls free in the dark hours before dawn when they had wordlessly made love again.

She looked around the room. Now there was an easel at the bedside and brushes scattered on a chipped dinner plate on the floor. The old floorboards creaked underfoot as Kaia got up. Joni Mitchell greeted her with a long, strangled meow and rubbed a whiskery nose on her ankle.

Wrapping her arms tighter around herself to ward off the January chill, Kaia walked around the easel and looked at the painting. It was only in its beginning stages, but it clearly depicted her asleep in Sam's bed, the dawn light just touching the edge of her hair and turning it to fiery gold. The suggestion of the cat curled at the end of the bed gave the painting a most intimate touch, as if to say this was not just a modeling session, but a comfortable morning-after between lovers. If only that were actually the case.

"Sam?" she called out again, looking over her shoulder and into the rest of the house.

There was no freshly brewed coffee. No pancake breakfast. No kisses in the kitchen. No fire in the woodstove.

No Sam.

She shivered as she walked into the living room with the cat following behind. Outside, in the cold gray water by the dock, the *Angeline* was gone. Perhaps he had taken a trip to shore to get something from Penfeld's market. Or maybe he had to work, and was out fishing.

She spent the next few minutes searching for a note on the kitchen counter, the fridge, the bedside table in the bedroom, but found nothing. He didn't have a landline for her to try calling his cellphone, and, anyway, she didn't have his number memorized.

Kaia sighed and put on the kettle to make a fresh batch of coffee in the fancy pour-over contraption she found on the counter, then busied herself with building a fire in the woodstove, taking a shower, and making the bed. She toasted some bread and fried an egg. She fed Joni Mitchell and cleaned her water bowl. She swept the wood chippings from the hearth. Snooped around Sam's bookshelf and examined his paintings. Bundled up and walked around the circumference of the island, stopping at a north-facing promontory that afforded a view of Wapomeq Bay.

Sam's boat was nowhere to be seen. The January days were short, and the afternoon sun had already crested the frosty hill behind Quolobit Harbor as Kaia stood on the edge of the dock on Thursday Island. It was well below freezing outside, and the wind bit her cheeks and the tip of her nose and made tears blur her eyes as she squinted landward.

It didn't seem right that Sam had left her here without so much as a note. Then again, she didn't really know the man at all. He'd acted strangely the night before, getting up and suddenly needing to leave Foley's Point for no apparent reason. Still, it wasn't as if she felt that he didn't care about her. In fact, it was the opposite. She'd never been with someone more attentive. The painting of her and the lovingly wrought details of it were further proof of his feelings.

Kaia sighed and was about to turn for the cabin again when she got the idea that she could just swim back to Foley's Point. She laughed aloud.

Of course, the thought hadn't come to her immediately—because why would it? She'd been a siren for less than a week. She'd also only known

Sam for less than a week. That thought, paired with his sudden and unexplained absence, was sobering.

She frowned, crossing her arms over her chest as she assessed the water beyond the dock. It was deep gray-green, so dark it was almost black, and despite the fact that it was cold enough to kill a regular person, it did look inviting to her.

Why should she stay and wait? Sam had left her literally on a deserted island for a whole day without giving her any way of contacting him, and with very little to eat. She was hungry for something other than eggs and bread, and she did not like the feeling of waiting around for a man.

The frigid wind lashed at her back and thighs as she undressed. She left her things heaped just inside the door of the cabin, and dove in. The transition was painful, but it was a little like waxing—the more you did it, the more you knew what to expect, the less it hurt. Sort of.

Kaia found her bearings and set off on a course toward Foley's Point, knowing better than to make any noise. *Wouldn't want to call forth the Evil Ones from the Deep!* She found herself flinching with fear as soon as she left the island's sheltering presence and entered the open water.

But the water was clear, cold, and quiet as she pulsed her fanned fin through it, feeling the regular ripple of muscle along her scaly tail. She lifted her head regularly to make sure she stayed on course, heading toward the cove on the northern side of the Point. She was squinting against the wind and wiping frigid saltwater out of her eyes with her webbed fingers when she noticed something glinting in the water, moving towards her. She spun to the right and caught sight of a boat traveling at high speed, water purling from its prow.

Shit.

Kaia dove down, far into the dark, as the white hull passed over her. Heart pounding, she snuck back toward the surface and kept her head and tail safely out of sight until she could pause and look around, making certain there were no other boats nearby. All was quiet again, still and green. She sighed a flurry of bubbles in relief and continued toward the brown, belt-like fronds of kelp near the shore, where she remained in the water from the neck down as she transitioned, breathing the winter air in eager lungfuls, hoping not to be seen.

CHAPTER TWENTY-EIGHT

Using the sealskin, Violet had commanded Sam to park the *Angeline* in the boathouse, out of sight, then climb up to the cupola, where she waited for him. All the pain, all the jealousy—it ignited and burned up into pure triumph the moment she saw him duck through the door.

Eyes dark, lips slack, he appeared drunk. "Why... why am I here?" Sam asked as he stepped into the cupola, his gaze scanning the space, passing over her, not noticing the sleek pelt she held in her arms.

"Because I need you," Violet answered, drawing him to a chair in the center of the room. "Stay," she commanded under her breath to the sealskin as she laid it in the trunk on the floor and locked the lid. She gazed over her shoulder as she walked out the cupola door, locking it before descending the stairs to make her preparations.

After several hours, Sam was still waiting for her, just as she had commanded him. She was nearly ready. She would make him forget that redheaded tart. She would make him truly hers.

Outside the room, Violet now stood with her back to the cupola door, a teakwood box clutched in her hands. Emory, her twin, her other half, stood beside her as they conferred silently between their halved mind.

Do we have everything we need?

The moon was full and edging toward waning—perfect for their intentions of increasing Sam's devotion to Violet and stripping away his attachment to anyone else. To invoke the elements, they had a small leather satchel of dirt for earth, incense for air, a candle for fire, a bottle of seawater for water, and salt for casting the circle. They had geranium and rue and ginseng for increasing Sam's lust and their own control, as well as a spray bottle filled with birch infusion for asperging to banish Kaia's influence over Sam. And, most importantly, they had wine to offer to the horned demon Baphomet, whom they would summon for aid.

Yes, we have everything.

Emory smiled and shrugged out of her satin robe as Violet did the same, letting the garments pool on the rough wood of the landing.

Violet paused for a moment, considering what they were about to do. *It's not twincest,* she told herself. *Not when we share a consciousness.* Emory gave her a sly smile.

Violet turned the doorknob and entered the circular cupola with Emory behind her. Sam sat precisely where she had left him, on a wooden chair in the center of the sparse room.

"Hello, Sam," they cooed in unison. Violet felt a rush at just how synchronized they could be.

She set the teakwood box and bottle of wine down on the trunk and dragged it closer to the center of the room as a makeshift altar. She hadn't had need of magick yet in this lifetime, and had not created a proper space for it. That would have to change, apparently. For now, the trunk would do.

Emory stroked Sam's cheek as he stared vacantly at the floor, not noticing the two slender, naked women moving around him, one dark, one light. He had not removed his coat, nor moved an inch as far as Violet could tell. Her command over him was even stronger than she had hoped.

The sun had already fallen behind the hill above Quolobit Harbor, and the snow-dusted peaks of the roof took on a sugared aspect around them. Violet began casting the circle with a line of poured salt as Emory pulled Sam to his feet and undressed him. She set the chair and his clothing outside of the circle, leaving him to stand naked in its center, silent and obedient.

The twins shared a smile, one reflection to another. They worked in tandem, Violet lighting candles, Emory calling to the elements and making offerings. In a shallow silver bowl they burned the herbs, and soon the air was filled with fragrant smoke. The sharp scent of birch cut through it as Emory misted Sam's body with the asperging spray.

Violet began the incantation to summon the sacred demon Baphomet.

CHAPTER TWENTY-NINE

DECIDING SHE NEEDED to talk to someone about all the weird shit that had been going on, Kaia took a hot shower, dressed as warmly as she could—sparing a regret for the boots and sweater she'd had to leave back on Thursday Island—and drove herself to the hardware store on Milk Street. Felicia Dunne was at the door in oversized pink glasses and furry boots, sprinkling salt on the granite step. She looked up at Kaia, her hot pink lips curving in a broad smile.

"I thought I'd see you again," Felicia said, holding open the door. "Looks like we're supposed to get hit with a blizzard. You're going to need some snow boots."

"I… had some," Kaia said as she stepped into the warmth of the hardware store, her thin, pointless canvas sneakers slapping on the old floorboards. She turned to Felicia, hands shoved into her coat pockets, unsure how to begin. "I need to talk to you, Felicia."

Felicia drew in a breath, then nodded and turned to lock the door, flipping the sign to *closed*.

"Come on upstairs," she said.

Felicia's second-floor apartment was airy and welcoming. From the small kitchen window a blue-black streak of ocean could be seen glimmering in the last light of day, past the peak of a fancy Victorian house on Main Street and the spires of hemlocks.

Felicia pushed aside a big stew pot and a stack of cast-iron pans to set a kettle on the stove. She pulled a can out of the cabinet and started scooping out something that looked more like roots dug out of the ground than like coffee, dumping the stuff into a grinder.

"Tell me the other bitch looks worse than you." Felicia cast Kaia a shrewd eye.

Kaia laughed, then put a hand to her tender cheek, where the three-inch scratch was scabbing over. "A siren attacked me while I was in the water," she said loudly over the grinding. "I fought her off. The other day I caught her spying on me from the woods, and the other night she broke into my house. I don't know what she wants."

Felicia stopped the grinder and spun around, putting her hands where her high-waisted jeans ended and her cropped sweater revealed a strong abdomen with skin rich as earth.

"I think I really hurt her," Kaia added.

Felicia frowned. "Good." She went back to grinding.

When Felicia was finished with the grinder she dumped the dark, crumbled contents into a French press.

"So, are you... ?" Kaia stammered. *Like me?* she wanted to ask.

Felicia lifted her graceful, arched brows. "Am I what, sweet pea? Makin' you coffee? Why, yes, ma'am." She spun around again and attended to the grinder. "Coffee with chicory roots, like we do in New Orleans, where I'm from. Doesn't taste as weird as it sounds, I promise."

Kaia wriggled her way into a chair at the round oak table. Maybe it was rude to ask someone point-blank if they weren't human.

She thought she'd try another tack. "So, beside me, are there other... you know?"

Felicia snorted. "Fishies in the sea, and wolves, and foxes, and lions, tigers, and bears, oh my? Yes."

Kaia gulped, looking down at a crayon drawing in front of her. It was of a wind turbine, with dead fish floating around it and a fisherman in his boat below, throwing up his hands in distress. She was about to ask if there'd been any progress on the town's wind farm vote, but Felicia interrupted her thought.

"There are ghosts and gods and witches and demons and spirits and you-name-it." Felicia sat at the table. "Anything we have a story for has a foothold in reality. You can bet on that."

A chill spread across the skin of Kaia's forearms as the kettle began to pop and gurgle on the burner.

"Now, where I come from, New Orleans," Felicia went on, "we've got a diverse array. The Big Easy is known for being a melting pot. You've got the Africans, the Spanish, the French, the Native Americans, all boilin' down together. Pissin' each other off, but lovin' each other, too. And that's where things get interesting. I met a Latina vampire carrying on a love affair with the ghost of a dead African slave who used to be a lycan—that's a werewolf. She was beside herself to find a way to travel back in time, and she met a Choctaw shaman who gave her a flower to eat and next thing you know, the blood-sucker was gone from the room like that."

Felicia clapped her hands together and Kaia jumped back against the chair, startled. Part of her mind still bucked against all of this absurdity, but another part cowered in a corner and waited for the rest to come out, knowing it was all real.

"How do you know all of this?" she asked.

"Reading books, mostly. But, like my mother and her mother and her mother before her, I'm a hereditary witch," Felicia said. "Our tradition comes from a variety of places—all over, really. My mother taught me, and hers taught her. My mother gave me my sight, which she got from her mother, and so on. I suppose that means Claudette and Tessa will have it too." Felicia rolled her eyes. "If they ever learn to use it. Tessa I don't think I need to worry about, but Claudette, oh, that girl." She shook her head and turned her eyes upward in silent prayer.

"So you're... you're a..."

"I'm a seer and a witch," Felicia clarified, pushing her big bright glasses up higher on her nose.

"Okay," Kaia said. At this point, a witch seemed normal compared to a siren.

The kettle began to sing and Felicia poured the boiling water into the press. "But you shouldn't forget that you're not alone out there," she warned as fragrant steam purled upward, filling the cozy kitchen with the scent of coffee. "I don't know the clan of sirens in Wapomeq Bay personally, but I do know they're not friendly."

Kaia gulped. "Do they really call themselves a clan?" There was something violent and primal about the word she didn't like.

"I wish I knew more about them," Felicia admitted. "The siren clan has been mythologized here in Quolobit Harbor for centuries, of course. It was my Joe's grandmother who told me about them."

Kaia grimaced.

"My Joe, he's a marine. Away on duty. That's why you haven't met him yet. He'll be back in March and you can meet him then."

Kaia opened her mouth to say she wasn't planning on being around that long, but the way Felicia smiled gave her pause.

"Life never was too easy here in Quolobit Harbor," Felicia went on, calmly pressing down on the plunger of the coffee press with one hand while she whisked something in a saucepan with the other. "Fishing's an unpredictable industry, and these northern winter nights get awfully long. Not everyone can handle it. Sure, some folks make shit up to stave off the crazies. But, I'll tell you—the stories people've been telling in Quolobit Harbor for centuries aren't all fairy tales. Besides, I believe this place calls to the other kind, whatever you'd like to call 'em. Folks like yourself. There's something here that draws them in."

Kaia realized she'd been holding her breath. She released it as Felicia set down a cup of hot chicory and coffee in front of her. It looked and smelled like regular coffee, as far as she could tell. Felicia bustled over with the saucepan and topped it with steaming milk.

"There now, just like Cafe du Monde," she cooed.

After stirring in sugar, Kaia blew on the top of the coffee and sipped it cautiously. It was hot, creamy, nutty, and delicious. She let out a low hum of approval.

"Good, isn't it?" Felicia said.

Kaia nodded. They drank in silence for a moment.

"I guess I shouldn't swim anymore," Kaia said, at last. "I mean, I've lived this long not even knowing what I am—"

"You'd deny yourself the joy of being who you really are?" Felicia scoffed. "Honey, please don't. If that doesn't make *you* sick, it'll make *me* sick."

"But what if the siren shows up again?"

"I'll tell you what," Felicia began, cradling her coffee mug in her hands, "you're stronger than she thinks you are. If you can't flee, then you fight. Take something out there with you next time you swim. I've got an old speargun belonged to Joe's daddy laying in the garage. Next time she comes at you, chase that bitch down and show her who's boss."

After several cups of café au lait, Kaia left Felicia's house with the speargun and several sachets of angelica root and cedarwood to scatter around the outside of the house for protection.

CHAPTER THIRTY

IT WAS A dream; it had to be a dream. The room around Sam shimmered, undulating and glistening like he was underwater. Part of his mind fought it, tried to pull free, but the larger portion of his consciousness was static as a stone, not wanting to take action. He was being pulled in two directions, caught in a riptide.

Violet and Emory moved around him, both of them naked, their long hair streaming down their backs—Emory's pale blonde, Violet's dark as aged mahogany. They spun and chanted, lifting cups of dark liquid high into the air. The octagonal room smelled of strange things—earthy and pungent. Smoke stung his eyes.

Sam looked down and saw that he, too, was without clothing. He wanted to move, to walk out of this strange room with its glistening black walls, but he could not. His feet were pinned to the floor, which was scattered with colorful blankets and embroidered pillows. He wanted to cry out, to scream, but he could barely breathe. He felt like he was moving through water, swaying like a kelp frond rooted to the ocean floor. He hadn't felt so helpless since the first day he had come to land.

Violet and Emory began to sing together with one voice. A cyclical, crooning chant. He could understand enough to tell that they were communicating with some being whose name he didn't recognize, holding up their cups of wine and chanting in unison. His ears rang and his head spun, but when Violet held a cup to his lips he opened them and swallowed. She sipped next, her eyes smiling up at him as Emory imitated her. Violet's twin moved with such a precise impersonation, it appeared as though the two of them truly were mirror images of each other.

Emory moved closer to him on his left side as Violet moved in on his right. Their hands pressed him into a pile of cushions on the floor, where he knelt before them. He was utterly helpless as they lowered him onto his back amid the scattering of silk pillows.

Though he was terrified, his body responded as Emory began to stroke his rising cock and Violet bent to tongue his mouth. He was hyper-aware of each physical sensation—Violet's silky hair touching his chest, her hot, slick tongue on his lips, Emory's firm grip and his own pulse against her palm, the brush of her thigh on his. He searched for a distant part of himself that could fight this, but could not find it. Whatever it was that had frightened him a minute ago had melted away, washed from his mind by pure, driven lust.

"Baphomet, we summon thee," Violet whispered into Sam's ear.

"Baphomet, join us," Emory crooned.

Sam wanted to ask who the hell Baphomet was, but he couldn't speak. He couldn't even breathe for a moment, as if all the air had been sucked from the room. And then, when he did inhale, his body was filled with an atomic blast of energy. He was no longer himself—he was now covered in thick, black hair from the thigh down; his feet were gone and replaced by two black hooves, hard as granite. His head, when he glimpsed his reflection in the windows, was heavy with horns, thick and curving upward.

"Kiss me when you arrive," Violet commanded him, and he did.

Sam—or whoever he'd become—gorged himself on Violet's wine-sweet mouth. He gripped Emory's hair and pushed her mouth down over the head of his cock, which was engorged far beyond its normal proportions. Violet watched her twin.

"Are you jealous, child?" Sam asked in a voice that was not his own, feeling the weight of his horns as he turned his head to look at her.

Violet's lips twisted into a smile. "Only a little."

He guided her to her knees near his furry right hip, opposite Emory, and watched as Violet, too, bent to lick his cock. It had to be twice the size it normally was, he thought, distantly, thinking that this was by far the craziest dream he'd ever had. Together their tongues, soft as velvet, stroked the length of him. He reveled in the twins' worshipful attention, the pleasing sight of them—two halves of one being.

"Emory," he said, his voice feeling faraway and foreign. The pale blonde looked up, her full lips open and glistening. "Fuck me, Emory."

He delighted in the sight of Violet's brows sweeping together over her eyes, and laughed as her twin straddled him. Emory gasped as he gripped her hips and thrust himself inside her.

"Oh my fucking God," Emory panted, throwing her eyes to her sister as she rode him, rocking her hips and flexing her spine. "Why've you been keeping him to yourself all this time?"

Violet's gaze burned as she crawled towards him where he lay propped on a pile of pillows. He slipped a hand along her belly and between her legs, and as she kissed him he slid two fingers inside her.

Wake up.

It was a dream. It had to be. There was nothing real about this. He didn't have hooves and horns in real life. His dick wasn't *that* big. Violet had a voracious sexual appetite, that was real enough, but she'd never mentioned anything as kinky as a threesome—with her sister, no less. Even as he heard himself groan with pleasure as Emory writhed on his cock and Violet's hot, slick pussy tightened around his fingers, he urged himself to wake up.

You don't want this.

He screamed it inside his mind, but still he hooked his fingers inside Violet and pulled her closer, turning her around and guiding her hips lower over his face so he could taste her. Over the slope of her ass he saw her grab Emory's long blonde hair and pull it, forcing her head back. She bit and licked her other half's throat, lowered her head to her breasts and sucked on her nipples.

Wake the fuck up!

The demon, or whatever had overtaken him, wouldn't let him. He continued licking Violet, even as Emory thrust harder against him. He gripped Violet's thighs and spread them wide, lapping her from front to back in long, wet strokes until she was dripping onto his chest.

Sam found himself moving after a time, positioning Emory under Violet instead, commanding Emory to pleasure her sister. Violet's jaw dropped in protest, but she, too, went along with his wishes, widening her thighs and lowering her hips over Emory's face. He watched in satisfaction as Emory's pink tongue darted against the cleft between Violet's legs.

Stop!

His hands took hold of Emory's milk-white thighs, pushing them up to either side of her ribs, spreading her wide. He looked down at his own hand, rubbing where she was wet and swollen.

This is wrong.

He slid two fingers inside her, up to the hilt, and heard her moan. "Hold her legs," the strange voice inside him commanded Violet.

She obeyed and gripped both of Emory's ankles. Emory gasped as Sam slowly drew his dripping fingers out and slid them back in. As he did this, he looked up at Violet—or the demon in him did—watching her eyes widen.

"Do you feel that?" he asked Violet.

Violet nodded.

Inside, Sam was screaming in agony. He wanted out of this crazy dream, however insanely hot it might be. It was the subject of many a man's fantasies, but not his own.

Emory, meanwhile, was groaning rhythmically with his motion as Violet sat back on her heels and watched.

"Come here," he commanded her, motioning for her to bend over in front of him.

Emory sighed as he continued touching her before nudging the throbbing head of his enormous cock into Violet's wetness. She cried out, unprepared for Baphomet's girth. He threw back his horned head and laughed. The two halves of her cried out together as he thrust into each of them, pulsing to the edge, to the point of pain, and when he found his release, golden and burning, the demon felt them come with him.

Sam found himself back on Thursday Island, opening the door of his cabin as the wind howled at his back. It was as if he had just woken up to find himself turning the doorknob, looking over his shoulder at his boat moored near the dock, the small lights of Quolobit Harbor twinkling in the otherwise dark mass of land to the west. Heavy exhaustion weighed his limbs. Turning away, he puked into a large pot of shriveled basil stalks beside the door.

He stumbled into the house to find it completely dark. Joni Mitchell assailed him, clawing at his shins. He shook her off and poured himself a glass of water, sucking it down before holding a match to the lantern on the kitchen table. Dull, sinking dread filled him as he carried the lantern into the bedroom. There, on the easel, was the painting he had started of Kaia. It was the last thing he could remember before he had blacked out.

"What the fuck…?" he muttered, rubbing a hand to his aching head.

Last he could recall, he'd been standing right here with a paintbrush in hand, trying to get just the right blend of colors for Kaia's fiery curls. After that—he didn't know. The whole day was gone. At least, he hoped it had just been one day.

And Kaia—where the hell was she? With no boat, there was only one way she could've gotten off Thursday Island. He leaned on the bed and looked out across the water toward Foley's Point. A faint glimmer of light shone from the uppermost windows.

"Fuck!"

Sam fell onto his bed. It still smelled of her. He pulled out his cellphone and dialed the number for her house. It took some time, but eventually she answered, sounding sleepy and startled.

"Kaia," he said, practically sobbing her name. "What happened?"

Silence.

"Kaia?"

"You tell me, Sam."

He felt himself gag again and lurched out of the bed, headed for the bathroom. He made it to the toilet just in time, tripping to the floor and emptying himself of what looked and tasted like several bottles of wine.

"Sam? Are you okay?"

He heard Kaia distantly from his phone, tossed onto the bathroom rug. Kneeling back on his heels, he picked it up. "Ugh, yeah," he stammered, coughing. "Sorry. I think I'm sick."

"I can hear that." Kaia still sounded annoyed, but maybe she was softening. "Where'd you go? I woke up this morning and you were gone."

"I—I dunno what happened."

"Are you *drunk?*"

He covered his eyes as he flushed the toilet and sat on the edge of the tub.

"Sam."

"Yes," he said. "I think so. I mean, I don't know. I feel like I've been drugged. I can't remember anything after—after this morning, when I was painting you."

"Were you drinking while you were painting me? Did you suddenly feel the need to go on a binge? Did things get too real for you?" She sounded hurt, on the edge of crying.

"No," he replied dully, too zonked to get riled, even though he wanted to defend himself. "I hadn't even had my morning coffee yet. I just… found myself walking into the house a few minutes ago. I have no idea where the day went."

"Whatever, Sam," Kaia said, scoffing. "I'm tired. I was about to go to sleep." She hung up.

He deserved that. Sam sat with the phone in his hands, staring down at the screen miserably for several minutes, still not sure whether he might puke again. Joni Mitchell came in and mewed her concern. He stroked her between the ears until he felt well enough to stand and light the candles on the shelf beside the sink.

As he undressed he sniffed something strange coming off his skin—an astringent scent, something he couldn't define. His skin, when he rubbed his abs and chest, felt salty. His hair was laced with smoke. When he pulled off his jeans, he smelled sex.

He sank into the womblike warmth of the tub. When he began to scrub with a sea sponge, he found something tugging at his mind, caught like a hook. It felt like shame. But shame for what? He hadn't done anything wrong, as far as he knew, other than cheating on Violet with Kaia. But had it been cheating? He and Violet had never exchanged any promise. They had never even been to each other's homes, always holding their rendezvous in the back of Violet's shop. Their relationship had been purely physical and satisfying only to a point.

Kaia was another story. He could feel himself, even now, sinking into a state of hunger for her so bottomless it could easily swallow him whole, and he'd gladly let it. But he was screwing it up. He'd finally found someone who made him believe that this life was one he'd willingly live, a life he'd even choose over the other life that was rightfully his, but now Kaia was slipping away from him. Whatever had happened to him today, it had been his own fault, surely.

Leaning out of the tub to grab his phone, Sam called the Hook and Anchor pub.

"Harvey, hey, it's Sam Lowell," he said. "Was I in there today?"

Harvey laughed. "What?"

Sam had little patience at the moment. "Just tell me—did you fucking see me today?" he asked through his teeth.

"No, man," Harvey replied, affronted by Sam's tone. "You didn't come in here. Everything okay?"

Sam ended the call. He'd explain to Harvey some other time. Or not. It hardly mattered. He let his phone drop to the floor and sank into the tub again, shutting his eyes against his misery.

CHAPTER THIRTY-ONE

KAIA DIDN'T KNOW what to think.

She'd heard enough alcoholic's excuses from her father to know them all. *I only had a few. My buddy was buying. It was a good game. I had a rough day.* And yes, even *I feel like I've been drugged.*

But maybe she'd been too hard on Sam. He'd sounded so pathetic—his normally deep, smooth voice had been ragged and weak, on the brink of tears. Still, he'd left her alone on the island all day, with no note and no way to get home. Yes, she'd taken a big risk in swimming to Foley's Point—but she probably should have just stayed put. She couldn't blame him for her own choices.

Sleep wasn't going to come easily to her that night. She found herself torn between the old anger he had triggered and her memories of the night they'd shared, when he'd opened up an ocean of need inside her. She'd never even imagined it could be like that, never imagined she could give herself so completely to someone.

Kaia turned and gathered the down comforter tighter around herself to ward off the cold. She realized this was her first night in Maine sleeping without Sam Lowell nearby. He had made her feel safe. Relaxed. She ached for him—not just for the pleasure he could give her, but for the solid reassurance of his presence. Even as she tried to quiet her mind, some part of her brain was still aware of the speargun Felicia had given her, leaning between the bed and the nightstand, and the protective herbs she'd scattered around the house's foundation, anchoring her to the reality that she was a siren, and that she had enemies.

✥

Kaia woke to the phone ringing again. She shot out of bed and out of a dream of Sam being attacked by a humongous octopus and her needing to use the speargun to save him. She panted as she threw off the covers and picked up the bedside phone.

It was the realtor, Markus, returning Kaia's call. Relieved and a little disoriented, Kaia sat up and did her best to sound alert and adult as she spoke with him about her intention to sell the house on Foley's Point. A *heritage property*, Markus called it, and sounded enthusiastic about coming by for a visit later that afternoon, as long as the storm didn't get too bad.

"Storm?" Kaia said, rubbing her eyes.

"Yap. Nor'easter comin' in, stahtin' in the next howah or so."

"Oh, right," Kaia murmured, vaguely remembering Felicia mentioning a storm.

"Two feet, they're sayin'. Of course, they're wrong half the time." Markus laughed. "Could be four feet. So, I'll, ah, come by 'round two?"

"Sure, sounds good."

Ending the call with Markus, Kaia got up and showered. She dressed in a comfy pair of patterned leggings and an oversized sweatshirt, and ensconced herself and her banjo on the yellow velvet couch with a steaming cup of coffee within reach. She was picking and singing *Moonshiner* when there was a knock at the door.

Reluctantly putting down her instrument, she padded over, turning the cool doorknob and bracing herself for the blast of wintry wind. Sam Lowell stood on the porch wearing a parka and a black beanie, holding her clothes and boots. His face was grim beneath his dark beard, eyes solemn above purple rings of utter exhaustion.

"Thought you might want this stuff," he said gruffly, "with the storm coming, and all."

Kaia nodded and took the boots and clothes from him. Behind him the clouds were low and white and already filling the air with tiny flurries.

"Come on in, before I freeze," Kaia said, and stepped aside.

Sam entered and shut the door behind him. He stood looking down at her, unsmiling.

"You gonna tell me what the hell happened?" she asked, cutting right to it. "I need an answer. A real one."

Sam shut his eyes and sighed, then opened them again. "I don't know." He shook his head, gaze searching. "All I know is I spent half the night puking my guts out."

"Does this have anything to do with how you suddenly needed to go back to Thursday Island the other night?" Kaia asked as she set her things down on the hall bench.

"No." Sam lowered his brows in thought. "I don't think so. I just wanted to get back there. I wanted"—he paused, confusion passing over his face—"I don't really remember. My head's all messed up."

Kaia crossed her arms, keeping herself at arm's length from him, knowing that if she let herself get too close she'd give in to the warmth and comfort she'd find there. "Did you just freak out?" she suggested. "You've mentioned a bunch of times that you've never let yourself get close to anyone because you know you're tied to the ocean, and… you said I terrify you."

Sam snorted and leaned back against the door, tilting his head to expose the white, strong pillar of his neck. Kaia remembered kissing him there and felt her cheeks burn, her lips tingle. She tried to stop herself but the memories kept surfacing—Sam's hands gripping her thighs, his abs flexing as he moved in her, his jaw dropping open, brows knitting together when he came. Tears stung her eyes and she turned away, gripping the banister of the stairs.

Pull yourself together.

She was already more attached to him than she should've ever let herself be. There was little hope for them. Him: basically a confessed player. Her: still nursing a healing heart and only staying in Maine until she got the house on the market.

Tell him to go.

Struggling to keep her back straight and not collapse with the tears threatening to spill out of her, Kaia pulled herself onto the stairs. Sam would leave and she would go up to her bed and cry it out until she was empty, and then she'd meet with this realtor Markus, wait out the damned Nor'easter, then go home to Tennessee.

Say goodbye.

Sam's hand landed softly on her shoulder. "Kaia, please," he said. He was close behind her now, his warmth against her back, his face nestling into her hair, moving his hands to encircle her waist. "I'd never lie to you. Do you believe that?"

She did believe that. She bit her lips and squeezed her eyes shut. "Yes," she answered.

"I don't know what happened to me," he whispered, his breath hot against her hair. "I only know that it made me sick, and hurt me, and left me with no memory. The minute I came back to myself, you were the first thing I thought of. I'm sorry, Kaia."

She turned on the step and faced him, still not nearly at eye-level. His pleading eyes met hers and, though she felt the sincerity of his apology, she thought to herself that the smartest move would still be to tell him to go. They had shared one night together and yes, the sex had been life-changing—it seemed everything about their experience together was life-changing—but to keep going now would just be idiotic.

"There's nothing I wouldn't do for you, Kaia," Sam said, his hands brushing down the length of her arms. "Tell me what you need from me, and I'll make it happen."

I need you to leave.

She opened her mouth but couldn't bring herself to say it.

I need you to kiss me.

She couldn't say that, either.

Chapter Thirty-Two

"What the fuck," Violet said between her teeth as she and Emory stood at the second-story window of the master bedroom. "He was supposed to forget about her. Look, his boat's there at Foley's Point. *Again*."

Emory shrugged. She possessed the cooler, more collected half of Violet's mind. She was a drone, of sorts. Violet probably should've kept herself in one body. It had been an experiment, one she had thought about for several lifetimes before enacting. Now *she* was pure creative intelligence, intuition, passion, lust. *She* was liberated. Emory, on the other hand, was rational intelligence and practicality. In short, Emory was boring. Violet had kept only a small portion of her simpler virtues to herself and generally relied on her twin for things like paying the bills on time and doing taxes.

"Dammit!" Violet slapped the window frame as she stared out at the harbor, Foley's Point disappearing in the wash of snow.

Emory took her by the wrists and turned her away from the window. "Use the sealskin," she said. "It works."

Violet heaved an aggravated sigh and went up to the cupola. It still smelled of sex and burnt geranium, the floor scattered with colorful silken pillows. She felt a flush creep up her chest and cheeks at the recollection of what she and Emory had done with Sam. She hadn't expected the spell to work that well. Hadn't actually expected Baphomet to come. And he had, she was certain. Though she had seen no physical change in Sam, she'd felt the demon's presence through him.

Violet knelt at the trunk and used her key to open it. The selkie's pelt felt heavy and comforting in her arms as she lifted it out of the trunk and cradled it close. "Go home, Sam," she whispered to it. "Go home and forget about Kaia."

She stood and carried the pelt to the harbor-facing windows, where she could look out and see Sam's lobster boat moored off the southern side of Foley's Point. "Go home," she said, squeezing the pelt tighter. "Go home, Sam."

She stood there, commanding him repeatedly, waiting to see him rowing around the edge of the Point and getting into his boat, but he never came. Emory appeared at her side at last.

Hot tears of frustration and envy streaked Violet's face. "Why isn't this working?"

"It's just not," Emory said, her hands soft on Violet's shoulders. "Leave it for now. You need to eat something."

She let herself be pulled from the window. Kaia might hold a powerful sway over Sam for now, but Violet would find a way to fix that, and soon.

CHAPTER THIRTY-THREE

SAM STOOD CLOSE enough for Kaia to smell his sandalwood soap and the lingering woodsmoke on his jacket. She lifted her hands to his neck and slid into the warmth beneath the collar of his flannel shirt. He lowered his forehead to hers.

"The realtor's coming soon," she told him.

Sam sighed and stepped back. "I should go."

Kaia shook her head. *Make up your mind, dammit.*

Just then, the phone rang. Kaia groaned, irritated by its shrill sound raking through the silence of the house. As she went for the kitchen, Sam turned to the door.

"Wait," she told Sam. "Just… hang on. Okay?"

He nodded.

After taking the call, she came back into the hall to find him sitting on the stairs, his jacket unzipped, leaning with his forearms on his thighs. His dark, tired eyes looked up at her.

"That was the Markus, the realtor," Kaia explained. "He's not coming. Storm's getting too bad. Says he's got a crappy car, so…"

Sam lifted his brows expectantly.

"I want you to stay," she admitted.

A smile melted the tension from his face, softening all the hard angles. Kaia stepped between his knees and felt him wrap his arms around her waist, resting his cheek on her chest. His hair was thick and smooth under her fingers as she brushed it away from his forehead.

Whatever he'd been through, whatever had kept him from returning to her for a whole day, whatever had made his memory a blank, it had taken almost everything of him. She could feel it in the way he leaned into her, like he needed comfort, needed rest.

"Are you okay?" she whispered.

"I don't know," he whispered back, his voice choked. "I'm sorry."

Her fingers slid over his warm, damp cheeks. "Oh, Sam," she muttered, holding him closer, pressing her lips to his dark hair. "It's all right."

"I feel like I don't deserve you," he said, pulling back, his hands sliding down to rest lightly on her hips. His eyes brimmed with tears; the tip of his nose was tinged with pink. He swiped at his cheeks and shook his head. "I swear to God I don't know what the hell happened to me," he said, "but I keep getting this feeling, this feeling like I did... a bad thing."

Kaia shook her head and tightened her grip on his shoulders. Eyeing him face-to-face, she said, "Whatever it was, I know you'd never do anything to hurt me. I trust you, Sam."

He nodded, wiping a hand down the front of his beard. She wanted him more fiercely than ever. She wanted to kiss his tears, to undress him and comfort him the best way she could think of. Taking his hands in hers, she said, "Come upstairs."

The bedroom was lit with the cool, quiet light of snow. As she pulled him to the bed, the only sound that could be heard was the soft rush of ocean to land. She slid his coat from his shoulders and let it drop to the floor, then pulled off her sweatshirt as he began unbuttoning his flannel. He watched, his dark eyes glowing with desire, while she slid the top of her leggings down over her hips and wriggled out of them until she was in nothing but a pair of soft black briefs.

She stepped closer and felt the current of his body heat flow around her. Her hands drifted over his skin, pale and firm. She touched where he was marked with blue-black ink, ran her fingers over the tangle of Nordic knot-work and imaginary beasts coiling from his right pectoral muscle, over the round expanse of his shoulder, twisting down the slope of his bicep and his thick forearm and wrist, ending in a point over the top of his broad hand.

He had the arms and hands of a man who used his body for work, thick and capable. Appreciating his strength, she lifted his hand to her mouth and kissed the center of his palm, where a silvery scar slashed across his heartline and lifeline. She'd seen it the night she had arrived, when she'd impulsively grabbed his hand and commented on his callouses as a tactic to get him to tell her something of himself.

Despite knowing more about him than perhaps anyone else did, he was still a mystery to her. It frightened her, that part of him she felt lingering like a dangerous shadow in the faraway reaches of his spirit, but it drew her to him, too. She wanted that part of him, wanted all of his light and all of his shadow.

His lips were hot and warm in the crook of her neck, sending a shiver of pleasure over her skin. "I'd do anything for you," he muttered, his lips tracing a line between her ear and her shoulder. "Kaia, I mean it. I know we just met but I've never—"

She wanted to listen to him, but was too taken with the contours of his abdomen flexing down in a sculpted V toward the waistband of his jeans. She palmed the thick ridge straining against the denim of his jeans and shivered with delight when he gasped in response. Her fingers made quick work of his belt and the buttons of his fly. Sam gasped when she pressed her hand down into his boxers and closed her fingers around his cock.

"Oh God," he said, leaning back against the maplewood poster bed, chuckling. "You're making me dizzy."

His smile faded and he bit down on his lower lip as he hooked his thumbs into the top of his jeans and boxers and rucked them down a few inches over his hips, his dark gaze holding hers. Her knees quivered. She leaned against him, squeezing his thigh between her own for balance as she tightened her grip and looked down. He'd seen more of her than anyone else ever had, she was pretty sure. She wanted to see him the same way.

He was slipping his fingers into the back of her panties when she pulled away. "Not yet." She felt a smirk twist her lips as she nodded down at his exposed arousal. "You first. Everything off."

Sam chuckled bashfully. "All right," he said, and stood from the bed to step out of his jeans.

"I wanna see you," she told him as she sidled closer, touching his bent back, the soft fluff under his arm. "All of you. I wanna know all of you, Sam."

She ran her fingers up his thigh, palming the round firmness of his ass, then turned him away from her. He gripped the bedpost, leaning against it as she kissed him between the shoulder blades, where his scar broke along his spine.

She wanted to lay him out and pull him apart until he was weeping, to push her way into him until he was shaking and begging her for release. She wanted to make him cry, to wash herself in his tears.

Kaia stepped back, shocked by her own indefinable desires. She'd never felt anything like this before—this desire to tear, to break, to consume. It frightened her. It made her recall Felicia Dunne's words about sirens: *Some say you're dangerous. Dangerous to men, at least.*

Sam lifted his head and twitched it over his shoulder, then turned to face her. He held his cock in one hand, stroking up and down with a soft, even motion.

"Everything okay?" he asked.

Kaia nodded, finding herself feeling bashful now, caught thinking crazy thoughts. She wasn't dangerous. Just because she'd discovered something new about herself didn't mean she was suddenly a different person. Maybe it was Sam that made her feel this way. He certainly made her feel like she could go to the limits of her own soul. He drove her to the edge of her known territory, to see what was out there—only to find the infinite.

Sam continued looking at her, binding her to him with his gaze as he knelt at her feet, his knees resting on the wide floorboards. She gasped when he pulled her underwear aside and leaned closer until she could feel the heat of his breath on her sensitive flesh, the expectation as intense as the act.

"So beautiful," he told her, and brushed his lips over her.

He licked her softly and insistently, holding her underwear stretched tight against her hip till she felt it threading between her cheeks, nearly snapping along with her own endurance to sustain this level of pleasure while remaining on her feet.

"Sam," she whispered, voice trembling, toes gripping the floorboards. "I need you inside me."

He reached behind her and slowly, torturously, drew her stretched underwear off her bottom. Kaia's knees buckled and she groaned. He smirked, apparently delighted with himself now. Cupping her ass as he stood, he lifted her off her feet and onto the bed, crawling over her as he placed a trail of kisses along her sternum.

CHAPTER THIRTY-FOUR

SAM DROPPED HIS head to Kaia's shoulder. "Shit," he said. "I forgot condoms."

He felt her sigh. Her fingertips drifted up his sides.

"That's okay," she whispered. "I... I can't get pregnant."

Propping himself up on his elbows, he looked down at her face. Her eyes were wide and beginning to glisten. She pressed her lips together and swallowed, then said, "I can't have kids. I, um, I had ovarian cancer and, yeah. It was five years ago. I'm healthy now. Cancer-free!" She gave a shaky grin, then became solemn again. "It was a really hard time, obviously. I still have to go for routine screenings and the anticipation surrounding them can be, well, it can be a nightmare, but it seems like I'm doing great."

"Seems like?" Sam asked. Something about the way she said it didn't sit right with him.

Kaia shifted her weight, drawing closer to him. "Yeah, not that I want to bring up the past with you, 'cause it's not exactly a sexy conversation..."

"Tell me," Sam said, "if you want to."

"Going through surgical menopause definitely did a number on my, um, previous relationship," Kaia said. "It kind of made my sex life suck and I felt like it was all my fault and it made me really, ugh, I don't know, defensive and frustrated and—and then my ex started cheating on me and I blamed myself—"

"Not your fault," Sam growled, feeling a surge of protective anger.

Kaia smiled wanly. "I know. I know that now."

"Yeah?" He kissed her forehead, and Kaia wrapped her arms around his neck and drew his mouth to hers.

"I never thought I could feel this way again, Sam," she whispered. "Honestly, I never thought I'd feel this way *ever*, with anyone, but you... you're amazing."

Sam couldn't help smiling. "You're amazing, too," he said, brushing her bright curls away from her cheek.

"I know I maybe should've told you about it already but—"

"No," he said, shaking his head. "You didn't have to tell me before you were ready."

"Well, I'll admit it's not something I like to dwell on," Kaia said, pressing her lips together in a firm line. "It was a horrible experience and I spent a long time grieving the idea of being a mother and being terrified about the cancer coming back in another form, but I'm through that now and I don't want it to define the rest of my life."

The idea of Kaia being sick, going through pain and grief, made him wish violently that he could have been there to support her. "You don't have any scars," he said.

"Oh, I do," she said, wriggling a little as her hands drifted to her belly. "But they're subtle. It was a laparoscopic surgery."

Sam let his body down beside her, wrapping an arm around her waist as he propped his head on the heel of his palm and gazed down at her. She pointed to two little places on either side of her pelvic bones, where there were subtle shadows on her skin about the size of two dimes.

"They went through my bellybutton, too," she told him. "You can't see that one."

Goosebumps on her skin told him she was cold, so he grabbed the rumpled bedcover and tossed it over their bodies.

"Kaia," he whispered, pressing a kiss to her temple as he drew his body close alongside hers. "I'm sorry."

She turned to face him and smiled. "Don't be." Her fingers were soft in his hair, her smile fading. "I should've told you sooner. I didn't tell my ex, not right away. I lied about the scars, said they were from ovarian cysts, nothing too serious." She nodded, pressing her lips together as tears filled her eyes. "But he found out the truth and, well, he wanted a family. He told me it didn't matter, but it did. Then, of course, he got together with Darla and"—she drew in a long breath—"they're expecting a baby later this year."

"Shit."

"Yeah," Kaia replied, and let out a shaky laugh. Her hands found his face and drew him closer. She kissed him softly, and whispered, "So, no condom, no problem. I want you, Sam."

"I want you, too," he told her, running his hand over the softness of her low belly. He rested his hand over the ridge of her pelvis, where one of her scars was. "And anyway," he whispered as he nuzzled against her neck, "I'm pretty sure if you and I had a kid he'd be a sea monster."

"Kraken baby," Kaia said. She laughed and turned, twining her legs through his, coiling her body against his.

She was so smooth and soft, so warm. He felt the blood coursing through his veins focus its flow and in a breath he was hard again, aching for her. He lifted her thigh over his hip and reached between their bodies to guide himself inside her. Finding himself surrounded by nothing but her sweet giving warmth, he let himself thrust steadily as he cradled her closer. It felt so good, being together without anything separating them. He was very likely to come in the next thirty seconds if they kept it up like this.

Kaia let out a low moan, squeezing her eyes shut even as he felt her fine muscles squeezing his cock. Her eyes now opened wide and she groaned a loud and profane affirmation as he pounded into her, faster and faster, until he felt his joints shaking, his head and his cock exploding.

Sam growled as they fell apart, collapsing into the pillows. "Sorry," he breathed. "I wanted to make that last longer."

Kaia laughed. "I think that one holds the record for my fastest orgasm ever."

"Really?" Sam brightened at the thought.

She nodded and turned to tuck herself into the crook between his shoulder and his chest, where she fit perfectly.

"Were you playing the banjo when I knocked on the door earlier?" he asked, after a while.

"Mmhm," Kaia hummed against his chest, her little fingers moving over the short, dark hair that grew in tight whorls against his skin.

"I've got an idea," he said. "I'll make breakfast while you play me something."

Kaia's smile broke over him like a wave of sunshine and melted away whatever it was that had happened to him the day before and the bad, lingering feeling that had followed.

⧽

Sam cracked an egg into butter bubbling in the black iron pan. He glanced over his shoulder at Kaia, sitting at the long, battered oak table in the center of the kitchen, picking on her banjo. She was good. Really good. And he'd thought her voice was her talent. After a long instrumental intro, she broke into song and her voice filled the room.

"*I been a moonshiner,*" she sang, "*for seventeen long years, I spent all my money on whiskey and beer, I go to some hollow and set up my still. If whiskey don't kill me, I don't know what will.*"

Sam leaned against the counter and watched the clever fingers of her left hand moving over the banjo frets, hammering here, pulling away there, moving with mind-boggling speed and accuracy while her right hand beat a constant tempo against the strings. When she sang, her eyes went faraway and her face became placid, and she was more beautiful than ever.

The eggs started to fizzle and pop behind him and he reluctantly turned toward the stove again. She finished her song with a flourish of lightning-fast notes on the banjo just as he was plating the eggs and toast.

"This looks amazing," she said, raking a hand through her unruly red curls as Sam set her plate in front of her. She placed her banjo on the table and began tucking into her breakfast eagerly.

Sam smiled as he sat catty-corner to her. "When did you start playing?" he asked.

"When I was seven," she answered, one cheek stuffed with food. "My dad and I used to go on these fishing trips in Kentucky and we'd eat at a dive bar that always had live music. Mountain music, my dad called it. Banjo, fiddle, mandolin. I liked the banjo the best and begged him to let me get one."

"Sounds like your dad is a good guy," he said.

Kaia chewed and nodded, narrowing her eyes. "Yes and no. He's an alcoholic."

"And your mom?" he asked. "Do you... remember her?"

Kaia gulped down her food suddenly and diverted her gaze as she took a sip of the coffee Sam knew to be scalding. Eyes widening at the boiling heat in her mouth, she gulped and sucked in a long breath of air.

"Shit. Sorry. That was really hot, wasn't it. Ice water?" Sam suggested, getting up.

She was silent as he cracked the ice and ran the tap.

"I don't really remember her," Kaia said when he set the frosty glass in front of her. She stared down at her plate. "But I think she was like me." Her storm-cloud eyes lifted to his. "I think she was a siren."

Sam nodded as he sat again, cutting into his eggs with his fork.

"And if that's the case... then I don't understand how she could've drowned to death." Kaia chewed on her plump, delicious lower lip. "And if what my dad has said about their love is true, then I don't believe she would've willingly left him. Which means... well, I don't know what it means exactly, but I haven't been told the truth."

"Did you talk to your dad yet?" Sam asked. "Ask him if he knows about... you?"

Kaia shook her head. "I tried calling him, but he was wasted. I just hung up. But I suppose I should try again. I just don't know how I'm gonna feel if it turns out he's been lying to me all my life."

The kitchen was surrounded by silence, even the crashing of the ocean buffered by the densely falling snow outside.

"Do you remember your mother?" Kaia asked suddenly, leaning toward him.

Sam swallowed his bite of food and washed it down with a cautious sip of coffee. "I remember her," he said, at last, hoping his voice wouldn't betray his emotion. "I remember her smell. Her face. She was... gentle. Attentive."

And where had she gone? Why hadn't she come to land with him when it was his time to become a human? He had been plagued by these questions all his time on land.

"The day I changed," Sam swallowed, lowering his brows over his eyes in hopes they wouldn't fill with tears, "we were hunting and we got separated. I can't even imagine what she went through, after I was gone. I've wondered why she didn't come to land. Why she didn't look for me. I guess it's possible she wasn't a selkie, but just a normal seal. But still, I never understood why she didn't try to find me." The conclusions he'd come to were not ones he could bring himself to utter aloud.

Luckily, he didn't have to say more. Kaia reached over and rested her hand on his. She gave him a soft smile and they continued eating in comfortable silence.

"How's the painting going?" Kaia asked later as they finished drying the dishes. "Getting geared up for your big show?"

Sam chuckled. "I don't know how big it'll be. It's winter in Quolobit. There's nobody here to come." He lifted his shoulders and slid a plate into the shelf. "Doesn't bother me. I've got a lot of work to do, though. I need more stuff."

Kaia smirked. "Well, I think you got a good start on that painting of me," she murmured, turning to stand on tiptoe to nudge a mug into its spot in the cabinet.

His eyes traveled down the curve of her back, over the swell of her hips and her perfectly round ass in tight leggings. Unable to resist, he reached for it, cupping her between her cheeks. "Since I'm here, maybe I should do some study sketches of you," he said, pressing his lips into her hair.

She arched against him, gasping slightly as he squeezed. "What do you think?" he asked. "Would you sit for me?"

"Sit?" Kaia asked, a little breathless. "You sure that's all you want to have me do?"

He growled against her warm skin. No, that certainly wasn't all he wanted to have her do.

"Maybe we can start in the living room," he suggested, reluctantly pulling his hand out from between her warm, soft cheeks. "I've got some paper and pencils hidden in the desk in there."

Despite the snow, there was decent light hitting the couch, where he set her up for a portrait. Of course, he wanted to tell her to strip down and pose nude for him, but he didn't think that'd be fair. He *had* asked her to take off her shirt; that way he could get the lines of her shoulders and neck.

"What do you think?" he asked, turning his back as he went to the credenza along the wall and selected a record. "How would you feel seeing your face on the walls at my show?" He looked over his shoulder and gave a playful grin.

"I think I'd like that, very much," Kaia declared as she settled onto the couch, a soft wool blanket drawn about her bare shoulders.

"Good. 'Cause I think I'd like that, too," Sam said.

The fire popped in the hearth as the stereo crackled to life with the energized, fresh first notes of the *Rumours* album by Fleetwood Mac. Sam sang along in his tuneless way as he cut his first lines onto the page using light, fast strokes.

Curve from forehead to chin. Line of the neck. Yoke of shoulders. Slope of brows. Shadowed circles for the orbital cavities. The suggestion of a mouth—the mouth that he was dying to capture.

Kaia hummed along as the record switched to the second track and Stevie Nicks began to croon *Dreams*. Her features became clearer in his drawing, lifting out of whispered graphite. He traced the slightly downward curving line where her lips met. God, that full upper lip. That plump lower one. He struggled to maintain focus. She giggled.

"What?" he asked.

"Lemme see."

"Not yet."

Sam kept working, cross-hatching in the light, exaggerating the chiaroscuro that highlighted her round, beautiful face.

Freckles!

How could he forget? Yes, he had to include a few of those, too. He glanced up at her and committed a constellation on her cheek to memory before transferring it to the page. By the time *Songbird* came on, he had a decent sketch.

Her eyes widened, her mouth falling open as he turned the pad toward her. "Sam," she whispered, "that's so beautiful. And really freaking good. Like, Leonardo da Vinci good."

He snorted. He was hardly that talented, but he did have to admit, he'd captured her well and his touch had somehow improved dramatically.

"Guess it helps when you've got a muse," he said, angling the portrait now so he could look at it, too.

The record hit the end of side A and the room was enveloped in quiet once more. Sam looked up at Kaia. Her eyes were soft and sweet, her lips parting, the blanket falling from her shoulders. He made a low noise in his throat at the sight of her breasts. She unfolded her legs beneath her and stood from the couch, stepping towards him.

Sam set the drawing down on the coffee table as Kaia approached where he sat on a stool beside the hearth. His hands found her bare, silky waist as she straddled his hips and lowered herself onto his lap. She kissed him with eager, sucking lips, her hands gripping the hair at the back of his head.

"I don't think I've ever been anybody's muse before," she whispered against his mouth.

His heart started pounding as he spread his hands under her bottom, pulling her closer. She arched her back, growling as his fingers pressed into the seam between her legs. Lowering his lips, he took one nipple between them. She smelled of honeysuckle and tasted of vanilla and he was suddenly out of his head and desperate for more of her.

"I'm going to taste every inch of you," he told her, inhaling the warm scent between her breasts.

Chapter Thirty-Five

"But first, I've gotta get a shower," Sam said, suddenly pulling away. "I'm covered in bacon grease."

Her heart was keeping a steady, up-tempo rhythm against her chest and she was aching between her legs. She wasn't sure she could wait that long.

"Fine," she said, standing up. "I'm coming with you."

Sam smiled up at her as his fingers began to lift the hem of his T-shirt. He stood and pulled the shirt away, revealing his hard, lean body. She started unbuttoning his fly while pulling him upstairs.

The shower screamed to life as the plumbing lurched. Sam shoved his jeans down over his hips and stepped out of them as Kaia watched. When he stepped into the steaming shower and offered her his hand she took it and followed. He let out a groan of pleasure as the water struck him, throwing back his head of dark hair into the spray.

"Feels good?" Kaia said, sidling closer and rubbing his chest with a bar of soap.

Sam smiled down. "Not as good as that bar of soap in your hands."

She pushed the suds down through the tight curls below his navel, sliding lower. He let out a low groan and leaned against the tiled wall as she stroked him.

She felt the mischievous urge to push him to the brink and leave him aching. Tightening her grip, she pressed him against the wall as the hot water fell over them. She was sure she was about to be victorious when he stopped her, pulling away and laughing.

"Give me that goddamned soap." He wrested it from her fingers with one effortless grab and used it to perfunctorily wash the rest of his body, scrubbing his face, his pits, his butt. "Keep going like this and I might be out of commission. Now," he said, when he was apparently finished, "it's your turn."

She laughed at the ticklish sensation of his soap-laden hands scrubbing beneath her arms, then began to pant as he rubbed her breasts, her back. He gathered more soap between his palms before slipping one hand behind her.

Sam smiled like a devil and slipped his other hand along her belly, gliding down between her thighs. His slow, deliberate rubbing was making her so delirious she couldn't even move. His dark, wild eyes held hers. "I can't get enough of you, Kaia. I want everything."

She let out a moan but managed to say, "I want that, too. Everything and forever."

CHAPTER THIRTY-SIX

EVERYTHING AND FOREVER. It was what he was afraid of. And what he wanted most.

If Sam could have Kaia, he could deal with life on land till the end of his days. She really made him almost forget the bone-deep longing for the ocean he'd carried around for fifteen years. Almost.

His head was still spinning from yesterday. There was no rational explanation for his behavior, for his forgetting. And if there was no rational explanation...

No. This had nothing to do with the supernatural. Nothing to do with his sealskin. Impossible. The thing was probably gathering dust under somebody's bed. Or buried in a landfill and not rotting because it was magickal, because the creature it belonged to was still alive. He was damned lucky it hadn't been cut into pieces to make some stupid garment or throw pillow. That would've been the end of him. Felicia Dunne had been straight-up when she told him that without his sealskin, his life-expectancy was bleak.

"What is it?" Kaia asked, toweling her hair, standing stark naked in the bathroom door.

He felt himself stirring at the sight of her. Could he ever get his fill of this woman?

"Sam?"

"Huh?"

She giggled, cheeks coloring at his wandering eyes. Her laugh and her smile faded, though, and she leaned against the doorframe. "You look… troubled, darlin'."

He sighed at the sound of her calling him that. "Just thinking about yesterday. I'm worried that what happened to me had something to do with my sealskin."

"Oh."

"Yeah." He glanced in the mirror and smoothed a hand over his beard before bending to pick up his discarded clothes. "I'm getting this feeling, you know, like it's not natural, whatever happened."

"You mean… "

"Yeah, like it was a… magickal occurrence."

She lifted her foxy brows. Gave her head a little shake. "Sorry," she said. "I'm still getting used to the reality of this."

Sam nodded. He understood how she felt.

She stepped closer, a soft hand on his arm. "Well, there's nothing you can do about it right now, is there?"

He shook his head. There wasn't.

"I have an idea." Her lips brightened into a smile. "I bought some snacks the other day. We can have a VHS tape marathon and pig out on nachos. Sound good?"

He pulled her close and wrapped his arms around her bare waist, nuzzling against her neck. "Will you be wearing this outfit the whole time?"

She laughed, and the sound blew away his fears.

CHAPTER THIRTY-SEVEN

THE MINUTE SHE saw the *Angeline* finally leaving Foley's Point the morning after the blizzard, Violet lifted the sealskin to her lips again. "Come to me, Sam," she commanded, and smiled as she watched the small craft change course.

It proved to her what she'd thought impossible: that Kaia had used some form of protective magick to guard her property. The perky bitch was perhaps smarter than Violet had thought. If Kaia had used a protective charm, that put to question why she had done such a thing. Was she a witch who cast protective wards over her home by habit? Maybe. Did she know Violet's secret? Impossible.

When Violet was sure the *Angeline* was making its way to her property in the center of the harbor, she ran downstairs and past Emory in the kitchen. She went barefoot through the snow until she came to the land's edge, where she flipped the switch that would open the boathouse door. With a high ceiling to make room for fishing instruments and a deep bottom carved out of the rock, it was perfect for Sam's lobster boat.

When the *Angeline* was safely inside, Violet flipped the switch to close the door. Her feet burned from the cold as she watched Sam walk out to meet her. His eyes were vacant, pupils dilated, his gaze directionless.

"Carry me to the house." Violet wrapped her arms around his neck and felt him lift her off the cold, hard ground.

CHAPTER THIRTY-EIGHT

KAIA STARTED TIDYING up the minute Sam left, needing to pull the house together before the realtor showed up at half-past ten. As she swept and scrubbed, her body felt light. Felt *whole*. More whole than it had since the night she had first changed into a siren. She'd been so afraid of herself in the days between, so afraid of what was waiting just under her skin. Afraid of the other siren who'd attacked her.

In fact, now that she was thinking about it, she hadn't seen hide nor hair of that siren in days... somehow that wasn't comforting. Kaia felt her good mood plummeting. She squeezed her eyes shut at the image of the siren's face as blood plumed around her. Had Kaia killed her? God, she hoped not. She pressed the heels of her hands to her eyes and fought back a sudden sob.

No, no, no. This was no time for a breakdown. She had less than forty-five minutes to get dressed, tidy up the bedroom and the living room—both of which had been destroyed by her and Sam's lovemaking—and clean up the mess from dinner and breakfast in the kitchen.

Sam had offered to help, but she'd told him to go home and work on his paintings. She'd vacuum the popcorn strewn across the living room carpet. She'd wipe up the coffee smudges on the counter and the stove. She'd scrub out the pot they'd used for cooking chili. Make the bed. Put dirty clothes in the hamper. Wipe curly red hairs and globs of toothpaste out of the sink. She had nothing better to do.

"Dammit!" She grunted as she moved her fingers too hard over the scratch on her face, opening it up. Blood, scarlet and oily, streaked her fingers.

Did you kill her?

Kaia dampened a washcloth and pressed it gingerly to the cut on her cheek for a few minutes. Then, groaning like a beast, she swiped clothes off the floor and chucked them haphazardly in an empty drawer that would have to serve as a makeshift hamper. She stubbed her big toe on the door-frame of the bedroom and let out a roar as she soldiered onward, down the stairs, into the wrecked living room. She gathered nearly a half-dozen used glasses and mugs, wondering how two people could go through so much dishware, and was working up a sweat vacuuming when she just had to stop.

"To hell with it," she grumbled, kicking the vacuum off. She brushed her hair out of her face and went to the window overlooking the bay.

The water was dark and peaceful as a holy place. It called to her. And, yes, her white-haired nemesis called to her, too. At least, Kaia hoped she did. She hoped she was alive, because she could not bear to live with her-self if she was a killer. That was so, so very far from who she wanted to be.

The windowpane was cold when she pressed her fingers to it. Her breath fogged the glass. The coolness of it felt good on her bruised, broken cheek when she pressed it there and shut her eyes, listening to the constant crash and hiss against the rocks of Foley's Point.

"I hope you're out there," she whispered to the siren. "I hope you're okay."

Kaia pulled away and looked out at the bay again, eyes centering on Thursday Island. The *Angeline* wasn't there. Maybe Sam had decided to go into town to the post office to pick up the art supplies he'd ordered. He'd mentioned something about that. Or groceries. He couldn't exactly drum up the essentials out there on Thursday Island, could he?

With a sigh, Kaia turned from the window and wheeled the vacuum cleaner to its home in the hall closet, before rolling up her sleeves to tackle the kitchen.

Chapter Thirty-Nine

By the light, Sam judged it to be midday. He was tied to a chair, bound by wrists, ankles and neck with a thick rope. The room was well lit by windows encircling its octagonal circumference. He was high up, and could see only the dark spires of snow-dusted hemlocks and the white chevron of a gull circling the gray. There was something familiar about this place. A smell, or…

He head the sound of a door opening. Footfalls ascending steps. The creak of the wood floor under a person's weight behind him. Then he smelled the perfume he knew so well: grassy vetiver and sweet jasmine warmed with a hint of ginger, grounded in a whisper of earthy patchouli.

"Violet?" His voice broke when he said her name.

There was something else, something indefinable in her perfume. Something he frankly did not like. It was in all the perfumes she created, and he could never quite put his finger on it. But whatever it was, it made him want to gag.

She sidled in front of him, black hair swinging to her waist. She wore a loose black dress, a pair of fur-lined moccasin boots over wool stockings, and a silver skeleton key dangling between her breasts on a delicate chain.. Her makeup was perfect, as usual. She didn't look like a person you'd expect to tie somebody to a chair and leave them in a basement. Or an attic. Or whatever this place was.

The cupola, Sam realized. The circular room that crowned the Wilde's magnificent Victorian on Main Street.

"Why am I here?" he asked.

"Sam, we need to talk." Violet frowned and went to sit on top of an old trunk nearby.

"That's fine," he said. "How 'bout you untie me? And tell me, Violet, how the fuck did I get here? 'Cause I've got no memory of it."

She lifted her arched brows and twitched her lips into a fleeting curve. "No, of course you don't. And you won't remember being here, either, when I'm done with you."

"*Done with me?*" He pulled against the rope, feeling it grate against his wrists, pull at the sockets of his shoulders. He was beginning to sweat. "Why the *fuck* do you have me tied up?"

Was this some kind of sexual fantasy of hers? Sam hadn't known Violet to be particularly kinky. Other than raking her nails down his back and pulling his hair, she'd never shown any inclination toward this type of sexual play. He had a bad feeling it wasn't about sex at all.

Violet cast her baleful eyes upon him. "Stop struggling, will you? It's not just rope that binds you to the chair. You're spell-bound, Sam. You're not going anywhere. Not till I say."

Sam stilled. "You're a witch," he said, not so much a question as a realization.

Violet lifted a shoulder. "Among other things," she purred.

"What do you want?" he asked, fighting his instinct to struggle against the ropes.

"Let's talk about how you've been cheating on me."

Sam slumped against the back of the chair. He should've seen this coming. Well, not this, exactly. Not being held against his will, possibly drugged, possibly abducted.

"Hey," he said, suddenly connecting the dots. "This isn't the first time you've done this to me, is it? Two days ago, I don't know what happened, but I lost track of an entire day. Felt sick as a dog afterwards when I came back to myself. Was that you?"

A lurid smile spread over Violet's lips. "It's really a pity you don't remember that day. I suppose I could reverse the forgetting spell…"

"Violet! This is—this is crazy." He tried kicking out his legs, only to find that the rope binding his ankles was attached to his neck. Gagging, he felt the blood squeeze through his eyeballs and nostrils.

Violet approached him and stuck her cool fingers under the rope around his neck and loosened it, clucking. When he turned his head toward her wrist to bite her—his instincts were an animal's, after all—she slapped him. Hard. His beard protected him from some of the sting, but still, his left eye was tearing and he tasted blood.

"Fuck!" he shouted, spraying saliva. "Fuck you!"

Violet laughed and stepped away, shaking her head. "We'll get to that eventually."

"Violet, look," he began, trying for a rational tone. "I get it. I've been dishonest with you. You're hurt. That's… that's understandable. But this? This is crazy."

Violet leaned down and put her hands on his thighs. "You want to leave me, Sam? For *her*? Just say it. That's all I want. I want to hear you say it."

Sam kept his mouth clamped shut as Violet's fingernails pinched through the denim covering his legs. He had to think clearly. Play his cards right. She was telling him she wanted honesty. He'd give her that.

"We never had a commitment, Violet," Sam said between his teeth. "Our relationship was just physical, wasn't it? You don't even know me."

She pushed off him, laughing bitterly. "Oh, I know you, Sam. I know you better than you think. Better than *Kaia* ever could."

Sam didn't like the sound of Kaia's name on Violet's tongue. He wanted to tell her to leave Kaia out of it, but something told him that if he were to give an order of any kind, he could bet that Violet would do the exact opposite. She wanted to be in control. *That* was what he needed to give her.

"You know, you're probably right," he said, then stopped himself from speaking more.

Most humans, Sam had observed, were not comfortable with silence. If he didn't talk, she would. And then he could hopefully figure out how to use her words against her.

A raven squawked outside. The wind whistled under the eaves of the cupola. Violet sighed.

"See, I'm confused." She lowered her brows and shook her head in puzzlement. "I've met her, Sam. She's nothing special. She's not even that attractive. I mean, she's… stumpy."

Sam swallowed the metallic taste of blood in his mouth from where Violet's slap had cut the inside of his cheek on his teeth.

"I'd use the words *petite* and *curvy*, but okay," he said.

Let her have control, dammit.

"*Stumpy*," he echoed. "Sure. She's not as beautiful as you."

Sam's head spun with the lie. Kaia was the most beautiful woman he'd ever seen. Still, he had to play Violet's game if he was going to get himself free.

"And there's no way she's as intelligent as me, either," Violet added, widening her eyes. "That hillbilly accent? Does she think that's cute?"

I do.

"I don't think she can help it," Sam said. "Just like me. I know I talk like a Mainer."

Violet snorted. "You do," she agreed. Her brows lowered in thought. She sat on the trunk again and stared at him. "Is that what it's about, then? She's easier for you to relate to? Blue-collar upbringing. No college education. Working a string of shitty jobs. Failing to make it as an artist. She grew up in a ranch house that might as well have been a double-wide." Violet rolled her eyes.

Sam frowned, wondering how Violet had gotten this information about Kaia.

"Oh, I know all about her. It wasn't hard to find her social media accounts online. Not that she has any following to note. She doesn't even post regularly, but there was enough information on there for me to get the picture. So? Is that it? Do you feel like I'm too good for you, and she isn't?"

Sam nodded. That would work. "Yes," he said. "You *are* too good for me, Violet. Where did you really think this relationship could go, huh? Did you think you could take me out to dinner with my dirty hands and my Downeaster accent and introduce me to your father? Me, the lobsterman you're dating?" He laughed. It did sound ridiculous. "Did you think your family would approve of me, pay for a big wedding and invite all their friends in the one percent to meet their poor son-in-law? Did you think you wouldn't be *embarrassed* by me, Violet?"

She pursed her lips, eyes burning into his. "I don't have a family," she said. "This?" She held up her hands and gestured to herself. "This isn't even my body."

Sam's head spun. He didn't get her meaning. He hoped his silence would draw her out.

"I've been on this earth a long, long time, Sam. Imagine if each day in your life was a lifetime in itself. That's how long my time has been."

He swallowed, fearing her more as he looked up into her cold gaze.

Violet stood and paced to the window. "I know you've had your share of lovers. Last summer alone there were five that I counted. That loud blonde, Amy, who you picked up at the Hook and Anchor. The single mom, what was her name? Oh, Therese. The one on vacation with her parents and her kids. Boy, was she miserable. And before that, scores. I wonder if Kaia knows about your track record."

Sam gritted his teeth. He wanted to defend himself, to say he'd always been honest with those women and told them he didn't want a relationship. And most of them had been fine with that. They'd just been passing through, looking for a little summer excitement.

"Of course, there was that one a few years ago... Riley Patterson." Violet laughed, slapping her thigh. "Remember her?"

He did.

"Skinny little waif of a thing," Violet continued. "Got a summer job on the ferry boat. You'd end up the days at the Hook, and, well, one thing led to another and eventually she was sleeping out on Thursday Island. And when summer ended she was heartbroken."

Even though she'd promised she wouldn't be. Yes, Sam remembered Riley. He remembered her letters sent from her university campus. Her emails. Her phone calls. All unanswered. She'd stopped trying to reach out to him eventually.

"Poor Riley," Violet sighed dramatically. "Of course, there was Paige Mather and Larissa Moody and Rosalee Thompson, too," she added.

Sam felt like he'd just been slapped in the face. Those were girls he'd been with when he was a teenager. How did Violet know about them? He certainly hadn't known Violet at that time, no more than to see her on the street, the strange girl living alone in the big house with a live-in tutor who homeschooled her.

"Oh, I know about those poor girls, too," Violet said. "I saw the tall, dark-haired boy who worked with his dad on the fishing boat. I made friends with the biggest gossip in Camden Hills High, Chrissy English. Remember her?"

Sam didn't.

"I didn't think you would," Violet admitted. "Chrissy had the *biggest* crush on you. But you never noticed her. Not for a moment. Oh, and who could forget your first? Tara. Wasn't that her name? Wasn't she... older?"

Sam shook his head. He didn't want to be reliving any of this. Violet, however, was hell-bent on dredging up his past, holding him accountable for every woman he'd ever been with, as if each one had been a betrayal against her.

"Tara came to Quolobit Harbor your second summer," Violet said. "Her family rented the house on Foley's Point, didn't they?"

They had.

"She was eighteen and you were what, sixteen?"

Something like that. Sam was struggling to keep up with her. She remembered more about his life than he did.

"And her parents were lushes and her little brothers were assholes and she was always hanging around downtown by herself and you'd drive around together in her parents' big old Buick station wagon." Violet laughed, like it was her own fond memory. "They were the kind of rich people who wouldn't buy themselves a decent car. Tara was wearing cute clothes only because she'd earned the money herself, babysitting. And Tara... she took your virginity in that Buick. Didn't she, Sam?"

Yep.

"And then, at the end of summer she left you heartbroken." Violet sighed. "And that's when you started breaking hearts of your own, one after the other."

"How in hell do you know all of this?" Sam asked.

Violet shrugged, sitting with her legs crossed atop the old trunk. "Just paid attention, that's all."

Sam shook his head. This was more than *attention*. This was *obsession*.

"And, you know, I get it," Violet went on. "After having your heart broken you learned not to trust women. So you never let anybody in. And you were an animal, Sam." Her mouth opened, then curved into a smirk. "I mean, you left all those ladies *destroyed* for other men. Poor Riley wasn't the only one who couldn't get over you."

Sam frowned. He had to defend himself. "No, you're wrong about that. She's the only one I ever heard from afterwards. I swear."

Violet laughed. "Um, no. You're the one who's wrong. The only reason you haven't had droves of women weeping at your feet and begging for more is *me*. And you're welcome, by the way."

Sam shook his head, beyond confused.

"I made sure they forgot about you when they left Quolobit Harbor, Sam," Violet explained. She crossed her arms over her chest. "I did that for you. I knew you wanted it that way."

He was floored. Shocked. He would have called her a liar, only he knew she had ripped an entire day out of his own memory. If she could do that to him, she could surely do it to others.

"Riley slipped past me, and I'm sorry about that one," Violet admitted. "She left a week early because her grandmother died, if you remember."

He did, vaguely.

"Anyway, it caught me off guard. I didn't have time to prepare the spell that would make her forget you. Needless to say, that was the last time I was so careless." She gave him a trite smile, as if he ought to thank her.

But he didn't want to thank her. He wanted to rip her to pieces.

"I waited, Sam," she said, eyeing him. "I waited for you. Till I thought you'd be ready for something real. Ready for me."

Sam almost laughed, but thankfully managed to control himself. Violet wasn't his lover. She wasn't his friend. She was his stalker. And she was batshit crazy.

Imagine… if every day in your entire life was a lifetime in itself. That's how long my time has been.

What did that even mean?!

"So what is it about Kaia?" Violet asked with a tone of curiosity. "Why her?"

Sam shook his head in terror. No. If Violet could make women forget him, she could do the same to Kaia, if she chose. And if, God forbid, she found out that Kaia was not a human woman but a siren…

"Kaia's nothing to me," he said. "Just another fling."

Violet laughed ruefully. "Just had to make your mark on her, huh, Sam? Claim all the pretty ones that come into town?"

He nodded. "Something like that."

"Oh, how I love your insatiable virility."

Violet's smile was fading. He sensed he was treading on dangerous ground.

"And me?" she whispered, lips trembling. Her dark, full lashes swept over her brilliant green eyes. "What about me, Sam? Was I just another fling?"

Chapter Forty

Kaia watched the realtor's car slip and slide out of the driveway as he left Foley's Point. Her heart sank, when it should have been singing.

One point two million. *Million.* That was how he'd told her they should price the place. It was more, by half, than what she had expected, what she'd hoped. It frightened her, that big number.

A terrible quiet stole over her as she turned from the kitchen door and went to the sink, looking out the window at the rugged coastline where she had dragged Sam Lowell to land her first night in Maine.

One point two million was a number she couldn't ignore. With that money, she could buy three of her own houses—two for herself, one for her dad. She could go back to school and get her music degree.

So she'd agreed to put the property on the market. Markus hadn't even had to take photos; the ones on his rental site would do just fine for his web listing. He had shaken her hand and said he'd come by with a sign in case there happened to be any random January tourists looking to buy a place for their next summer retreat.

"You never know," Markus had said to her. "The place could be sold by this time next week. I've seen it happen that fast."

Kaia swallowed the heavy, dull queasiness rising inside her and clung to the edge of the sink, watching the waves roll in. Bittersweet tears started rolling down her cheeks. Her mother would want her to have the money, to have the best life she could. But her mother would also want Kaia to live the truth. And the truth was that she was a siren.

If only she had known. If only her father had told her. Maybe then she wouldn't have stupidly jumped into the water and stirred up this conflict with the other siren. Maybe then she wouldn't have another person's lifeblood on her hands.

Angry, she picked up the phone and dialed the number for her father's house. She needed answers. She wanted to hold him accountable for the secret he'd kept from her. The secret that had been under her skin all this time.

It rang and rang.

Eventually, Kaia hung up. She leaned against the fridge, defeated.

She pulled her arms around herself, wanting to be held. Another self had been living inside her her whole life, a self that was wild and strange, a self that could kill. She wasn't sure she could live with herself if she had killed the siren. She needed to know. She needed to know who she really was.

Kaia picked up the phone and dialed the number from the scrawled note Sam had stuck on the fridge. She also needed someone to talk her out of swimming into the dark womb of Wapomeq Bay.

His phone went straight to voicemail.

"Dammit." Kaia slammed the phone down on the receiver and stalked into the living room to look out at Thursday Island. Snow was coming in again, covering the island in a white haze. It was nothing more than a blurry smudge in the paleness. No sight of the *Angeline*.

She decided to try finding Sam in town, the only other place he could possibly be. After suiting up in her warmest clothes and letting the old truck run for ten minutes before dashing out to it, she took the road through the forest between her property and the main road. She went slowly, eyes on the quiet pine tree trunks and their whispery dead branches. A raven flew across her path and she watched it alight on a branch, unsettling a fine powder of snow that fell on the windshield.

When she got there, Kaia found Main Street deserted. Felicia Dunne's shop was closed. There was no one except for Harvey in the Hook and Anchor. The *Angeline* wasn't moored near the wharf and the harbormaster hadn't seen Sam all day.

She had never felt so desperate for human company. For a reassuring word. Out of her mind and wishing that for once something could just be easy, she wiped the threat of tears from her eyes and turned the truck back toward Foley's Point, taking Main Street slow.

Then she saw the lights on in one shop and settled her foot onto the brake.

CHAPTER FORTY-ONE

SAM HAD PROMISED Violet she wasn't just another fling, but she didn't believe him. He had also said Kaia was unimportant to him, but she didn't believe that, either. Violet needed to know for sure. And she had a way to make him tell the truth. She just needed to find the jar of white chrysanthemums.

As she stood on a stool and reached for a jar atop the highest shelf her fingers found the cool glass, which kept slipping out of reach.

"Dammit!" Violet cursed and shifted her weight on the stool. Her foot slipped.

"Everything okay?" a soft, drawling voice said behind her.

Violet spun around on the step stool and lost her balance. All she saw as she toppled to the floor was a wild head of bright red curls flying toward her. She landed partially in Kaia's arms, partially on top of her as they both fell to the floor. Kaia made a little *oof!* as they landed, then began to disentangle herself.

"You all right?" she asked, brushing a springy curl from her eyes.

Violet felt a splinter lodge itself into the palm of her right hand where she had jammed it into the old floorboards, its sting a physical reminder of the pain Kaia Foley had caused her heart. She sat cross-legged and pinched at the splinter, using her fingernails to push it out of her flesh. She hissed as the narrow needle of wood surfaced from her skin and pushed out a bead of scarlet with it.

"I'm sorry for startling you," Kaia said.

"Oh, I think I was going to fall either way," Violet replied, dryly.

Kaia smiled a wide, sincere smile. She shrugged. "You seemed pretty focused on finding whatever it was you were looking for up there. Guess you didn't hear me come in."

Kaia stood, dusted off her bottom, and grabbed a deer antler sitting on a display table. She climbed the step stool and hooked the antler around the jar, using it to pull the jar closer to the edge of the shelf. She hopped off the stool and gave the jar to Violet.

Violet pulled herself to her feet and set the chrysanthemum jar down on the front counter. Turning to face Kaia, she put on a smile and stepped toward her, running her fingers across her soft, peachy, freckled cheek.

"I love the light of snow, don't you?" Violet said, eyes taking in Kaia's face as she touched it.

Such an open, innocent expression. It was no wonder Sam wanted her, if she was being honest with herself. Violet's anguish drew in on itself like a great wave gathering before the rush to shore. If she was to win, she had to play from multiple angles. Bewitching Sam wasn't enough.

"Hey, I've got an idea! There's nowhere to go, nothing to do," Violet said as her thumb traced the curve of Kaia's cheek. "What do you say we do that photoshoot for my website?"

CHAPTER FORTY-TWO

KAIA DIDN'T WANT to go back to Foley's Point. She didn't want to think about letting go of the house. She didn't want to think about what she'd do with a million dollars. And she *definitely* didn't want to think about the siren she might have killed.

"Sure," she said to Violet, trying not to pull away from her touch too obviously. Some people were just touchers, she told herself, though for some reason she wouldn't have imagined Violet to be one. "I don't have anywhere to be."

Violet smiled, seeming delighted. "Great. Let's go upstairs. The light's better up there and that's where I keep my inventory."

After Violet locked the front door, Kaia followed her up the narrow, dark stairs at the back of the shop. Tall windows on either end of the building let the soft, grayish light of the snowy afternoon into the open room. A long table sat in the center, scattered with chemistry vials and vessels. A crazy bronze contraption that looked like a miniature whiskey still sat at one end.

"I use that to make my own essential oils," Violet explained.

"That must be why it smells so amazing in here," Kaia said.

The shelves were far less tidy than those downstairs, though they still appeared organized. Everything was labeled in neat, sweeping script—the kind of handwriting people had had a hundred years ago.

"I'm thinking we'll do all of my tinted lip balms," Violet said in her low, smoky voice as she set a handful of things down on the table. "And the mineral highlighter."

Kaia busied herself admiring the workshop as Violet laid out the cosmetics and got her camera set up.

"You must be so proud of your business," Kaia said, sniffing a vial of rose oil. "Oh my God, that smells amazing."

"Do you like that?" Violet asked. "I made that using wild roses I collected along the coast here. There's nothing like them. Best-smelling roses in the world. I made my first perfume using that rose oil as the main note and all of my other perfumes have it as a base."

"Wow," Kaia said, impressed. She sat on the stool Violet had set out for her, beside the table. "And this is all you?" she asked. "I mean, it's your business and you make all this stuff, on your own?"

"I have a few employees to help out in the store and my sister sometimes comes in to help me make big batches of stuff when I need her. But, for the most part, it's just me."

"You're so independent," Kaia said.

Violet lifted her perfect, arched brows. "I've learned it's wisest to rely only on myself," she said, and handed Kaia a face-wipe. "Just wipe off any oil and I'll put on a moisturizer, then we can start."

Kaia did as bidden and wiped her face with the cucumber-scented wipe. Violet began with combing her brows, then applied clear mascara.

"You sure you don't want to use black?" Kaia asked skeptically. "My lashes are orange."

"Yes, and I want to keep them that way," Violet said as she leaned close and flicked the wand over Kaia's lashes. "This'll just make them look wet. Like you've just come out of the sea."

Kaia swallowed as her heart started pounding. She gripped her thighs and told herself to calm the heck down. There was no way Violet knew. No way.

Violet applied the mineral highlighter on Kaia's cheeks and eyelids next. Then she applied the first of the tinted lip balms, a bright coral color.

"That looks incredible on you," Violet said as she offered Kaia a hand-held mirror.

Kaia admired the color on her lips as Violet turned on her camera.

"Tell me something about yourself, Kaia," Violet said, looking at her through the lens. "What do you think of our little town?"

Snap, snap, snap, went the shutter.

Kaia smiled.

Snap.

"It's beautiful. The houses are all so old and charming. The shoreline is stunning," she said. "I can't wait to see what it looks like in summer."

Snap.

Violet's head popped up above the camera. "Summer?" she asked. "So you think you're staying, then? Did you decide not to sell?"

Kaia's smile fell. "No, actually. I put the house on the market this morning. I don't know why I said *summer*. I—I don't know what my plans are," she stammered.

Violet approached with another wipe and removed the lip balm from Kaia's lips, then applied the next color—a sheer, juicy magenta that smelled of ripe summer berries.

Behind the camera again, Violet asked, "You don't seem overly eager to get back to… where is it you're from?"

"Nashville," Kaia replied. "Yeah, um, no. I'm not eager to go back. I… met someone here."

Snap. Snap. Snap.

"Oh?" Violet's voice was muffled behind the camera.

"Yeah, this guy, Sam. Sam Lowell?"

"Oh, Sam," Violet said. "Lobster Sam."

Snap.

"Yes," Kaia replied, laughing. "Lobster Sam."

"When did that start?" Violet asked.

"Pretty much the day I arrived," Kaia said. That was the truth, if she was being honest. The energy between her and Sam had been obvious to her from the moment they had met. And now, knowing their connection had the power to make her feel good in ways she had never thought would be possible for her, she couldn't imagine it ever ending between the two of them. "It's only been a week but already I feel like… like he knows me better than anyone else ever has. I feel like I've finally found someone I could trust. Someone who wants to share himself with me, completely."

Snap. Snap.

All business, Violet came around the tripod and wiped at Kaia's lips. She was a little rough, and Kaia spun an eye up at her.

"Do you know Sam?" Kaia asked.

CHAPTER FORTY-THREE

ALL VIOLET HAD to do was gain Kaia's trust. Ask her to the house. Give her wine with a few drops of the snapdragon and dogwood essence she had prepared, speak the Incanta Oblivio—and Sam would be gone from her head forever.

"Everybody knows everybody here in Quolobit Harbor," Violet answered, affecting a neutral tone with great effort.

Kaia was visibly tense. She knew there was someone else in Sam's life. Knew she was the other woman. Bitch.

Violet applied the last of the tinted lip balm to Kaia's full, disgustingly pouty lips. She pictured the things she did to Sam with those lips and wanted to slap Kaia. But that wouldn't do. She must save her rage and her lust for Sam, and Sam alone.

"I have to warn you," Violet began as she angled herself behind the camera again. "Sam Lowell has a reputation for being something of a lady-killer."

"Oh, he's told me."

Violet paused before taking the shot. She watched Kaia's expression for pain, jealousy, bitterness. The dumb bitch chuckled. Violet pressed down her finger and got the image of Kaia laughing and rolling her eyes, lips painted perfectly pink.

If she had any idea what Sam was up to with me and Emory two days ago, that grin would be wiped off her face for good.

Violet suppressed a smug smile as she pictured Sam, naked and sweating, pounding into her while pleasuring Emory at the same time. She recalled, with vivid clarity, the sensation of him through their shared consciousness. It was better than anything she'd ever experienced. She only regretted not having thought of sharing him with her split half sooner.

"You must not be the jealous type," Violet said, and snapped another picture.

"Me? No," Kaia replied. "And anyway, why would I be jealous of the women he was with before me?" A brief sadness passed over her face. "People are going to love who they're going to love, and no amount of wishing otherwise will make it different."

Love. Had she really just used that word?

"Do you think Sam loves you?" Violet asked, biting back a sardonic laugh as she took another photo.

Kaia's lashes brushed over her cheeks, hiding her soft blue eyes. "I think so," she said, like it was a prayer. "And I think I love him back."

Violet removed the camera from the tripod and turned her back to Kaia as she scanned through the photos. She needed to change tack. Casting a forgetting spell on Kaia might not be enough, if she already believed there was love between them.

Using every ounce of her willpower, Violet squeezed her eyes closed and let her breath come in deep, ragged swells until tears stung her cheeks.

"Violet?" Kaia asked behind her. "Are you okay?"

"I bet Sam didn't tell you about me, then, did he?" Violet asked, sniffling as she spun around. She wiped the tears from her face and forced a pained gasp.

Kaia's mouth hung open. Her large, round eyes bored holes into Violet's face.

"We've been seeing each other a few months now, and…" Violet let herself descend into a fit of sobs. She covered her face and heard the sound of Kaia standing from the stool. "He told me it wasn't serious between us but I couldn't help it, Kaia. I hoped."

"Oh… I'm so sorry," Kaia murmured, her unsteady footsteps hesitant on the floor.

"He's at my house right now," Violet said, uncovering her face. "We just—" She exploded into tears. "We just, *you know.* And two days ago he spent the whole day with me, making love. I bet you didn't know that, either."

"What?" Kaia gripped the edge of the table, her face turning pale.

Violet nodded and stepped closer. "He's been lying to both of us."

Kaia shook her head as her eyes, too, began to glisten. "No, that can't be true. The things he said... the way he..."

Violet laughed bitterly and nodded. "Oh, I know all about it," she said. "The things he's made me do with him... the thing he's made me *want* to do... he's claimed me. Completely."

"Me too," Kaia said, her voice thin.

Violet put her hands on Kaia's shoulders. "I think we should go confront him, together. He's at my house, waiting for me to come back."

But Kaia shook her head and began pulling away. "No," she said. "That won't help anything. I'm so sorry, Violet. I—I should go."

"Wait!" Violet reached for her wrist. "I was going to pay you for the photoshoot. Just come over and I can write you a check."

"No, it's fine," Kaia said, pulling away as the tears began to dry on her cheeks and a hardened, cold look came over her face. "I don't want your money."

"At least let me give you something." Violet panicked, needing to give something to Kaia to bind her to herself, even just temporarily. She needed to maintain the connection they'd begun to ensure she'd have a window to use the Incanta Oblivio on Kaia later. It had to be something personal. Something Kaia would keep close. There—perfume. Violet took a vial of the precious wild rose perfume that had been her first creation. She handed it to Kaia.

"As a symbol of my forgiveness," Violet said, going for a pleading tone. "Don't blame yourself, Kaia. This is Sam's fault, not yours."

Kaia looked down at the vial in her hand and smiled sadly. She shook her head again and said, "I'm sorry." She closed her fingers around the perfume and, with a ragged sigh, left.

CHAPTER FORTY-FOUR

"OKAY," KAIA SAID to herself, grabbing handfuls of her hair as she turned around in the kitchen after getting back to the house on Foley's Point and crying her guts out for the better part of an hour. She had tried calling Sam's phone again. Straight to voicemail. She could barely believe that what Violet had said was true, yet it all added up: Sam's unexplained absence two days ago, his avoidance of her calls today. He had said he was seeing someone but that it wasn't serious. Kaia should've taken that as a red flag. She should have known.

"Stupid!" she yelled, and kicked the fridge. It was harder than her toe. *"Dammit!"*

She limped to the table and held her head in her hands.

What have I done?

She'd lured a man away from his partner and possibly killed a fellow siren—was she nothing more than a force of destruction? Was this all some kind of twisted karmic joke?

She pictured Violet confronting Sam at this very moment. Maybe she should have gone with her. Maybe—but no. Kaia was the other woman. The relationship between Sam and Violet, however depthless Sam had claimed it to be, had months of history to it compared to the five days Kaia had spent with him. She didn't have a right to be at Violet's house. Nor could she control what happened next between Violet and Sam. She couldn't even say what she wanted the outcome to be, not now. Even if Sam were to choose her over Violet, Kaia wasn't sure she'd want him.

But at least she could find out if her siren nemesis was alive or dead. At the very least, she could clear or condemn her conscience on that matter.

She opened the back door and braced herself against the biting wind and the sting of snow. Her footsteps crunched through snow and frosted grass as she trudged toward the rocks, toward the shore. She ought to bring the speargun, she knew, but that would only make the sirens see her as a threat.

She trembled as she undressed, leaving her clothes on the dry, thorny branches of a dormant rosebush. The ocean felt like a thousand shards of glass cutting her as she entered it and breathed it in, letting it consume and transform her. Gliding silently out toward the darkness beyond, she let her tail propel her onward, away from land, away from the known.

PART THREE

CHAPTER FORTY-FIVE

VIOLET RETURNED TO the cupola after what had seemed like an hour or two, bearing a tray with a jar of white flowers and a carafe made of double-walled glass and filled with steaming water. Entering without a word, she cast Sam a dark, accusatory look and sat on the floor in front of him.

"What's this?" he asked as she dropped a handful of the dried flowers into the hot water.

The flowers, once wilted and withered, now began to bloom, revealing pale pink centers as they unfurled in the hot water. Violet watched intently, ignoring him.

"Hey, it's friggin' cold up here," he said, and struggled against the rope binding him. "I'm hungry and I gotta piss."

She pursed her lips together and held her hands over the steaming carafe, saying in a quiet voice, "In grief and darkness, pain and ruth, I bid thee, flower, tell me truth."

"What?" Sam said. "What are you saying?"

"In grief and darkness, pain and ruth, I bid thee, flower, tell me truth." Ignoring him completely, Violet quietly repeated her little poem.

Sam considered hurling himself over to one side and trying to break the carafe on the way. If he could get a shard of glass—but no. The glass was too thin. It wouldn't cut through the thick vinyl rope that bound him.

"Violet, please."

"In grief and darkness, pain and ruth, I bid thee, flower, tell me truth," she went on, holding her open hands in the steam that rose from the carafe.

The steam had been white, normal as any steam from freshly boiled water. But now, as the flowers continued to bloom, it took on a subtle purple glow. At first, Sam thought he was seeing things.

He blinked and shook his head. Nope. Purple steam.

An odd scent filled the room, like a pungent, earthy flower, half-rotten. It filled Sam's nostrils as Violet wafted her hands in the vivid steam, sending it out into the room. The eerie, purple mist spiraled around him, brushing his face with its warm, odorous touch. He couldn't help but inhale it.

"In grief and darkness, pain and ruth, I bid thee, flower, tell me truth," Violet said, again and again, till his head was filled with the words.

This was no ordinary flower or steam. There was something intoxicating in it. It gave him a spacey, relaxed feeling similar to weed, only there was also something darker in it, something dream-like and frightening. He felt himself plunged into that place between sleep and wakefulness, where his human imagination could hold him hostage and plague him with scene upon scene of the strange desires and fears that prowled his subconscious.

Sam drew in a deep breath and felt the room spinning.

It dawned on him: he'd been here before. Not just in this mind-state, but in this room. With Violet. Against his will. Tied to the chair, just like this. The recollection was strong, but rooted in a memory just beyond his grasp.

"Now," Violet said, ending her chant. "Tell me the truth, Sam."

He aimed his unsteady gaze on her, seeing her face in the center of a blurry, spinning vortex.

"What am I to you?" she asked.

Sam swallowed the strange, floral taste in his mouth. "Right now," he said, slurring, "you're a pain in my ass."

Violet's expression hardened by some kind of micro-degree that Sam perceived through the swirling purple mist.

"Sam Lowell, tell me true," she said, "am I just another fling?"

Sam laughed. Something in this stuff made him giddy. "Yeah," he answered. "Isn't that all I was to you, Violet?"

"Yes," she answered. Her eyes widened and she clapped a hand over her mouth, as if she had not answered of her own free will. Lowering her arched, black brows, she added, "But I want more, Sam. I want more from you."

"And what is it that you want?" he asked, leaning back in his chair and balancing comfortably on the two back legs.

"I want you to love me, to worship me, to—" Violet shook her head and clamped her mouth shut. "I want you to be honest with me," she said, through her teeth, against her will.

"I love Kaia," he said. It was the truth, and he would have said it whether or not he was high on purple truth-smoke. "I want to spend the rest of my life loving her."

Violet shook her head. Clearly this little experiment of hers wasn't going as she had wished.

The idea suddenly came to Sam that if this smoke brought out the truth, he ought to use it to his advantage. "What did you mean when you said you'd lived as many lives as all the days in my life?" he asked.

"I'm a skinwalker." The words came out of Violet's mouth automatically. Her eyes went big again, expressing her distress at the sound of her own voice. Despite herself, she kept going. "I'm cursed to live again and again. In my first life, more than a thousand years ago, I was betrothed to a young lord. It was an arranged marriage, but as soon as I saw him, I loved him." She blinked rapidly, her cheeks turning pale. Her fingers gripped the skirt of her dress. "On the night before our wedding, I left my bedchamber to find him. My father's castle was large, and it was hard for me to find the room where my husband-to-be was sleeping, but eventually I did.

"I was careful to be quiet when I opened the door. I walked in and parted the bed curtains and there I saw him fornicating with my sister, their bodies tangled and sweating. His eyes were full of her. She was crying out his name."

Tears streamed down Violet's cheeks as she recounted this tale.

"The lord's sword was leaning against the wall beside the bed," Violet said, her voice trembling. "I drove it through both of them, then threw myself out the window, to the sea below."

Violet went silent, her gaze far, far away, as though she were once again in her first life, living through her last moment.

"Then what?" Sam asked.

Her lips parted as she drew in a long, shaky inhalation of the intoxicating steam. "The lord's mother was a witch, and a powerful one. It was she who cursed me to live forever, without ever finding true love."

"Does that mean you're reborn after you die?" Sam asked, intrigued. "How does that work?"

Violet shook her head and sniffled, swiping at her pink-tinged nostrils with the back of her wrist. "When the body dies, my consciousness goes on. I have to find a new body to inhabit. It's easiest if it's a body that is near death, passing through."

"And in this life you have a twin," Sam said, something tugging at his thoughts, telling him there was still more Violet hadn't divulged. "Does Emory know what you are?"

Violet's watery green gaze lifted to him. "I am her, too."

A chill crawled down his back. Sam knew he needed to keep the questions coming while the magickal mist surrounded them; otherwise Violet would use it for her own purposes.

"How is that possible?" he asked her.

Violet lifted her shoulders. "I decided I wanted to be two people instead of one," she said. "I thought I could accomplish more. Live more. Maybe figure out how to break my curse. When I entered the space between life and death after my last life, I found a set of twin girls who were caught there. They were three years old. Their parents were wealthy. The girls had been in a small plane flying out to the Orkney Islands to meet their parents, who'd been touring Scandinavia on their yacht. There was a storm and the plane crashed. It was perfect. I got two lives, and Kenneth and Margot Wilde got their daughters."

An image flashed before Sam's eyes: Emory and Violet dancing naked in the light of dozens of candles, lifting glasses of wine and calling out his name. Only it wasn't his name.

Stay focused.

"Why me?" Sam asked.

But it was too late. Violet had stood and was backing out of the room, moving out of the cloud of steam.

"Why Kaia?" she asked, from a safe distance. "What's so special about her?"

He held his breath, praying he could avoid answering. It came out of him anyway, like vomit. "She knows this secret I have, and I feel safe with her," he said.

"Why do you feel so safe with her, Sam?"

"I trust Kaia because she's like me"—he fought not to speak, not to give more away, but it was no use—"she's a siren."

Violet smirked. "I already suspected as much, but I am glad to hear you confirm it."

The sound of her laughter faded down the stairs, muffled and diminishing as she closed the door and moved through the house, leaving Sam alone in the dissipating steam.

✍

Violet returned a while later with a tray of food. She untied him and let him piss in an old-fashioned chamber pot. Sam wondered what her plan was for when he had to do more than urinate, but hoped that by the time that happened he'd be out of her house.

"Look, I don't know what you're hoping to accomplish by keeping me up here," he said as he eagerly bit into a chunk of buttered bread dipped into the beef stew she'd brought him. "I'm sorry I hurt you, Violet, but you keeping me here isn't going to change the circumstances."

She had killed before. She had admitted it. Jealousy was like a rabid dog that had chased her through all her lives. He would have to tread carefully.

"I thought we were friends," he said, honestly.

She sat atop the blackened old trunk, the only piece of furniture in the room besides the chair she had tied him to. Arms crossed, legs crossed, she rolled her eyes at him.

"I mean it," he said.

"Yeah. Got that." Violet scowled.

"Does my friendship mean nothing to you?" he asked. "Lovers come and go. But friends… friends stay forever."

He thought he saw a glimmer of tenderness break her stony façade.

"I don't want to stop being your friend, Violet." He set down the half-eaten bowl of stew on the floor and began to stand. "This thing with me and Kaia, maybe it'll just be temporary." Now that he wasn't under the influence of that horrible steam, he could lie.

Violet rolled her eyes again. "Oh, I'm *sure* it's just temporary," she said, and drummed her fingers on the sides of the trunk.

He took a step toward her. "Why's that?" he asked.

"Well, see, I was with Kaia when I left the house earlier," Violet said, a smug look on her face. "And she and I had a little heart-to-heart. Sisters before misters, you know, that kind of thing. She knows about *us*, Sam, you and me. She knows you've been playing us both. Lying to her and going behind her back to see me."

"But—"

"I was kind before, making you forget. This time, I think I'll let you remember."

"Remember what?"

"Take off your clothes, Sam," she said, in a loud, commanding voice.

Sam felt the sound of her voice hit him like a wave. Unbidden, his hands went for the buttons of his shirt. Feet kicked out of boots. Next thing he knew, he was standing naked before her.

A smile crept over Violet's lips. He heard footsteps behind him on the stairs leading up from the lower stories of the house and turned. Emory's blonde head appeared out of the darkness of the stairwell, the smile on her face matching her twin's perfectly.

"Come here, Sam," Emory said. "Kiss me."

And he did.

❧

Night had fallen by the time Sam walked out of the Wilde mansion. He was covered in sweat and bone-tired, his legs and arms barely strong enough to carry him to his boat, but he made it to the *Angeline* and out of the harbor. He saw no lights in Kaia's house as he passed by Foley's Point. It was just as well. He couldn't show his face to her now. Not after all he'd just done with the Wilde sisters.

He cut the motor in the middle of the bay, halfway between the harbor and Thursday Island.

He cursed and fell to his knees, letting himself curl into the fetal position on the deck. He let the swell rock him as he wept, the smell of Violet and Emory seeping from his skin. Violet was clearly a powerful witch, able to command him at will. God only knew what crazy spell she'd put on him to make him do that. Maybe it'd been something in the stew. After the steam of truth, he should've known better.

He slammed his fist into the deck, feeling the cleansing pain radiate up his wrist. After all that pleasure—pleasure he hadn't merely *endured,* but, despite his will, *enjoyed*—he needed something to hang on to. He banged on the deck again, screaming.

CHAPTER FORTY-SIX

TWO WEEKS LATER

"Hey, have you heard from Kaia Foley?" Sam asked Felicia Dunne as he stood at the counter of the hardware store. "She told me you two were friends."

Felicia frowned as she picked up the lamp oil Sam was buying and scanned it into her register. "Yes, I thought so. Sweet girl. But nope, not a peep," she said. "Seems odd to me she'd up and leave without saying goodbye. There's that *For Sale* sign up at the end of the drive out to the point. News around town is that she put the house on the market and headed back south."

"Yeah."

He'd heard the news, all right. Foley's Point was on the market. It was all anybody was talking about. At Penfeld's Market. At the Hook and Anchor. And he'd heard it plenty from Violet, too, who continued to summon him and force him to satisfy her and her other half on a daily basis. Sam handed Felicia the turpentine next, avoiding her gaze. Though he couldn't say it to Felicia, it made perfect sense to him that Kaia had left Quolobit without a word.

"Hey." Felicia put a warm hand on his wrist, turning her sympathetic eyes to him. "Are you all right, Sam?"

"Me?" His heart was broken. His pride was crushed. His dick was sore. "I'm fine."

Felicia shook her head. "Don't lie to me," she clucked. "What's got you so down? Is it the wind farm they're going to set up? You worried it's going to cut into your business?"

"What?" Sam felt like he'd just been slapped out of his daze.

"The wind farm," Felicia said. "Town council voted to go ahead with the project, starting this spring."

"What?" Sam repeated. "No. No fucking way."

Felicia frowned and nodded. She handed him an issue of the Quolobit Gazette. There it was on the front cover: an image of a towering wind turbine rising from the water.

"They're going to drag up some old sunken military ship that's been down there since the forties, right where they want to build. It's all in the article. They say it'll put a halt on all fishing in Wapomeq Bay for the rest of the year. They're going to offer some kind of compensation to the fishermen in town, but... who knows if their word is good. You know how those corporate assholes are." She gave a disparaging grunt. "I never liked that Wilde family."

Sam shot his eyes to hers.

"I mean no offense," Felicia said, holding up her hands. "I know you've been dating one of their girls a while now. It's their father I'm talking about."

"Their father?"

"Kenneth Wilde," Felicia said. "He's the owner and CEO of Maracor, the company that's going to build the wind farm."

Sam could only shake his head. "I didn't realize that," he whispered.

Felicia pursed her lips together. "Mm. Well, now you do. Go on. Paper's free. It's yesterday's."

"Thanks, Felicia." Sam sighed. He gathered his bag of supplies and slid it wearily off the counter, tucking the paper beneath his arm as he turned for the door.

"Sam." Felicia's voice stopped him. "What's going on? You're not yourself," she said, leaning over the counter. "Haven't been for a while now. You've got a look about you like..."

He stepped closer. "Like what?" he asked, hoping she saw everything that was at war inside him. Hoping she could help get him out of it alive.

"Like you've been bewitched."

Sam nearly collapsed with relief. He set his bag back on the counter and glanced around the store, then took a deep breath.

"Can you help me?"

❦

An hour later, after pouring out his story to Felicia, Sam left her store with his lamp oil, some protective herbs, and an assurance that Felicia would be conducting a magickal ritual for protection on his behalf. "Oh, and by the way, Sam," she said as he was about to leave, "I put up one of your posters in my window."

He turned back to her with a questioning gaze.

"For your show?" Felicia said, her brows lifting above the large frames of her tortoiseshell glasses. "Your art show? Isn't it tomorrow?"

"Oh, yeah." Sam shuffled toward the door, noting the poster Violet had created for his show and plastered all over town. He couldn't care less about it now.

"The girls and I can't wait!"

"Thanks, Felicia," Sam said. "Thanks for everything. I'll see you there."

He left the store and walked down Milk Street, toward Main. With a brief gaze up at the towering Victorian where he'd been spending too much time with the Wilde sisters, he turned toward the wharf, toward the *Angeline*, toward home. He had yet to complete the one painting he wanted to set as the centerpiece of his show: the one of Kaia asleep in his bed. He still needed to do some work on the rumpled bedcovers. That kind of work was tedious, but if he flubbed it the whole painting would look amateurish. Her face, though—he had captured that perfectly. Eerily. He had put off finishing the rest because he didn't want to look at her.

And because he did.

He had emailed her, called (hoping she'd finally gotten a new phone), and stalked her social media. Nothing. His truck was still at the Point where she had left it, but he couldn't bring himself to go get it. He had hurt her, and now not only would she not be there to play at his show, but he would likely never see her again.

His plan was to bring the two paintings he had done of Kaia with him the next day and put them front and center when people walked in. They were intimate and raw. They were his best work. And they were all he had of her.

He wanted to use them against Violet. To show her that, no matter how much control she had over his body, she couldn't touch his heart.

CHAPTER FORTY-SEVEN

DARKNESS SURROUNDED HER.

The metallic taste of Kaia's own blood filled her mouth, circulating in the water she floated in. She had memorized the dimensions of the iron walls that enclosed her, knew she had to be mindful of where she was letting her tail go if she didn't want the tips of her fins to snag on rusted debris littering the room. She couldn't tell how much time had gone by. It could have been hours, days, weeks. It seemed that for every minute she spent in her siren form, time meant less and less to her.

She'd done a lot of stupid things in her life. She'd been too trusting, always. A *Pollyanna*, one particularly nasty schoolteacher had once called her. A blooming idiot. She'd gotten herself into plenty of scrapes. But this was the worst.

When she had gone in the water and transitioned, she thought she'd swim out and call to the siren using the strange, high-pitched screech that came out of her mouth in this form. She'd called and called, swimming farther into Wapomeq Bay. She went past Thursday Island, putting Sam behind her because that was the best thing she could do for herself, the only thing. She'd been betrayed before; she knew the deal: the sooner she cut the ties he had on her heart, the quicker she'd heal.

No, she wouldn't let herself think about him. Not even for a minute. She had ventured far out, far past where she had gone before. Her voice carried even farther. And, eventually, she was heard.

The white siren appeared out of the deep, ghostly and sleek, eyes glowing with eerie phosphorescence. She was flanked by three others—one muscular female and two large males.

They attacked, slamming into Kaia with their tails and scraping with long, untrimmed fingernails. The water was soon clouded with blood. Kaia let herself sink, in too much pain to continue fighting back. She thought they'd leave her to die. Then the white one articulated a command in a series of chirps and her three companions took hold of Kaia and began dragging her down.

She distantly thought she probably should try again to fight them off, to escape, but she couldn't bring herself to do it. She felt too weak. Too helpless. So she surrendered. Her eyes adjusted to the darkness—did that mean they glowed, too?—as they reached the belly of the bay, where there wasn't enough light for plant life.

They had brought her to an old, sunken military ship, tilted on her beam ends and grounded in the sand. *USS Davis* was painted in chipping red paint on her side. As they approached, Kaia counted six other sirens swimming around the ship, some working on a repair, others scouting.

So this was where the colony lived.

Clan, Kaia reminded herself. That was what Felicia Dunne had called it.

The white siren went ahead as Kaia's captors dragged her closer to the *USS Davis,* then into a quarterdeck door in the top deck. It was all strangely quiet… haunted.

Plunged into the darkness of the ship's hold, they followed the trail of the white-finned one and came eventually to a large room at the ship's stern. Furniture fuzzy with decades of sea debris had shattered in the collision and now lay heaved to one side of the room, where it had landed when the ship settled to the ocean floor. The white siren floated in the center of the room, gesturing in some form of sign language to another siren.

This one had a powerful tail of midnight blue that deepened to black at the fins. Her abs and arms were toned and muscled, and laced with silvery scars. Battle wounds. Judging by her face, she had to be somewhere in her late sixties, Kaia noted with surprise. Her silver hair was cropped close to her head, highlighting brilliant blue eyes that now landed on Kaia and shimmered with their own inner light. This was their leader, then.

As the leader approached, the white siren turned to her. Finally able to look at her nemesis, Kaia noticed that she did have a nasty scar on her side where Kaia had sliced her with a shell, but it was healing well. Very well. In fact, it looked like it had happened more than a month ago, not just a few days. Clearly the siren possessed some kind of accelerated healing. Did they all? Was it the same for all of them? And to think that Kaia had been so wracked with guilt she had gone on a suicide mission!

As the leader lunged forward and took Kaia's face in her webbed hands, Kaia felt her heart pound against her ribs. Pointed teeth revealed themselves between the siren's parting lips. Were her own teeth like that? She made the mistake of running her tongue over them and found that yes, they were. Bleeding from her mouth, her face, and somewhere on her tail, she felt herself becoming weaker in the siren's grip.

The leader-siren flung out a hand in some sort of gesture and said something, letting out a stream of bubbles.

Baba baba was what it sounded like.

Kaia felt herself swooning, about to faint. Aware of the shadows of at least a dozen others behind her, she knew there was no escaping. She met the siren's gaze.

To her surprise, there was kindness there. Sadness, too. And hard, undeniable determination. She felt the siren's grip tighten around her arms. The leader then gave a nod to the white siren, who began signing something to the others.

It wasn't traditional sign language—not that Kaia could recognize. The gestures were slower and larger. Fit for water. Hands were placed in angular gestures at different heights, switched in swooping motions. It was complex and lyrical, and as Kaia glanced around she saw the others nodding and making gestures of their own. It seemed that what the sirens lacked in verbal communication, they more than made up for with signing.

Soon there were ten sirens floating in a line. All male, Kaia noted, as the leader angled Kaia toward them. She gestured for Kaia to look at them, drawing her closer and bringing her to the first siren in the line, an older male with a gray beard. She watched Kaia's reaction. Confused and terrified, Kaia shook her head.

Is this a lineup?

She pointed to the white female siren.

That's the one that attacked me.

The leader tightened her grip and shook her head, firmly pushing Kaia toward the next male in line. He reached out for her, opening his scary, pointy mouth. Kaia felt her tail slip against his as she pushed herself away, back into the arms of their leader, who released a series of laugh-like chirps.

The white siren darted forward and pushed Kaia into the third male in line. His hands closed around her waist.

Oh, I get it. They want me to choose one. They want me to... mate?

Kaia pulled away, shaking her head.

"No!" she tried to say, letting out a stream of bubbles. It might have been garbled, but they got the message.

The dark-tailed leader let go of Kaia and gestured for her to be removed. Kaia fought against clawed hands that grabbed her by the arms, bucking with her muscular tail as they dragged her through the door. She scraped herself on the corroded metal doorframe and screamed as they pulled her into a corridor and shut her into a cell.

And there they'd left her, sending in males one at a time to try to woo her. She had rejected all of them, and, thankfully, the males had respected her wishes. Still, they kept coming, over and over. After several rounds of this, Kaia could tell they were as tired of it as she was. When guards came to unlock the cell and her suitors communicated that she'd been unresponsive, the white siren would come in and beat her up. Now her body was covered in gashes and bruises. It stung every time she moved. Her head throbbed.

Kaia wished she knew how long it had been since she had left land. Long enough for them to come in about a dozen times to give her raw fish to eat. That could mean anything between four days, or two weeks. She had no idea. She was starving, that was all she knew.

Her stomach growled as she twitched in the confines of her cell. She wanted land. Wanted to feel the wind. To see the sun. To sit by a fire and eat something warm and soft. Like bread... buttered bread. And a cup of coffee. *Coffee.* That would explain the headache, Kaia thought, bringing her hands to her head. If she was still having headaches from lack of caffeine, that meant it had been less than two weeks, she figured. She hoped.

Just then the door opened. In came yet another male. He was thrown in, seemingly against his will. The metal door was slammed shut, the lock pounding into place like a gunshot. The male flinched at the sound and curled into a ball.

Haven't seen you before, Kaia thought.

Despite his non-threatening body language, Kaia backed herself up against the wall and folded her arms over her bare chest. She still wasn't used to the nakedness around here—the way all the females' breasts were uncovered, the way males showed their arousal without shame through the narrow vent at the front of their tails.

This one sank to the floor of the cell without even looking at her. In the gloom, Kaia observed that though his ribs showed beneath his pale skin, his arms were thick with muscle, and inked with what looked like old-time military tattoos. Lank blond hair floated at his shoulders, cropped unceremoniously. He tilted his handsome, unshaven face up toward her, revealing one black eye. There was something searching and pleading in his gaze.

Kaia held up a tentative hand in greeting. The siren blinked, then offered a curt smile. He saluted her sarcastically.

Whoa. That was... awfully human.

She pointed to her own eye, then to his bruised one. He jerked his head toward the door and the guards outside it, then shook his head in response.

The siren moved his ink-black tail and floated upward. He moved closer, eyes taking in Kaia's injuries. When she flinched at his nearness, he lifted his hands, signaling his neutrality. She floated nearby as he pressed a finger to the wall of the cell and began to draw something in the silt that coated it.

Stick figures—a man, a woman, and beneath them, a smaller one. A baby. He circled the little one for emphasis. His eyes searched hers again.

Kaia laughed grimly and shook her head.

Can't, she wrote in the dust. *Barren.*

She hated that word, but it was the quickest way to explain herself. The male began scratching something else into the dust.

TOMMY.

He floated backward and pointed to his chest. Kaia wrote her name beside his and then offered her hand to shake. Returning to the wall, she wrote: *Prisoner?*

Tommy nodded.

ESCAPE, he wrote.

Kaia nodded, her heart beating faster.

TRUST, he wrote, and moved his index finger back and forth between them.

She nodded again. Tommy gave one short nod in return and lifted his eyes in thought. His movements were quick and efficient as he turned to her and opened his mouth in a grimace, gesturing with a hand. He pointed to her and repeated his strange antic.

You want me to scream? Kaia pointed to herself and opened her own mouth, repeating Tommy's gesture.

He nodded.

She let out a searing, high-pitched shriek, then looked at Tommy for approval. He circled his hand, widening his tired blue eyes, telling her to keep doing it. She screamed and screamed until they heard the metallic clinking of the door being unlocked. Tommy grabbed her and covered her body with his. She felt him press firmly against her, his mouth landing halfway on hers as his hands gripped her waist, and he thrust against her as though they were going at it. It all happened too quickly for her to take in what the hell was going on, but when the door squealed open, Tommy turned toward it snarling, baring his sharp teeth and his half-erect, unsheathed penis from the vent in the front of his tail.

Tommy lunged toward the guards and they pushed him back into the cell, chirruping between themselves as they threw the lock again. He remained facing the door for several moments, his hands pressed against it, his muscled, finned back facing her. Eventually, he turned back to her and wrote again on the wall.

SORRY.

Kaia shook her head at him and rested a hand on his shoulder. *It's okay,* she said, but he was already swimming away from her, down into the far corner of the cell, where there was a pile of rubble. He looked over his shoulder and gestured for her to keep making noises.

Oh geez, Kaia thought with dread, but she began groaning as Tommy rifled through the mess of broken furniture and rusted tools. She thought she might as well make it sound real, so she increased the rhythm of her cries, raising her voice in pitch until she was keening.

Tommy looked over his shoulder and grinned, giving her a thumbs-up. She almost laughed, but there was really nothing funny happening. At last, he dislodged the metal leg of a chair. He wiped their scribblings off the wall, then held his finger up to his lips.

Kaia quieted and swam close to Tommy as he approached the door. They waited. The *USS Davis* was quiet. Tommy's hand was firm on her hip as he positioned her behind him. At the sound of movement outside the door, he lifted the chair leg, jagged edge up.

That's gonna give somebody tetanus was Kaia's last thought before the door swung open. Tommy lunged for the guard, thrusting the chair leg into his belly and up under his ribs and ripping it out again, sending a cloud of blood and chunks of tissue into the water. The siren gave a low grunt and went motionless, floating up toward the ceiling. Tommy wasted no time, grabbing the other guard by the neck and pulling her into the cell, threatening her with the chair leg. She held up her hands in surrender as Tommy shoved Kaia out the door. As he shut and locked the door behind them, Kaia felt her stomach twisting in terror.

There were at least two dozen other sirens that she knew of in and around the *USS Davis*. Was Tommy planning on fighting them all? If so, there was no way they'd succeed in escaping without getting killed.

TRUST, he'd told her.

When he grabbed her hand and looked back at her, she squeezed his fingers in hers and followed, moving swift and silent as they traced their way out of the hold. They burst into the open water and were immediately spotted by an older female siren repairing a fishing net. She looked up at them slowly. Kaia met her eyes and waited for her to react, but the old one only blinked her eyes once, then turned them back to her work, knotting the rope with quiet, firm fingers as if to say it wasn't her fight.

Tommy tugged at Kaia's hand. They began swimming upward, toward the glimmering surface far above.

"They're going to come after us," Tommy said as they burst into the air. It was a relief to hear his voice—to hear any voice. "Ah, goddamn it feels good to talk again."

The sky was cloudy and wintry. The wind blew harsh, far colder than the water, as it swept over their heads. Still, it was a welcome sensation.

"They're hunting now," Tommy said, "but when they come back, they're going to be out for blood."

"How many are there?" Kaia kept her head low enough that she could still respirate through the gills at the back of her ears and not instigate a change back to her frail human form.

"Twenty, all told." Tommy's eyes scanned the water surrounding them.

Kaia spotted land and felt her heart swell. "Let's at least get to my house," she said. "We can make a plan."

Tommy gave her a nod. "You lead the way."

Kaia looked over her shoulder several times as they made their way to Foley's Point, hauling themselves to shore where she and Sam had lain together her first night in Quolobit Harbor. There, they rolled with their backs to each other for privacy as they coughed, sputtered, and wheezed their way back to two-legged humanity.

"Sweet Lord, thank you," Kaia heard Tommy muttering to himself. "I never thought I'd be so happy to see my balls."

She chuckled to herself as she got to her hands and knees first, skin prickling in the frigid air. "I would've thought you'd be more excited about the legs," Kaia said as she stood, feeling pretty thankful herself. Glancing back at him to see that he was now standing facing away—slim, pale, very much naked, and *human*—she said, "Follow me."

The snow was bitterly cold underfoot as Kaia began tromping up to the house. It was significantly deeper than before, too—and Sam's truck was encased. There'd be time to deal with that, she told herself. They needed to get into the house first, into the warmth.

After dressing in jeans and a sweater, Kaia grabbed the speargun she'd left leaning beside her bed. She should've had that with her when she went into the water; maybe then this whole thing wouldn't have happened. She wouldn't leave herself unprotected again.

She found Tommy in the living room building a fire, dressed in a pair of Sam's boxer shorts and a flannel shirt he'd left here. Seeing Sam's clothes stung. Images of the flannel landing softly on the floor, the boxers inched down over his sculpted hips, were too much to handle.

Tommy turned to her, eyes scanning her clothes. "I found some galoshes I can fit into in the hall closet, but I don't suppose you've got any socks and trousers for me lying around?"

"Sorry," she said. "I can make a run for the thrift store. Do you think there's enough time?"

Tommy lifted his brows. "Hope so. They hunt for a long while—sometimes days. I don't know. I could never keep track of time when I was down there, and they've never taken me hunting with them."

Kaia wanted to ask Tommy more, to learn why he was being held prisoner, but if he was going to stay on land he'd need pants, plain and simple. And they'd need something to eat other than a package of stale crackers or the moldy leftovers in the fridge.

"All right," she said, setting the speargun down on the coffee table. "I'll leave this here, just in case. I won't be long. Half an hour at the most."

"Let me help you shovel out," he said.

"But… you don't have any pants."

He stood, his mouth a grim line. "I'll survive."

⊷

Kaia's hands shook as she put Sam's rumbling truck into gear. She'd have to find a way to give the damned thing back without speaking to him. Tears stung her eyes as she bumped along down the drive, the snow making it impossible to go faster than five miles per hour.

No, she would not let herself cry. Not for Sam. He was a liar. He'd used her. Betrayed her. He'd made her think they could have something real together, something lasting, and she'd been a fool to believe him.

Had it all been for the sex? Was that all Sam had wanted? Because if that had been it, he could've just said so. She'd probably have slept with him anyway. But that hadn't been how he'd acted. He'd acted like it was real for him, like he wanted to be with her for the long haul. He'd even been upfront with her about the other woman he'd been seeing.

I could never love her, he'd said, *not like I could love you.*

Lies.

"Dammit!" Kaia cried, slamming her palms down on the wheel as a sob came and ripped through her chest. "Fuck you, Sam!"

She wept till she got into town and found her way to the thrift store parking lot, then scraped her face dry on the cuffs of her jacket. After buying clothes for Tommy, she ran into Penfeld's Market and grabbed two frozen pizzas, a package of pre-made hot wings, a garden salad for good measure, and a bottle of wine for afterwards.

Afterwards... after whatever was about to go down. Her hands wouldn't stop shaking. It wasn't just food she needed, but a good cry and a long night's sleep. The last thing she needed to do right now was fight off twenty bloodthirsty sirens.

"Kaia?" A friendly voice greeted her in the booze aisle. "I thought you went home to Nashville."

Kaia turned to see Felicia Dunne with her daughters, one the lanky teenager with long braids, the other a bashful little kid with an afro hiding behind her mother's hip. Felicia gasped when she saw Kaia's bruised face.

Kaia's eyes darted to see who might be within earshot. She stepped closer to Felicia, into her aura of patchouli and summer sunlight. "I didn't go home. I was... abducted by the sirens."

Felicia clapped a hand over her mouth, eyes going wide beneath her big, tortoise-rimmed glasses. She shook her head back and forth. "That was two weeks ago, Kaia," she gasped. "Are you all right?"

Kaia gave a shaky laugh, unable to answer. Felicia's older daughter narrowed her eyes at her.

"So you *are* a siren?" the girl whispered. "I thought so."

"Claudette!" Felicia chided.

"It's okay," Kaia said, praying Felicia's kids were trustworthy. "Yes, that's me. Kaia the—the siren."

Felicia gathered her daughters closer and whispered. "What did they want?"

"I really don't know what their end goal is, but they tried to force me to, um, procreate," she stammered. "I escaped with another prisoner, Tommy. He's at my house now. They're coming for us, Felicia. I don't know what to do. Maybe I *will* go back to Nashville."

Felicia scoffed, rolling her eyes. "Please don't do that," she said, resting a warm hand on Kaia's cheek. Her littlest daughter peered up at Kaia from behind the wooly billows of her mother's coat. "Listen. I've got an idea. That sunken ship they live in? It's getting pulled up, and soon. Town council voted *yes* on the wind farm and that's the spot Maracor wants to build in. Your enemies are about to be homeless. There are scores of people in this community who want to fight this thing, but there just hasn't been anybody to organize them."

"We're gonna fight the wind farm," Felicia's little one chimed in assertively. "Do you want to protest wif me and Claudee, Miss Mami Wata?"

"Tessa, hush." Felicia leaned closer. "You need to tell the sirens what's coming, and convince them you can stop it. You'll organize a protest committee and stop the construction. In return, they leave you the fuck alone."

Knowing what she now did about the way the siren clan operated, Kaia doubted whether a negotiation would be possible. Still, it was either that or fight them—and who knew where that might lead? Kaia shivered at the thought.

"Thanks, Felicia. That might just be the only non-violent solution here. What've I got to lose? I'll try it."

On her way out of the market, a poster caught her eye. It depicted one of Sam's paintings, a storm.

"Hey, what's the date today?" she asked the cashier.

January thirty-first, she was told. Sam's show was tomorrow. Kaia shook her head and walked out of the market, into the bracing cold where Sam's rusted old pickup was waiting for her in the lot.

"Pizza's in the oven. Should be ready in ten minutes," Kaia said as she came into the living room. She found Tommy hunched over on the couch, staring at a Led Zepplin album cover as the record, forgotten on the turntable, hissed at its end.

"Pizza?" Tommy looked up at her, bleary-eyed. "Didn't have you figured for a wop."

"Ex*cuse* me?" Kaia demanded, offended at the slur.

"All that red hair and them freckles, you look like a Mick to me," Tommy said, eyes trailing down to the record cover again.

His broad thumbs traced the edges of the cover's design. Something that glittered fell from his face and splattered onto the lettering of the album. Kaia sat beside him, setting the bag of clothes on the table.

"Tommy? You okay?"

He sniffled and shook his head, then got up and turned the record over, setting down the needle as the beat of *Immigrant Song* began, followed by Robert Plant's feral cry.

"What is this?" he asked, turning to Kaia. "This music... it's crazy."

Kaia quirked a brow. "Are you saying you've never heard of Led Zepplin?"

Tommy grunted a bitter laugh. "I've heard of a Zepplin, all right, but after the *Hindenburg* disaster..." He trailed off, looking down at the record spinning. The music was loud and grating, and his face contorted into a grimace. Flicking the needle off the record, Tommy stopped the sound.

Kaia looked up at him, confused.

"*Hindenburg*?" Tommy repeated, lowering his brows. "Happened in New Jersey about six, maybe seven years ago? Almost forty people killed?"

"It sounds... familiar?" Kaia said dubiously.

Tommy scoffed, shoving his long, surfer-boy hair away from his face. "You live under a rock or somethin'?"

"Uh, no," Kaia replied, standing. "Do *you*?" She rested her hands on her hips. "Who's never heard of Led Zepplin?"

Just how long had the sirens kept him prisoner? Kaia was frankly afraid to ask.

Tommy bit his lips and sighed. There was something edgy about him, something unsettled and unhinged, and Kaia was pretty sure it wasn't just because of the siren clan. If she wasn't mistaken, he'd already been crying when she'd come in. She picked up the bag from the thrift store.

"Hey, why don't you put on some clothes and come into the kitchen and eat?" she suggested.

Tommy nodded, taking the bag from her. He went into the hall bathroom and appeared in the kitchen several minutes later dressed in a pair of slightly large jeans and an old-man cardigan, eyes large and childlike, taking in all the appliances.

"I know—pretty vintage, right?" Kaia said, licking her fingers as she set out a platter of hot wings.

Tommy picked up the cardboard box the frozen pizza had come in and eyed it suspiciously. He turned it over and examined the back. Tapping it, he asked, "This, uh, 'best by' date. What's this mean?"

Fearing the pizza was spoiled, Kaia leaned over to read the date. "Oh, it's fine," she said. "Says we've got till June."

Tommy tapped the box again. "No. What's... what's this year?" His voice trembled. His eyes were glistening. "Because I know the roaring twenties have already happened and I'm pretty sure I haven't gone back in time..." Tommy swallowed. "What year is it, Kaia?" he whispered.

"2020," she told him quietly.

Tommy sank into a chair, letting the pizza box fall to the floor. His breath came in swift, heavy swells filling his chest as he began to shake his head slowly back and forth.

"No, no," he murmured, eyes filling with tears as he gripped the table's edge.

Kaia bent to pick up the pizza box and put it in the recycling bin before pulling the pizza from the oven. Best not to push Tommy to talk, she thought. Whatever he was going through, it seemed he had just as much reason to hate the siren clan as she did.

"I thought it was nineteen forty-four," he told her simply, as she put a plate of pizza in front of him. "I knew time worked different down there, but..."

Kaia didn't meet his gaze as she sat herself down at the table and took a bite of blessedly cheesy, garlicky, saucy pizza. She cared about Tommy's situation, but that didn't negate the fact that she was desperate for food.

"Nineteen forty-four. That's the year it was when the clan took me," he muttered. "My plane crashed in the North Sea between England and Germany. I was in the Air Force. Fighting Hitler." Kaia looked up at this. Tommy's face took on a grief-stricken, bewildered expression. "My wife, my Olivia, she was born a hundred years ago and... so was I."

Kaia swallowed and looked at Tommy as sobs began to shake him. "Oh, Tommy," she said, and got up. She sat in his lap and wrapped her arms around his shoulders as he wept, letting him rock her, rocking him back. "I'm so sorry."

CHAPTER FORTY-EIGHT

FROM WHERE SAM stood in his bedroom, painting in the last light of day, putting final touches to the crumpled bedsheets, something caught his gaze. He turned away from the canvas and the bed beyond it—the bed he'd shared with Kaia, where he'd lumped together pillows beneath the covers to give himself something to work from in her absence.

Looking out the window, he saw lights in the house on Foley's Point. Lights that hadn't been on the night before. Or the night before that. Or any night since Kaia had left.

He didn't think twice about pulling on his boots and his jacket and heading out for his boat. So what if Violet saw him going over there? So what if she wanted to summon and torture him? She'd do it anyway. But if Kaia had returned to Quolobit Harbor, that mattered. He had to see her. He had to try to explain himself, however unbelievable his story might be.

The January evening was bitter cold as he pulled his wool cap close over his ears and started the *Angeline's* engine. His stomach coiled into a tight knot as he steered toward Foley's Point. He'd have to own up to his mistakes. He'd have to tell Kaia he should have broken things off with Violet before letting himself get involved with her. That would be easy enough to say. Easy enough to believe. But the fact that he'd been bewitched and sexually tortured? Not so easy to say. Not so easy to believe. And he wasn't even sure it had been torture. He'd enjoyed it. All of it. Immensely. Like a drug addict enjoys a hit, and feels helpless and disgusted with themselves afterwards.

His heart began a low, thumping beat in his chest, heavy and fearful. There was little chance he'd get Kaia back. Little chance she'd feel anything for him besides hatred. Violet had seen to that. Still, he had to try.

He threw down the anchor at the Point and got into the skiff, praying he wouldn't be thrown overboard by the rough incoming waves as he rounded the peninsular edge of Kaia's property. The lights were blazing in the house, and Sam pulled the oars hard, hoping to God it was her in there and not just the realtor or the cleaning lady. Of course, if it *was* somebody else, there'd be another vehicle on the property. As of the moment, it was just his old truck and, if he wasn't mistaken, someone had recently removed the snow from it.

Pulling the rowboat up to land, he clambered up the icy, jagged rocks, using his gloved hands so he wouldn't fall on his face. He was winded by the time he got up to the back door of the house, where he paused on the steps and took a moment to catch his breath before knocking.

That was when he heard the sound of an unfamiliar man's voice. Not Kaia. Someone who had no right to be there. A trespasser. *Fucking squatters.*

"Shit," he muttered to himself, backing cautiously away from the door. He jammed his hands into his coat pockets, but he had stupidly forgotten his cellphone in his rush to get to Kaia.

Moving low, he scrambled back down the rocks and rowed hard out to the *Angeline*. Breathless from the exertion, he unlocked the glovebox in the wheelhouse. His fingers closed around the heavy, cold metal of his handgun.

He'd had to use it only once, on a porpoise that had been badly injured, run into by some asshole and left screaming on one of the tiny islands peppering the coast. Now, as he checked the chamber and flicked the safety, he hoped he would only have to use it as an intimidation tool, nothing more. He'd confront whoever was in there, get them to surrender, and call the cops from the house phone.

This time his heart was racing like hell as he rowed back to shore again. Sweating now, he took off his gloves and gripped the handgun as he slowly worked his way up to the house. He leaned against the back door and listened. The man, whoever he was, was still talking in the kitchen.

Gritting his teeth and gripping the gun firmly in his right hand, Sam turned the knob and swung the door open. There was Kaia, sitting on some guy's lap at the kitchen table, their arms around each other. Holding each other close.

Chapter Forty-Nine

At the sound of the door swinging open, Tommy jumped up from under Kaia. He overturned the chair as he lunged toward the door, sliding a knife out of the knife block on the counter with a swiftness that could only mean he'd already scanned the room for potential weapons. In the commotion, Kaia wanted to hide under the table, but it wouldn't be fair to leave Tommy to fight the sirens off all on his own.

"Drop the knife," said a low, growling voice.

Kaia stepped to the side and saw a man standing at the door, pointing a gun right at Tommy. The man's thick, black beard was frosted with ice. His dark eyes burned beneath an ice-encrusted black wool cap.

"Sam?" Kaia said, stepping closer.

"Drop the fucking knife!" Sam shouted.

His face was different than she remembered it. Harder. Colder.

Turning toward Tommy, Kaia stammered, "T-Tommy. It's okay. I know him."

Tommy's head twitched minutely in her direction, but he still held fast to the knife, his fit, muscular body coiled to spring.

"Kaia," Sam growled through his teeth, "tell your boyfriend to back the fuck off."

Kaia angled herself between them, anger prickling over her skin. "Both of you! Stop!" she shouted.

Tommy's eyes swiveled to her. "You know him?" he asked.

"Yes," Kaia replied, exasperated. She put her hands on Tommy's arm, gently forcing him to lower the knife.

Sam lowered the gun and clicked the safety into place, then placed it on top of the ancient refrigerator. "Who's *he?*" he asked.

"Tommy, Sam. Sam, Tommy," Kaia said, glancing back and forth between them just to be sure neither was about to lunge for the other's jugular. Her heart was thudding in her throat.

Sam's eyes finally found hers, and in the next moment he stepped toward her, cupping her cheeks with his cold, damp palms. "Your face," he said. More like cried. Tears filled his eyes as they searched her features, taking in the bruises and scrapes. "What the fuck happened?"

Despite how badly she wanted to wrap her arms around Sam and bury herself in the warm expanse of his chest, Kaia pulled away, putting him at an arm's distance.

"I was abducted by the Wapomeq Bay clan," she replied. "There's twenty of them. Tommy was also a prisoner, and he helped me escape." Tommy's bloodshot eyes met hers in solidarity. "And they're probably coming for us."

"Not *probably.*" Tommy set the knife down on the table and crossed his arms over his chest. Kaia wondered distantly if Sam recognized the flannel shirt that Tommy was wearing, and what he thought about how he'd seen them together when he bursted into the house. A small part of her hoped he was jealous. Well, maybe not a small part. A fairly large part. "They're *definitely* coming for us." Tommy paused, tension flickering in the jawline under his reddish-blond beard. "I didn't get the chance to explain everything to Kaia yet, but they're—*we're* going extinct."

"And what? What are you saying?" Sam demanded, kicking the door closed behind him. "They wanted Kaia to be a brood mare?"

Tommy nodded. His pale blue eyes met Kaia's with sympathy. "We're a dying kind," he said. "And Frances, the leader—"

"She has a name?" Kaia interjected. "Do they all have names?"

Tommy chuckled, but none of the tension left the room. "Yes," he replied. "Frances, the one with the short silver hair and the dark blue"— he gestured toward his legs—"you know. That's their leader. And she's your grandmother."

Kaia felt the room sway like she was on a ship. She grabbed the back of a chair and leaned on it.

"And the one you fought with, the one who brought you down to the *Davis?*" Tommy continued. "That's Zoe. She's your sister."

Kaia shook her head, feeling flashes of hot and cold sweep through her body. *Grandmother. Sister.* The floor wobbled beneath her feet as she stared at the uneaten pizza on the table. Sam was suddenly by her side, his hands on her shoulders.

"Don't touch me," she hissed, gripping the back of the chair so hard her knuckles went white.

"Kaia," he pleaded. "Can we talk? Privately?" His hands remained on her shoulders, warm and reassuring.

"Fine," she snapped, reaching for a slice of lukewarm pizza and dragging it off the plate. "Let's go into the living room. Tommy, you'll keep watch?"

He nodded, picking up the knife. "I'll be outside," he said.

Sam cast Tommy a suspicious glance before grabbing his gun off the top of the fridge and following Kaia out into the living room.

She bit into the pizza, desperate for food no matter how rubbery and tasteless it was, no matter that there were more serious matters at hand. Chewing as she sank into the couch, she eyed Sam. He crouched to add more wood to the fire before taking the chair across the hearth. He looked stiff in his coat and cap, the gun gripped between the chair arm and his right hand.

"I want to explain myself," he told her, his dark eyes resting on hers. "I need you to know I never lied to you."

She lowered her gaze to the half-eaten piece of pizza in her hands. She wouldn't let him see her cry. Wouldn't let him know how he'd broken her.

"I should've cut it off with Violet the minute I met you," he admitted, his voice low over the steady crackle from the hearth. "Because I knew right then that I loved you." His eyes brimmed with tears as he leaned towards her, the firelight dancing off his cheeks. "The minute I heard your voice, I knew you had this power over me," he explained. "And the way I want you, I'd give up anything else—everything else."

Kaia laughed then, but she also started to cry. She shook her head and swallowed hard, trying to gain mastery over herself. It seemed that any show of emotion at all would reveal the cracks in her, making her vulnerable to him yet again.

"But you *didn't* give up everything else," she argued. "Violet told me you were with her that day you disappeared and left me stranded on the island. Sam, you just said you'd never lie to me. So tell me the truth. Were you with her that day?"

She didn't want to hear his answer. She wanted to go on believing that what they had shared together was pure and sacred, and that it belonged to them, and them alone. She wanted to believe that the man who had pulled her from all-encompassing numbness and fear that she'd never have fun in bed again would be hers, forever.

He dropped his head between his sinking shoulders. At last, with a sigh, he answered. "Yes."

"And, that day, did you... did you and Violet... " She couldn't even say it.

"Yes."

Kaia sank deeper into the couch, covering her face with her hands. She couldn't bear to look at him. Couldn't bear to hear his voice. Even hearing him breathe hurt her.

"Go," she said from behind her hands.

"Kaia—"

"Go, I said," she repeated more firmly.

"Please, Kaia," he pleaded, his voice cutting through her, filling her with pain the way he had once filled her with joy. "She's—she's a witch. I didn't go to her because I wanted to. I didn't even know I'd been there that day till she told me. She's jealous of you and she's torturing me because of it."

A stream of hot tears slid between her face and her hands. Strangled sobs choked her.

"Get out," she whispered shakily.

"Kaia, look at me," Sam implored. "Please? Violet is a *witch*—a bad witch. A witch and a skinwalker. She forced me to be with her. My heart is yours, Kaia, believe me. I need to find a way to stop her from destroying my life. Please, I need—I need you." His last words were uttered in a broken whisper.

Letting her fingers trail away from her swollen eyes, she gazed at him in the firelight. Tears burned molten lines down his cheeks, reflecting the light from the hearth.

"Do you believe me?" he asked.

Did she?

Was Violet a witch? A skinwalker, whatever that was? With all her herbs and potions, her silvery skeleton key necklace, sure, Kaia could believe Violet was a witch—but the kind that read tarot cards to sort out her personal problems and cast little spells for success on the full moon.

"Do you believe me?" Sam persisted.

But look at you, siren, said a sly voice inside her. *You never would've believed your kind existed until you found out what you yourself are.*

"Ugh," Kaia groaned, wiping her face on her sleeves. "So, what, you're saying this was all against your will? She put some kind of spell on you?" She laughed bitterly. "You have to admit, that sounds kind of ridiculous."

"I know," Sam said. "But it's the truth."

"Okay. Look, I want to believe you. It's better than—than the alternative of you doing this of your own free will. But it doesn't make *me* feel any better. It doesn't make it hurt any less to know that you were… *with her.*"

A swell of nausea threatened to rise in her throat, surprising her. How had she become so attached to a man so quickly? Was she that desperate? Or was it the fact that they had a special bond, a bond she'd never felt with anyone else? Either option sucked.

"And while I was gone?" Kaia asked, her voice feeling raw in her throat. "Have you been with her in these past two weeks?"

Sam leaned back against the chair, crossing his arms over his chest. His expression was closed as he stared at the fire. "She has a way of making me come to her whether I want to or not. It's like she's inside my head. I have no control."

Kaia shook her head, her anger returning and taking the place of the whimpering, quivering grief that wanted to swallow her. She was thankful for it.

"*No control?*" she parroted, sneering. "Am I supposed to believe *that,* too?"

Sam shut his eyes, sighing heavily. "I don't expect you to," he said. "But I'm telling you the truth, Kaia, I swear it."

She let out a short, angry laugh. "I don't know what you want from me, then. You say you have no control, that she can summon you whenever she pleases, that she's a witch and a—a whatever you called it—"

"Skinwalker."

"Yeah. Whatever," Kaia scoffed. "But where does that leave us? She can have you whenever she wants. Am I supposed to live with that?"

Sam shook his head slowly, his face lined with despair. "No," he muttered, his voice cracking. "I don't expect you to be with me, Kaia. I just wanted you to know the truth. The truth about what happened, and the fact that I love you."

Tommy strode into the room, the knife he clutched glinting in the firelight. "They're here," he announced. "Swimming towards shore."

Kaia shot up from the couch as Sam stood, palming his gun in both hands. "I'm guessing it's gonna be a fight," he said.

"Probably." Tommy's sharp blue eyes zeroed in on Sam's gun. "But try not to use that thing, if you can help it. Their numbers are dropping and I don't want to feel responsible for cutting them down."

"Listen," Kaia said, holding up her hands to both men, who looked poised to fight with each other instead of the real threat that was approaching from the sea. "I want to try to negotiate with them. If they come up to land, we can at least talk. I need to tell them about the wind farm and the *Davis*."

Tommy made a questioning noise.

"When I was in town buying groceries I ran into a friend of mine and she said construction starts this spring," Kaia rushed to explain. "They're building a wind farm in Wapomeq Bay and the *Davis* is on their building grounds. They're going to pull her up. The siren clan is going to lose their home."

Tommy's brows lowered into two straight dashes. "I don't know what the hell a wind farm is, but pulling up the *Davis* is going to be a big problem." He nodded to Sam. "You hear about this?"

Sam nodded. "It's not gonna be good for me, either," he admitted grimly. "Fishing's gonna be screwed while they're building, and who knows how long after."

"There are a lot of people in the area who feel their voices weren't heard about this project," Kaia said. She drew in a shaky breath. "I'm going to spearhead a protest committee to stop the wind farm. In return, the sirens leave me alone and let me swim where I want."

A shriek pierced the air. Though Kaia hadn't heard anything like it before, she instantly knew that it was the call of the sirens.

"They won't want to to leave the water if they can help it," Tommy said. "They're going to wait for us to get in, then attack. But if we don't get in, they're going to come to land. Believe me, if they do that, they'll be out for blood."

"No," Kaia said. "We don't want that. Let's meet them in the water, see if we can get them to communicate peacefully." She strode to the hall.

Sam was right behind her, putting a heavy hand on her shoulder.

"Don't go out there," he said. "Kaia, please."

The truth was, she didn't think she could live without the ocean. She wasn't sure she could live without Sam, either, but she had no control over that situation. And it wasn't just that she wanted to be able to swim free of the fear that someone might assault her—she truly didn't want the sirens to lose their home. If there was something she could do to make good with them, she'd do it.

She pushed past Sam and through the kitchen with Tommy at her heels. The cold air burned her face as she entered the winter twilight. The pines and hemlocks howled in the wind. The ocean slammed itself into the black rocks of Foley's Point, sending up hissing fans of spray unfurling into the air. It was a dark, violent sort of night. The kind that would have usually made her want to stay at home, curled up on the couch with a cup of tea and a bingeworthy show—but here she was, walking out into it, about to strip down to nothing but her bare skin.

The sirens' calls grew louder as she made her way down to the water's edge. It would be hard to get in with the water as rough as it was, but if the sirens really were hell-bent on a fight, there was no way she'd be a contender in her human form. Tommy and Sam appeared at her side as she peeled off her leggings and underwear, leaving her in nothing but a bra. Awkward, to say the least.

Tommy didn't seem to notice—he was too busy undressing himself—but Sam gave her a glance so sorrowful and woebegone that it almost made her regret the way she had dismissed him inside.

No time to think of that now, though, she told herself, and turned toward the waves. The iron-blue water was illuminated by half a dozen pairs of eyes, faces phosphorescing under the surface. At the sight of them, before the water hit higher than her knees, Kaia felt her skin begin to tingle with the change.

You were born for this, she told herself.

Chapter Fifty

Sam felt helpless watching Kaia plunge into the water, surrendering her delicate, pale body to the furious waves. Tightening his grip on his handgun, he centered his gaze on the sirens' glowing eyes. Her wild-eyed, jumpy friend Tommy dove in after her, his wiry frame glimmering in the wintry moonlight as his body began to shift even before he was fully submerged.

Sam had to admit it: he was jealous. Jealous of both Kaia and Tommy and their ability to be in the water. Also jealous that they could share that, and whatever else they had clearly bonded over. Of course, he had no right to be jealous. No right to even ask what their deal was. After what he'd done—what had *happened* to him—it was understandable that she'd put some distance between them. Besides, right now there was more than his wounded ego at stake.

He turned his focus to the action in front of him. His heart pounded, sweat prickling his skin even though it was far from warm outside. The water in the cove on the northern edge of the point churned as the sirens fought. Sam gritted his teeth, the bitter wind stinging his eyes, drawing salty tears from them.

"Dammit!" he cursed, nearly throwing the gun down on the rocks.

There was nothing he could do to help her, not from here. As he hung his head, about to turn away from the water, a hard, cold hand grabbed him by the shoulder. Sam whipped around, confronted with a massive, bearded, naked man with glowing eyes, and a fist connecting with his cheek.

CHAPTER FIFTY-ONE

THIS WAS NOT the negotiation Kaia had planned when she'd been walking on two legs on dry land. Tommy had been flanking her in the water the whole time, doing what he could to defend and not maim, and she'd tried to do the same, but it seemed something else had taken over her—a primal need not only to fight, but to kill and consume.

Her mind was a blissful blank, her heart wild with blood ecstasy as she bit into a siren's arm and tore with razor-sharp teeth. The siren screamed in agony; then Kaia felt a blow strike her back. She doubled over, surrounded by a swath of silky, white hair.

Zoe.

Her enemy.

Her sister.

Kaia whirled around, teeth bared, and met Zoe head-on. She had her hands around Zoe's throat when a cutting shriek shot through the water. The sirens stopped fighting, backing off from Kaia and Tommy as their leader, Frances, appeared.

Stormed was the word Kaia would use to describe Frances's entrance into the cove. Frances's eyes blazed with white-hot fury, glowing in the dark water as kelp bands swirled around her, disturbed by the powerful fan of her tail as she pulled herself to a halt. In a single, unmistakeable gesture, she pointed upward.

Kaia followed the others as they ascended, breaking the surface into the air. Their heads bobbed around Frances's, waiting for her command. Kaia looked over her shoulder, landward.

Sam was there at the shore break, fighting a huge, naked siren with a body like an ancient Greek olympian's. She had never seen this siren before. Sam was big, but this guy was bigger. He landed a heavy punch to Sam's face, causing him to drop his gun. It clattered to the rocks as the siren dragged Sam toward the water.

Feeling a surge of possessive, protective instinct, Kaia dove under again, fanning out her fin and pulsing once, twice, three times until she was right on them, in the breaking waves. The siren was pulling Sam into the water with him, transitioning into a form that could respirate in water even as Sam was beginning to drown.

Screaming, Kaia threw herself onto the siren's back and bit down on the thick pad of muscle above his shoulder. She felt him throw a sharp elbow into her gut in response. Despite the pain, Kaia gripped his steel-gray hair and plunged her teeth deeper into his flesh. He hadn't let go of Sam, but she'd make him. With one fierce lunge, she bit into his neck again and felt her needle-sharp teeth break the skin. She clamped down her jaw and pulled. Ripped. Flesh and tendon and blood spewed out of the siren's throat as he let out a strangled cry. Kaia wanted more of him. Wanted to eat his heart straight out of his chest.

She was gripping his hair and yanking his head backward with sickening ease, ready to take more, when she noticed Sam's body, floating upward. His limbs were slack, hanging down as his body arced toward the surface, his dark hair waving in the sea's current.

"No," she moaned, letting forth a stream of bubbles in the bloodied water as she let go of the siren, surrendering his body to the water and to two of his brethren, who now gathered him and pulled him into the deep.

The others were there then, grabbing her. They would rip her apart. They would kill her in retribution for what she had just done. Their voices surrounded her, wailing their grief and rage. And Sam was losing moments, the few moments that could mean the difference between life and death. It was exactly like the night they'd met, only this time she was even more afraid, even more helpless.

Kaia screamed as three more sirens began dragging her away from the surface, away from Sam. He would die, and she would be their prisoner. She couldn't let that happen.

Spiraling her tail, she threw two of them away from her. They released their hold, and she darted for the third, grabbing the female by her hair as her companions lunged. Tommy was there suddenly, throwing them off her.

Another sharp scream burst through the water. Frances's face was white with rage as she swam into the melee. She released another noise, this one a low, haunting howl that made Kaia shiver down to her bones and the fighting go quiet around them. Frances met her gaze, and Kaia burst away.

She found Sam tossing in the waves. The water tasted of his blood. He was heavy and cold as she pulled him onto the rocks.

"Sam," she cried, brushing his hair from his face as she climbed on top of him. "Sam, please. Don't go."

She smacked his cheek, shook his shoulders. Pushed him onto his side, pounded his back, waiting to hear the retching gasp for air. Nothing.

Panic struck her as she pulled him toward her again to check for a pulse, for breathing. Nothing. She'd never been trained in CPR, but she'd seen it enough times to hope that she could do it right. She folded her hands over his sternum and pushed all her weight into the center of his chest, over and over and over, until she had nearly exhausted herself. Moving to his lips, she blew into him, once, twice, then resumed pushing on his chest.

"Oh, Sam, come on," she cried, her voice breaking as she compressed his chest.

If he died, if he left her without the chance to tell him she loved him, she wasn't sure she'd be able to live with herself. Yes, he had hurt her. Wounded her immensely. He had broken her open and poured himself inside, filled her with a feeling of life she had never known. And then stolen that away.

But she had believed him when he'd said that Violet had used her dark magick to lure him to her. The memory of his face when he had walked through the door the day after he'd left her stranded on Thursday Island—it had not been the look of a guilty man. It had been an expression of fear. Of confusion.

"Come on, Sam," Kaia grunted, pushing into him again.

Tommy's hands pulled her shoulders. His distant voice urged her to stop. *It's too late*, he was saying. *He's gone.*

"No!" Kaia screamed, pressing with all her weight into Sam's chest.

She felt something break inside him. A gurgling sound, then water, rushing from his mouth as Tommy pushed him to his side. Kaia fell onto her bare bottom on the icy rocks as Sam coughed and retched.

Empty. That was how she felt. Purged of all sense of self by blood and fear and grief. Redeemed by the sound of Sam's struggling body beside her.

✦

She'd taken a life and she'd saved one, or at least that was what she was telling herself—even as she felt a dark chasm opening in her chest where her heart should be, even as her body trembled uncontrollably with shivers that rattled her bones.

"What was his name?" Kaia asked. "The siren that attacked Sam... Did I kill him?"

She sat on the edge of the couch, ears pricked for any sound from upstairs, where Sam was recovering in the big master bed with Tommy keeping watch. Frances sat on the chair across the blazing hearth, dressed in a pair of Kaia's pajama pants and a loose tee, with a blanket drawn around her shoulders. Zoe, also dressed in borrowed clothes, bloody and brooding, stood behind Frances. Kaia didn't trust her. Never would. There was something feral and cold in her eyes. Sharklike. Even now, while she was standing with bare feet on the hearthstone, wiggling her chilled, pink toes, anybody would see that she was simply not quite human.

After Kaia had resuscitated Sam, Frances had called off the rest of the sirens and, to Kaia's surprise, followed them onto land, saying they needed to speak, not fight. That Kaia could agree with. Unfortunately, Frances had insisted on bringing Zoe with her.

"His name is Alexander," Frances said, her voice soft and wooly, like she hadn't used it in a long while. Was that an Irish brogue Kaia detected?

Alexander. Someone had given him that name. Someone who had loved him. And even if he had been ready to kill Sam, Kaia should have found another way, should have…

"He's alive, for now—barely. Time will tell. You may be a killer yet, my girl." Frances's brilliant blue eyes were tired beneath the silvery fringe of her short hair. Zoe bared her teeth behind her. "Alexander is your father." Frances pressed her delicate lips together as she examined Kaia, waiting for a reaction.

"No," Kaia said weakly. She shook her head as a flash of panic raced over her skin. "Hank Foley is my father."

"Hank Foley," Frances began, pronouncing his name with great distaste, "took your mother in after she left us. She was already carrying you, Kaia, when she went to live on land with him."

Kaia shook her head again, but couldn't make any words come.

"It was because of *you* that my mother left," Zoe put in, speaking for the first time. Her face contorted with bitterness as she glared down at Kaia.

"You talk?!" Kaia balked, all of her sudden grief transforming to anger at the sound of Zoe's voice. "Why the hell didn't you say something when you were spying on me from the woods, or when you broke into my house?"

Zoe eyed her with an emotionless, cold-blooded gaze. "Because I thought you weren't to be trusted," she said in her rasping, monotone voice. "And I was right."

"Is… Alexander *her* father, too?" Kaia asked Frances, his name wounding her as she pronounced it. She bit back her tears, not wanting to show any weakness in front of the sirens. Zoe especially.

"No," Frances replied. "Your mother had Zoe long before you came along. As I am sure Tommy has indicated to you already, time does not work in the same manner for us sirens when we are in the water."

"Yeah, about that," Kaia started, wanting to hold Frances accountable for keeping Tommy prisoner for some seventy-odd years, wanting to shift the focus away from the terrible thing she had just done.

"Don't worry about me," came Tommy's soft voice from the hall. He walked into the living room, arms crossed over his chest. He met Frances's eyes. "I'll want to talk to you on my own, Frances, but later. Kaia has something to tell you that will affect the future of the clan."

Kaia felt anxiety skitter through her as she thought of Sam alone upstairs.

Tommy, noticing her gazing toward the ceiling, said, "He's fine. I got him a glass of water. His head's stopped bleeding, I just checked. All he needs now is rest, not some stranger standing in the door and making him jump every time the floorboards creak."

Kaia still wasn't happy about leaving Sam unattended with what was very likely a concussion. He had refused to go to the hospital.

"What is it you have to tell me, Kaia?" Frances asked, turning her glacial gaze to her.

"I want to negotiate terms," Kaia said, forcing her voice not to tremble. The man she loved had nearly died without knowing she loved him. She felt like she was crumbling inside. And worse still, she had almost just killed a man with her bare teeth—a stranger, yes, but he was her *biological father*. And he might die yet. She might now never get to know him. She opened her mouth to speak further, but all that came out was a rattling sigh. There seemed to be no strength left in her. She had no right to ask for a negotiation.

"Go on," Frances said.

Kaia forced herself to sit up straighter. "There's an energy corporation," she began hesitantly. "They want to—they're *going* to build a wind farm in Wapomeq Bay." Seeing the confusion on the sirens' faces, she explained, "They'll build massive turbines—windmills—six of them. Rooted in the ocean floor."

"Why?" Zoe asked, white brows lowering over colorless eyes.

Kaia felt a flood of loathing just at the sound of her voice. If Zoe hadn't been such an idiot and asshole and had simply spoken to Kaia from the start, maybe none of this would have happened.

"To harvest energy," she replied, working to keep the anger out of her tone. "For electricity. The wind, it moves the turbines and they, well, I don't know what the hell they do or how it works, but the point is they're going to drag up the *Davis* because it's sitting right where they want to build."

"Kaia will stop them," Tommy interjected, leaning forward from where he sat at the other end of the couch. "She'll gather a group of people to stop the wind farm."

"And in return?" Frances asked calmly, clasping her hands on her lap. Behind her, Zoe shifted her weight, clearly uncomfortable in her human form and just as wary of Kaia as Kaia was of her.

"I swim freely, and so does Tommy," Kaia said, lifting her chin. "You don't mess with us. Any of you." She pointed her gaze at Zoe. "Besides, what you wanted from me—to have babies? Well, I can't." Actually, she *could*, but that would require a skilled doctor and a state-of-the-art laboratory. Before her surgery, she'd had eggs frozen in the hope that someday, if she met the right person, they might want to try doing the whole Petri dish thing. That seemed pretty remote now. Regardless, it wouldn't work the way Frances wanted it to. "I had an operation years ago," Kaia said. "They removed my ovaries. I can't have a baby."

Zoe scoffed and turned toward the fire.

"What?" Kaia said.

Frances glanced up at Zoe, then responded, "Zoe is also… infertile."

Zoe turned and glanced over her shoulder. If Kaia wasn't mistaken, she was looking at Tommy, who simply sat with his fists clasped between his knees, staring at the floor.

"Tommy told you, I am sure, that our numbers are dropping," Frances said wearily. "There never were many of us sirens. Now, we are in danger of dying out altogether. There are others, other clans. But they are territorial, and far away besides. If we were to lose our home… I don't know where we would go. Some of us are old. Too old to migrate. We will take your offer, Kaia."

"Okay," Kaia said in barely a whisper, too relieved to summon the full sound of her voice. "Thank you."

Frances sat very still, her ice-blue eyes sparkling with what might have been the hint of a smile. Behind her, Zoe continued to pin Kaia with her cold stare.

"I… have questions," Kaia breathed at last.

Frances gave a nod of acquiescence. Kaia figured that would be the only invitation she'd get. Summoning what little courage and wherewithal remained within her, she asked, "What really happened to my mom? My dad, Hank, he always told me it was an accident."

Frances lifted her brows and drew in a long breath. "It was," she said, on a sigh. "One of our number was merely trying to pull her into the water. Alexander, if you must know." Frances paused and steadied herself, straightening her spine as the lines around her mouth deepened. "He never intended for her to... to snap her neck."

Alexander was responsible for her death.

This fact gave Kaia some small relief, a sense of vindication for what she had just done.

France paused, her gaze shifting to the embers in the hearth before returning to Kaia. "We gave her a proper burial. I can take you to her."

Lost, her father always used to say. *When I lost your mother...* He had never said *When your mother died.*

"Does my dad—does Hank Foley know the truth?" Kaia asked. "Did he know what she was? Does he know what I am?"

"No," Frances replied, pursing her lips. "And it must remain that way."

"Why did my mother want to leave the clan?" Kaia asked, sensing that she had to keep her questions rolling before Frances got fed up with dry land and returned to her home in the water.

"She wanted to raise you on land, away from us," Zoe said with a sneer.

"There was once a time," Frances cut in, "when our kind could pass more freely between realms. But men and their technology have made that nearly impossible now. They have made our very existence dangerous. Your mother yearned for the dual life that was in her blood. She wanted to know life on land."

"She wanted you to be better than we are," Zoe added. "Well, you aren't."

"She fell in love with a mortal. She loved Hank," Frances said evenly, ignoring her granddaughter. "Fiona loved him well enough to risk everything, including her life."

At the sound of her mother's name, Kaia felt something crack open inside her heart, letting all the sorrow she'd been holding at bay pour in. She could have drowned in it, easily and without resistance, had it not been for the creaking of heavy footfalls on the stairs. Everyone collectively turned toward the hall, where Sam was coming down with one hand to his head. Kaia stood and went to him.

"What are you doing out of bed?" she asked, her voice a thin rasp.

He had dressed in the clothing she'd bought for Tommy. The jeans were too short and fell above his big, boney ankles. The t-shirt was pulled tight against the broad expanse of his chest, showing an inch of skin at his hip when he moved. It made him look silly and vulnerable, and Kaia wanted to throw herself against him and wrap her arms around his waist, but she stopped herself.

"Going home," he said, with a dark glance to the three other sirens sitting in the living room. Frances and Tommy were quietly conversing. "I've gotta finish one of my paintings for my show tomorrow."

"You should rest," Kaia insisted.

"I should *leave*." He shook his head and heaved a heavy sigh, not meeting her gaze no matter how she angled herself. "I want to go home," was all he said, and padded into the kitchen, where the dryer was still going with his jacket and other articles inside it.

"None of that is dry yet," Kaia told him, pushing the machine door closed and hitting the start button again. "Stay, Sam."

She rested a hand on his arm, where his skin was still cool. Too cool. His face was already bruising around his eye and temple. The bandage on his forehead was thankfully still white, though.

"I want to go home," he repeated. "I don't want to be here. Do you... want to come with me?"

She pictured herself on the *Angeline,* crossing the bay where she had just been imprisoned, spending a night in the safety of Sam's arms. Sam's arms that had been around someone else, very recently.

"No," Kaia replied.

He nodded. "Okay," he said, simply, and humbly. "Just one more thing, then."

"Yes?" Kaia half hoped he'd ask her again. She might just say yes this time.

"Did you see that painting I started... of you? The one where you're, you know, in... bed?"

Kaia felt her cheeks flush and crossed her arms over her chest as she recalled the large oil painting of herself, drowsing face down in the early morning light, and the way it had made her feel to look at it—like the connection they had found together the previous night was nothing short of unbreakable. "Uh-huh," she responded. "What about it?"

"How would you feel about me, ah"—Sam scratched his head—"putting it up at the gallery?"

Kaia paused a moment, tucking a curl behind her ear. On the one hand, she couldn't believe the balls he had asking her if he could use it. On the other, she wouldn't mind Violet Wilde seeing that one in particular.

"That's fine," she said. "Thanks for asking."

Sam looked relieved. "And—and I just wanted to say, you're still welcome to play at the gallery for my show, if you want to. If not I, ah, I understand."

"I'll have to think about it." Kaia folded her arms around herself.

Sam nodded and, without another word, left the house. Before Kaia could process it all, Frances and Zoe appeared in the kitchen. Stark naked.

"We left the clothing in the other room," Frances said with complete dignity as she proceeded toward the door. She paused and turned to Kaia, giving her a nod. "I'll return soon, granddaughter," she said. "I wish to know you, and for you to know me."

"And you'll… you'll let me know what happens with Alexander?" Kaia croaked.

Frances paused. "You'll know," she said, like a threat.

Zoe only shot daggers with her gaze as she gave Kaia one last glare before following Frances out the door. Trembling, Kaia turned as Tommy came into the kitchen a moment later, eyes clearly searching the table for scraps of cold pizza and gummy-looking hot wings.

CHAPTER FIFTY-TWO

VIOLET STOOD IN the cupola, scanning the harbor. Kaia Foley was back, it seemed. She'd seen Sam's boat at the point for a short time. It had been moored there no more than an hour or two before returning to Thursday Island. The lights were still on in the house on Foley's Point, so Violet had to assume that Kaia had remained there, alone. Still, she was unsettled to think that Kaia had returned to Maine.

Violet had hoped her problem was solved, that Sam was hers and hers alone again. Of course, it could be someone else staying at the house on Foley's Point. There were renters during summers, she knew that. And Sam supervised the rentals for the Foley family, so it was possible he had been there helping them with something. Possible, but doubtful. It was the dead of winter, after all.

"Let's summon him." Emory appeared at Violet's side, wrapped in a long cashmere caftan. "I want him tonight," she said in a wheedling tone.

Violet scoffed. Nothing Emory said ever surprised her. She knew what she would say before Emory even knew she wanted to say it. If nothing else, this little experience with sharing Sam Lowell had revealed to Violet just how the connection between her and Emory worked. It was clear to Violet, at last, that hers was indeed the primary mind, the authority. Emory might not know what Violet was thinking or feeling, beyond what Violet wanted her to know. But Violet knew everything there was to Emory. And there wasn't much. Intelligence for numbers, yes. Business savviness. The ability to memorize huge tracts of legal text. And little else. But there *was* room for desire, it seemed.

"Not tonight," Violet said, just to exercise her dominance. She brushed her fingertips along Emory's collarbone as she turned and left her there to gaze at the darkened bay, and clutched the skeleton key hanging around her neck as she descended the steps to go to her bedroom. There would be plenty of time for fun with Sam tomorrow night, after his art show. After all, they would have to celebrate.

Chapter Fifty-Three

Both hungry for more than frozen pizza, Kaia and Tommy went to the Hook and Anchor and ate burgers without speaking, tucked into a dark booth at the back of the pub. Kaia thought she ought to feel so sick with what she had done to Alexander that she should have no appetite, yet the weeks of being half-starved in the belly of the *USS Davis* gave her physical needs precedence over her those of her conscience.

"Do you know him?" she asked Tommy, at last. "A-Alexander?"

"He's Frances's second-in-command," Tommy explained in a low voice. "Some say he wants to take her place. He spends a lot of time leading hunting parties. I wouldn't say I know him, no. His fists, yes. The man inside—if there is one—no."

They went on eating in silence for a time after that.

"You can stay with me as long as you like," Kaia told Tommy when she had finished her burger and all of the fries and found the fortitude to speak, and to think again. Tommy lifted his eyes from his nearly clean plate, one cheek stuffed with the last remains of his burger. "Unless... you want to go back to the clan?"

Tommy shook his head. His soft blue eyes were red-rimmed and glassy from physical and emotional exhaustion. His lips were chapped. His wheat-colored hair was tangled and salty. His beard was long and unkempt, giving him the aspect of a mountain-man Jesus. He looked like he hadn't slept in seventy years. "No way. They held me prisoner. Stole my life," he said. "I would rather stay here with you for a bit. If that's okay."

"It is," Kaia said, moved by the glimmer of tears shining in his eyes. "Oh! I know! We can look her up," she exclaimed. Tommy stared blankly. "Olivia, your wife. We can search for her online."

She had all but forgotten the laptop in the bottom of her duffel bag, which she had brought to Maine in case she got bored and wanted to watch movies. Now, the thought of being bored in Quolobit Harbor almost made her laugh.

Tommy's light brown brows gathered in confusion. "*Online?*"

⸎

As it turned out, the house on Foley's Point—though the plumbing was iffy and you had to light the stove with a match—*did* have WiFi. Kaia found Tommy's wife easily. Olivia had been the daughter of a wealthy steel magnate and the wife of the owner of a luxury resort hotel in the Allegheny mountains. The hotel, now on the historical registry, was still a popular destination for weddings and romantic getaways. The resort had a whole page of its website dedicated to Olivia, who had used the hotel to run a hospital for veterans in the aftermath of World War Two.

According to Olivia's brief biography, after the 'death' of her first husband, Tommy O'Holloran, she had remarried and gone on to have five children. She died at the age of ninety-one.

"Missed her by nine years," Tommy said. He was dry-eyed, but his hands trembled as they moved toward the black-and-white photo of the beautiful young woman on the computer screen, then closed into fists. "I wanna be angry. I wanna feel like she betrayed me by marrying that other guy. But she didn't. She thought I was dead. And I think she ended up happier than I would've ever made her."

"Oh, Tommy, don't say that—"

"Her father never wanted her to marry me—a rough-handed farm boy. We eloped, me and Olivia," Tommy told Kaia with a feral look in his eyes. "Just before I shipped off. We only had one weekend together before… " He dipped his head.

Kaia put her arm around his shoulders. "I'm so sorry."

"My mom and dad are gone, too," he whispered, the realization hitting him with another blow of grief that made a sob escape him. Kaia held him tight. Eventually his weeping passed and he lifted his head. "I had a brother and a sister. Can we look them up?"

It didn't take long to find that Tommy's siblings were also deceased, leaving children and grandchildren behind. "Maybe you could try to connect with your nieces and nephews," Kaia suggested. "Or... their kids?"

He shook his head and wiped his hands over his un-groomed face. "No," he said. "I'd rather leave it behind."

He got up and left the living room, climbing the stairs with heavy steps. A moment later she heard the door of the spare bedroom click closed, and she saw no more of Tommy for the rest of the night.

CHAPTER FIFTY-FOUR

TOMMY WASN'T AROUND in the morning, either. Kaia woke long after dawn, having slept considerably more than eight hours, and found the house empty. The truck was gone.

"Shit," she said, and would have maybe started to panic if she hadn't heard its loud rumble approaching from deep in the woods sheltering the land.

"Hope it's okay I stole your wallet and went to the store," Tommy said as he hauled in two armfuls of groceries and set them down on the table. "I used that little plastic card thing you've got to pay. I'm not in the habit of taking other people's money, but I didn't think you'd want cold pizza for breakfast."

Kaia laughed, hugging her sweater around her waist. "No, I really don't." She opened a bag to see a container of pastries, two navel oranges, and a carton of fresh cream. Another bag contained a loaf of bread, a dozen eggs, and several packages of deli meat. Her mouth watered. "Thanks, Tommy." She wanted to ask him if he was okay, if he'd slept well, but saw the look of raw determination on his face and knew that to ask would be to wound. She smiled at him instead and told him she'd get the coffee going.

Tommy didn't ask her questions, either, though she was fully aware that he noticed her restlessness throughout the day. She was still going back and forth on whether or not she should go to Sam's show. And whether or not she would accept Sam back into her heart.

᷍

"I decided. I'm going," Kaia announced to Tommy as she came into the living room, after showering and primping herself as best she could with nothing other than the cosmetics Violet had given her after their photoshoot.

It had irked Kaia momentarily to put on the makeup Violet had given her, but ultimately it was good stuff. She had even dabbed the wild rose perfume on her wrists and behind her neck, and rubbed a bit of it into her hair.

"Is that what you're wearing?" Tommy asked with a disapproving frown, turning from the hearth where he'd been tending the fire. "I mean, don't you have a skirt or something?"

Kaia looked down at her loose, bohemian blouse tucked into high-waisted jeans. "What's wrong with this?" she asked, then remembered. "Tommy. Things have changed," she said gently. "Women dress however they like, now. And most of the time that means... not a skirt."

His bloodshot eyes widened, then he dropped them to the hearthstone. "Right," he said. "I've got a lot to learn, huh?"

Kaia sat on a creaky wooden chair at one end of the couch and began tuning her banjo. As she started playing Tommy grew still, his hands resting on the iron fire poker across his lap.

"*Blue moon of Kentucky, keep on shining,*" Kaia began to sing. "*Shine on the one that's gone and proved untrue...*"

"*Blue moon of Kentucky, keep on shining.*" Another voice joined in, in harmony, soft but clear. "*Shine on the one that's gone and left me blue.*"

Tommy stood, still singing along as he went to the guitar case and lifted out the instrument. He quickly tuned it with expert ease and began to play along with her.

"Well, you sure know your way around that thing," Kaia said when they had finished the song. Tommy had impressed her with his skill on the guitar and the sweet, clear sound of his voice.

"You're not too bad yourself." His cheeks went subtly pink above the brush of his ruddy beard. "Used to play all the time with my grandpa. He was from West Virginia. I'm a bit rusty," he told her as he noodled out a final riff. "Nice guitar, too. I've always been partial to Gibsons myself." He put the guitar down on the couch, and Kaia felt the sadness returning to the room.

Then he said, "Guess I'd better get cleaned up if I'm gonna come play at this damn art show with you. You got a pair of scissors lyin' around here somewhere?"

Kaia grinned.

⮜

Kaia endeavored to hold her head high as she walked into the Water's Edge gallery with Tommy at her side, newly shorn and groomed. She had trimmed his hair so it was a little closer to the nape of his neck and not so uneven, and helped him cut his beard to a decent length, revealing a face that was damned handsome, if a bit gaunt.

There were already a dozen early birds milling around the gallery in snow boots and winter coats, taking in the turbulent, stormy paintings on display. A blonde woman was fussing over the wet floors and telling one of the catering staff to search for a mop in the closet. She looked so eerily like Violet that they had to be sisters—or even twins. Her icy eyes lit on Kaia as she loudly banged the snow off her boots at the doormat.

Ignoring the woman's scowl, Kaia took note of the paintings of herself, which Sam had positioned as the centerpiece of the show. In one she was portrayed from the shoulders up, gazing away calmly. In the other, she was sprawled face down in his bed, bare back and thigh and part of her butt, pink as though freshly smacked—which it probably had been—exposed in the sheets. And between them, in silver decal lettering on the wall, was the title of the show: *Song of the Siren.*

She tried not to blush, but failed. Tommy gave her a wry look, and though his lips twitched, she was grateful he didn't actually smirk.

She scanned the room for Sam and spotted him just as he looked away from a local who had been asking him about his paintings. He met her eyes with his cool, dark gaze, barely concealing the surprise he obviously felt at seeing her walk through the door. He was by far the best-dressed person in the gallery, though she knew that beneath the tailored suit he was hurting and scarred. His hair and beard had been freshly groomed too. He looked more devastatingly handsome than ever. A wild, feral sort of man—tamed, but barely.

Kaia swallowed the desire to walk right up to him and kiss him.

"Where do we set up?" Tommy asked as she ripped herself away from Sam's gaze.

"Oh, um, looks like it's over there." Kaia pointed to a corner, where Harvey from the Hook and Anchor had already set up a PA system. She looked at Sam again and found him still watching her. Sam's eyes flitted to Tommy. He offered a tight smile before returning to his conversation.

After setting up, Kaia began with a finger-picking rendition of the folksong *Moonshiner*. The song was like an old shoe her foot fit perfectly into; she didn't have to think about singing it, didn't have to worry about whether or not she could trust her fingers as they flew over the strings. And Tommy wove his way in beautifully. She caught herself smiling—actually smiling—at him as they parried back and forth together with riffs, as the vibration of his voice met and matched her own, a perfect harmonic fit. She had nearly forgotten just how good it felt to make music with someone who was on her wavelength, who knew the tunes in his bones, just like she did.

People floated into the gallery along with snow flurries—the cashier from Penfeld's Market, Felicia and her daughters, even Markus the realtor. Many of them gave Kaia and Tommy approving smiles, but most were clearly enchanted by the paintings on the gallery walls. Sam's cheeks were flushed while he was accosted by just about every human he'd ever known as they came to congratulate him.

Eventually, Sam found his way over when they were between songs. "You're here," he said. "I didn't think you'd come, but I had Harvey set up the PA, just in case."

"Wasn't gonna let you down." Kaia wanted to dive into the depths of his eyes, to hand him her broken, trembling heart, but she focused on retuning her banjo instead. "Looks like you've got a good turnout."

"I'm gonna go get us some drinks," Tommy said, giving Kaia a conspiratorial wink as he nudged past her and Sam.

Kaia felt simultaneously thankful to him for vacating and terrified to be alone with Sam and what was between them.

"Did your dad show up yet?" she asked, wanting to keep the conversation light.

"He's flying up from Florida and renting a car to drive north outta Boston," Sam said. *Bahstun.* Kaia forced herself not to smile at his cute Downeaster accent. "But nope. He's not here yet. I hope the snow doesn't delay him." He frowned.

"Hey," Kaia said, reaching up to touch Sam's shoulder. "He'll get here. Don't worry. And Sam… this is amazing."

Sam grimaced at her touch and flinched away.

"What?" she asked, withdrawing.

"N—nothing." He swiped his hand under his nose and sniffled, dark eyes meeting hers mistrustfully. "I, ah, went to Felicia." He pulled at the open collar of his shirt to reveal a hand-drawn sigil in permanent marker on the un-tattooed side of his chest. That little bit of skin sent Kaia's heart racing. She threw her gaze down to her boots. "She gave me some angelica root to keep in my pocket too. Violet shouldn't be able to get to me now." His eyes held a dark sort of hope that Kaia couldn't find a way to respond to. Sam blinked, then said, "So, ah, how d'you think… Tommy's doing?"

Kaia bristled. "Sam, are you jealous?" Because if he was, well, she could not abide that. Not considering what she still might put aside, what she might forgive. And she wouldn't lie to herself—the fact that Sam had been with Violet was hurting her something bad, whether or not it had been against his will.

"I'm not jealous," Sam whispered, leaning closer, close enough that she could smell his sandalwood soap and sense the warmth of his body heat radiating through his suit. He wrinkled his nose and squinted at her. "I know that what you and I had was more than either of us have ever had with anyone else, ever, combined, okay?" His dark eyes held hers. "I'm just wondering if we'll ever get past the mistakes I've made. And me—I might not be whole, but what I have left of myself I want to give to you," he said in a quiet rush. "I might not understand much about this life as a human, and nothing I do is without doubt and… and fucking fear"—he glanced around as if he was afraid at this precise moment—"but there is not a single grain of doubt in my heart about this, about how I feel for you."

Kaia opened her mouth to speak, but closed it again. Sam's eyes widened.

"And I'm sincerely asking you—how do you think Tommy is doing?" he asked. "He told me they kept him down there seventy years. This has to be a total mind-fuck for him."

"He's disoriented and grieving, but I think he's going to be okay. He's going to stay with me for a while." She watched him for any signs of jealousy at this announcement.

Sam nodded, his eyes scanning the thickening crowd. "Good," he said, without malice.

Just then, the blonde version of Violet came over and tapped Sam's shoulder. "Sam, there's someone I want you to meet," she purred, and drew him away without giving Kaia even the briefest of glances.

Sam slipped away as Tommy returned with two bottles of Smutty Nose Pale Ale and a plate of hors d'oeuvres. "I can see what you mean about the ladies wearing slacks," he said, licking his fingers as he shoved a miniature taco into his mouth, eyes scanning the thickening crowd. "But, I gotta say, the fashion today in general? It ain't flattering."

Kaia just rolled her eyes and took a healthy swig of beer as she perched atop her stool again and adjusted her mic.

"What's the story with you and him?" Tommy nodded in Sam's direction.

"Ugh." Kaia grunted. Her heart ached just looking at Sam. Thinking of how he had made her feel. Thinking of him with another woman.

"It's like that, huh?" Tommy gave her a salty grin, lifting his brows. "You don't wanna talk about it, no problem. What's next, captain?"

"I don't know," Kaia grumbled, crestfallen.

"I got one for you," Tommy said. "It was the big hit just before I went down." He winked as he started an up-tempo walk-down bass line in the key of G. "*Comin' in on a wing and a prayer*," he began to sing, in his old-timey, countrified style.

They were midway through the 1940s tune and Kaia was sincerely enjoying herself when Violet herself slid into the gallery, swathed in a floor-length dress of deep-rose-colored silk with a thick fur mantle clutched around her shoulders.

"Now *there's* a lady," Tommy leaned over and said between verses. Kaia rolled her eyes again.

Tommy's brows shot up. "No?" He continued strumming and began to sing the next verse as he looked from Kaia to Sam to Violet, putting the pieces together.

Kaia tried not to sneer as Violet's bright green eyes widened upon seeing her. Violet recovered from her shock quickly—too quickly—plastering on a smile as she greeted her sister and kissed the cheek of the tall, well-suited man Emory was introducing to Sam.

Violet then put her hand on Sam's sleeve and went in to kiss him, too, but something stopped her. Her eyes went wide for a moment as she took a step away from him. Felicia's sigils and herbs were working, it seemed, Kaia noted with satisfaction. Violet let out a little laugh, but her brows swept low over her eyes as she scanned the room.

"Hey, she ain't got nothin' on you," Tommy said, leaning in and whispering close to Kaia's ear.

As they continued to play and sing in harmony, Kaia kept an eye on Violet flitting around the room. Right as they finished, Violet sailed over, all smiles.

"Kaia, you look *cute* as always." She gave a cool smile. "Is that my lip stain you're wearing? Looks great. And you really do have the most beautiful voice," Violet went on, eyeing Tommy briefly. "I can see where Sam got his inspiration for those portraits." Kaia felt her cheeks burn. "Doesn't that suit look great on Sam? I had it custom-made by my father's tailor. It was pricey, but it'll never go out of style. Who knows, maybe he'll wear it for our wedding someday. Can you believe he didn't have a proper suit of his own? That old thing he had looked like he'd gotten it off the sale rack at Bargain Barn! Oh, excuse me, there's Mr and Mrs Winthrop. Daddy's friends." With that, Violet slid away in a whirl of bright-colored silk.

"*Daddy's friends*," Tommy parroted, showing his teeth in a snarl.

Kaia laughed, grateful for his camaraderie. Deciding she had to achieve a very specific level of intoxication on the drunk-sober spectrum in order to make it through the rest of the evening, she took another deep swig of beer before starting the next song.

CHAPTER FIFTY-FIVE

AFTER THE GALLERY had closed at the end of the evening, everyone headed over to the Hook and Anchor for an afterparty. Sam was happy to see Kaia sitting with Felicia Dunne at the corner of the bar, in the same spot where he had first seen her on the night she came to Quolobit Harbor. Kaia's eyes met Sam's, but just then a familiar man turned from the bar, his ordinarily unruly silver hair newly shorn into a close-cropped style Sam had to assume had been undertaken for the occasion. The sight of him nearly made Sam laugh and cry at the same time.

"That was one hell of a show, son," Samuel said, and pulled Sam into a hug. "You've been so busy talking to other people all night, I didn't have the chance to congratulate you."

"Dad, thanks," Sam said, trying not to sniffle too obviously. "It never would've happened without you."

Samuel gave him a questioning look, his white brows knitting together at the top of his nose, whiskers twitching beneath it. "What do you mean?"

"If you hadn't put the pencil into my hand that day and told me to draw a picture of what I wanted to say and what I felt," Sam explained, "I never would've found my... my voice as an artist."

Samuel smiled and patted a hand to Sam's cheek. "Proud of you, buddy."

Sam blinked away the sting of tears in his eyes.

"Thanks," Sam repeated, even though *thanks* wasn't nearly enough. He felt heat rise in his cheeks as he noticed Kaia and Felicia smiling mirthfully at him being patted by his father.

"How much did you make?" Samuel asked. "Did I hear they all sold?"

"I don't know yet, didn't do the math, didn't even set the prices," Sam replied. Emory had come up to him some time towards the end of the night and whispered that a single buyer had purchased all the paintings. "There's taxes, too, so who knows. I'm sure it'll be enough to keep me in supplies for the next year."

Samuel laughed and raised his pint to Sam. "A great start. I think you've got a few admirers to greet. Oh, and, ah, I told Harvey the first round is on me."

"Dad, no—" Sam protested.

Samuel held up a hand. "I insist. The town's gonna be paying me to do nothing over at that lighthouse, other than walk the occasional tour up the tower—"

"What?"

Samuel's blue eyes twinkled. "I'm here to stay," he said, and clapped a hand on Sam's shoulder. "Town hired me to be the lighthouse keeper."

"Seriously?" Sam said. "But what about the fishing tours in Fort Lauderdale? I thought you had a good thing going there."

"Florida's boring." Samuel took a swig of his beer, then gave Sam a nod. "Go talk to that pretty redhead you've had your eyes on all night."

Sam hugged his father again and began walking to the end of the bar, his heart heavy with trepidation, his tongue already tied in stupid knots. But before he could make it to where Kaia sat, Violet came into the Hook and Anchor with her father, Kenneth Wilde.

"Sam!" Violet called, and drew her father to Sam's side. "This is my dad, Kenneth Wilde."

Sam felt his insides quake beneath the cold and calculating gaze of the trim, scrutinizing man as he took his hand. "Sam Lowell," he said.

"I know," Kenneth replied with a tight smile as his dry, cold palm closed around Sam's. "Congratulations, Sam. I'd say your show was a success."

"Oh?" Over Violet's head, Sam saw Kaia and Felicia staring at him, watching his interactions with eagle-like focus. Beyond them, playing darts with Bobby, his sternman, was that damned blond siren stray Kaia had taken in, Tommy—also giving him a judging stare.

"My dad," Violet said, squeezing Sam's arm and demanding his attention. He resisted the instinct to take a step back from her as she leaned closer and spoke into his ear. "He bought out your show."

"What?"

Kenneth Wilde gazed at Sam, his eyes marked by little white lines that spoke of winter retreats to warmer climes. "I bought the whole show, Sam. Hope you don't mind."

"What? Why?" Sam asked.

There was an awkward pause in which Kenneth Wilde's icy eyes held Sam's. Then Violet let out a laugh.

"Because it's good work." Wilde clapped a hand on Sam's shoulder. "I'll make a pretty penny at a gallery I own in Boston. You'll gain a following, and Emory could set up another show for you here in Quolobit this summer when there'll be plenty of eager tourists and art aficionados in town, hunting down the famous Sam Lowell."

Sam blinked.

"My dad has a business proposal to make to you, Sam," Violet gushed.

"Me?" Sam asked. "I don't mean to be rude, it's just that… I'm a fisherman, Mr. Wilde—my life is, ah, out there on the water."

"Kenneth, please." The steely, reptilian eyes narrowed. "I'm about to launch a massive project here in Quolobit Harbor, and I'll need a community liaison," Kenneth Wilde said, glancing around the bar with the calculating aspect of a prospector surveying new lands which may yield great riches. "A local fisherman and celebrated artist would be just the person. You're the right age to appeal to the younger crowd, and your status as a seventh-generation fisherman will give you credibility to the old stalwarts. I want you on my team, Sam." Kenneth Wilde rested a heavy hand on Sam's shoulder. "And if it goes well, I could pave the way for your future."

Sam felt his face begin to burn when words wouldn't come to him quickly enough. Violet came between them with a gracious smile.

"Let him think about it, Daddy," she said. "Sam's had an intense night. There'll be plenty of time to talk about the wind farm later."

Kenneth Wilde nodded and moved to the bar, but Sam felt the man watching him out of the corner of his eyes as he pulled Violet aside and said, "Can we talk? Outside?"

As far as he was concerned, this conversation couldn't wait a minute longer. He drew her out onto the deck of the Hook and Anchor, where the star-strewn sky revealed the Milky Way in all its cold, distant glory. Violet, wrapped in her fur, followed him to the end of the deck, where he leaned on the railing and looked out at the great expanse of water.

She leaned her head back and inhaled deeply. "Ah," she said. "I love the smell of the sea, don't you?"

"Violet—"

"What's wrong?" she asked. "Need a breather from the madness in there?" A grin broadened across her mouth. "Want to sneak onto the *Angeline*? We can leave Emory out of it."

Sam sighed. "I need more than a breather, Violet," he said, striving to remain calm even though his heart was pounding and sweat was itching against his palms. "I'm not going to let you destroy my life. It's over between us. Got it? Whatever it is that you want—love, lust, the charge you get from seeing me on my knees—it's not going to make you happy. It's not going to take away the poison in your ancient fucking heart."

Violet, to his surprise, laughed. She reached up and ran a hand through his newly-trimmed hair. "Don't be crazy, Sam," she said. "You've been super stressed about this show; it was your first show and I get that, and we haven't had much time together. Things'll settle down now, and we can pick up where we left off. I can tell Emory it's just us from now on, if you want."

"No." He shook his head and pulled away from her. "No way, Violet. It's over."

"I need you more than you realize," she told him, her voice rising in pitch as her eyes grew wild, reflecting the smattering of stars overhead. "And you need me too."

Sam shook his head and stepped away from her. "I love Kaia. And even if what she and I had is now damaged beyond recovering, *she's* the only person I need. She knows things about me I could never imagine telling you, even if you hadn't started this crazy shit with Emory and—and fucking bewitching me. I'm sorry to disappoint you, Violet. I'm disappointed in myself for not cutting it off sooner, before it would cause so much suffering. I was weak."

"Sam Lowell, who knew you could be so eloquent?" She flashed him a biting smile. "You don't see it yet, but you will soon—you'll be tied to *me* for the rest of your life."

Before he could ask her to explain, Violet turned on her heels and strode off the deck and into the parking lot. He let her go. To chase after her would be to give her an inaccurate sense of the power she believed she held over him, and he wouldn't let her live under that illusion any longer. Sam turned to the ocean, lifting his face to the briny breeze, knowing that at least one part of him was freer than it had been.

CHAPTER FIFTY-SIX

"ALEXANDER WAS GOING to kill Sam," Kaia muttered. "And I almost killed *him*. And, like, maybe I actually did. The goddamn verdict is still out." She stifled a choking sob. "My biological father…"

Felicia made a sympathetic clucking noise and shook her head. "You didn't know who he was, Kaia."

Kaia let her head droop between her shoulders and instantly felt Tommy's questioning gaze from where he was playing darts. She offered him her best attempt at a smile, trying to say *I'm fine*. He nodded, his keen blue eyes lingering a moment to indicate he'd be at her side in a heartbeat if she said the word.

"Seems you found at least one friend down there," Felicia said.

"Yeah. He's good, Tommy. Right now, I'm finding it a little hard to get why I should do anything for the siren clan. Seems they're all assholes, except for Tommy. And you know, you might be crazy to think I could stop the Wildes from building the wind farm." Kaia had overheard Kenneth Wilde's conversation with Sam. "Seems like those folks've got this town by the balls."

"Not yet they don't, but they will if we don't do something about it," Felicia said, looking around at the storekeepers, fishermen, school teachers, and other stolid Mainers in the bar. "Cheer up, Kaia. I think you could gather a small army."

"I hope you're right," Kaia said. She sipped her beer, then lifted her brows as outside, Violet Wilde walked quickly past the windows.

"Looks like Sam finally said off with her head." Felicia craned her neck to peer out the window, and Kaia turned to see Sam standing alone at the very end of the dock. "I think you'd better go talk to him."

She wanted to talk to him, wanted to bring him to her bed and make each other forget that anyone, anything else existed. But that would be reckless, she knew. There was no way it could actually be healthy, no way it could be what it had been before. Her heart was too sore over what had transpired, and besides that, it was still scarred from the demise of her previous relationship.

Fool me once, shame on you. Fool me twice, shame on me.

"I don't know if I should," Kaia said.

Felicia's hand was soft upon hers, her amber eyes shining gently through the massive round rims of her grass-green glasses. "I think you need to let him—and yourself—know where you stand."

Knowing that her friend was right, Kaia heaved a sigh and slid off the stool. She shrugged her jacket around her shoulders, taking comfort in Felicia's compassionate smile. She realized, as she walked out into the cool night air, that her entire body was sore to the bones. She'd never been so tired, she decided as she walked slowly to the end of the deck, where Sam leaned on the railing, his face tilted up to the stars.

"They're beautiful," Kaia said.

Sam started and turned to her.

"The stars," she specified.

He looked up. "Oh, hm."

"There's no moon tonight." Kaia gazed out over the water, where nothing but reflected starlight sliced into the infinite blackness. "I saw Violet leaving. She looked... upset."

Sam sighed and shook his head. "I told her it was over between us, but I'll be honest—I don't know if she got the message." He turned to her again. He looked about as worn-out as she felt, but in the shadows around his eyes there was a softness that drew her to him. "I meant everything I said to you in the gallery."

"I know," Kaia said, though part of her still simmered with righteous indignation for what he'd put her through.

"From the first moment I saw you right there at the bar, the night you came to Quolobit Harbor, I knew I'd been living half a life," he said.

"And what made you realize that?"

"When I listened to you sing and I heard your voice, that's when I knew."

Her own heart ached as she remembered him crying while she sang that night. "Why did you cry?" she asked, looking up at him.

Sam smiled sadly. "Because your voice reminded me of a part of myself I'd almost forgotten. That night, I woke up. I realized I'd been avoiding real love because I was afraid it'd mean I'm just a man, no longer a seal, but somehow you made me feel that I can be both."

Kaia let herself wrap her arms around him. "Oh, Sam," she murmured, feeling his lips rest on the top of her head, feeling the warmth of his breath in her hair.

Stiffening, he pulled back.

"What's the matter?" Kaia asked as he recoiled.

"That smell"—Sam swallowed, hard, his eyes round with fear—"that's the smell of the person who stole my sealskin."

Kaia touched a hand to her neck, then sniffed at the inside of her wrist, where the vibrant wild rose perfume Violet had given her warmed her skin.

"Where'd you get that perfume?" Sam asked.

Kaia choked as the pieces began to fit together.

"Violet gave this perfume to me as a gift after I modeled for her. She said it was the first one she ever made," she whispered, sniffing her wrist again.

A look of dawning clarity came over his face. "Huh. So that's what she meant when she said I'd be tied to her for the rest of my life."

"She said that?" Kaia clutched at her neck, where the rose scent blossomed anew as her temperature rose despite the chill of the winter night. "You think Violet has your sealskin?"

"After what she just said to me, and smelling that on you, I'm sure of it." Sam laughed.

"That's terrible, Sam. Why are you laughing?"

"It's not terrible. It's great," Sam said, lifting his brows. He smiled. "I mean, it sucks that *I* don't have it, but at least now I know who does.

I've lived all these years on land not knowing where my sealskin was, not knowing if that person would take good care of it, or destroy me. Now I know. And I can get it back from her."

"Can you?"

Sam's smile fell. "I hope so."

Kaia gasped for breath and turned to take in the cold air that blew in off the ocean's surface. "And if you do, that means you'll go back to the ocean…"

His face crumpled in anguish. "Kaia—I—"

"I'll help you get it back," she said, and lifted her chin.

He shook his head, clenching his jaw. "Maybe it doesn't have to be like the curse says—maybe—"

"I mean it. I want to help you, no matter what the outcome," she said.

Sam paused before replying, his brows drawing together over his glimmering eyes. Then he drew her to him again, resting his cheek atop her head. They stood that way for a long while in silence before he asked, "Why?"

"Because I love you," she said, simply. "When your heart wasn't beating, and you weren't breathing, Sam, that was all I could think of. That you'd die without knowing what's in my heart for you. And I'm here," she said, her voice breaking as tears filled her eyes and she looked upward to stay them. "I'm here with you because I just… almost killed someone. Ripped his jugular out with my damned teeth." She contained a sob, barely. "And that man… he's my father." She felt Sam go still against her. "I think I need to be near you right now, Sam, because you make me feel safe, and free, and good. And strong. Stronger than I ever knew. And I need those things. I need to remember right now that I'm more than… a killer."

He gathered her against his chest as the weeping took her in earnest. "You did it to save my life," he said, pressing his lips against her hair as he wrapped his arms around her. "You didn't know who he was."

"Alexander," she cried, sobbing. "His name is Alexander."

"Alexander," Sam repeated. "And Alexander was most certainly going to kill me. In fact," Sam added, "he *did* kill me, Kaia. And you brought me back. Tommy told me. Tommy said he was trying to pull you off me, that he was sure I was gone, but you wouldn't stop. You didn't stop. You saved me, Kaia. And, I don't know if you want to hear this right now, but I'll always love you for that… and for a whole lot of other things."

She let a little sound escape her throat, something between a whine and a purr.

Sam's voice rumbled against her cheek. "Should we get out of here?"

There was a tremulous blossoming in her chest, something breaking open inside her heart. She pictured them getting into the *Angeline* and coursing through the starlit harbor, entering the cabin on Thursday Island without speaking, kissing their way through the kitchen, kissing against the bedroom doorframe, tumbling onto the bed.

"I'm sorry, Sam," she said at last, her voice choked as she stepped away from him and the night air hit her again. "I can't. It's too painful. I swear, I'm going to be here for you, to help you get your freedom from Violet once and for all, and maybe then—well, I just don't know. Maybe then you'll be gone."

"Or maybe not," he argued, eyes glimmering fiercely. He reached for her, but she inched back.

"Or maybe not," she whispered. A prayer. One she could not, in all reason, hope would be answered. She rested a hand on his arm, where his firm muscle was warm enough to make the winter seem to dissipate at her touch. "Time, Sam. I need time. I can only hope…" Kaia trailed off, unable bring herself to say the words that they'd be together again because in all honesty, she didn't know if it'd be possible.

He nodded, dipping his head as a sparkling tear fell from his eyes.

"And I'm not going anywhere," she said, moving closer again, taking hold of his other arm. "I swear, I'm going to see you free."

Sam pulled her to him, taking her into the shelter of his warmth. He pressed a kiss to her forehead, where she felt his tears cooling as they dropped onto her skin. "I doubt Violet even knows what love is," Sam said. "But I do."

Kaia felt his warmth surround her and let her eyes drift to the starshine on the surface of the ocean, fractured like a million diamonds. The world might be cold and harsh, but for now, for just this moment, she felt warm and held safe. She let Sam's words sink deep, letting the truth of them take root inside her soul where she could keep them always, no matter what was to come.

✧

Later that night, alone on the very tip of Foley's Point, Kaia stood looking out at the ocean. Wapomeq Bay was quiet and dark except for the lights of Sam's cabin on Thursday Island, sitting between her and the horizon. She crossed her arms over her chest and hugged herself to keep out the cold. It was fierce when the wind blew, yet it didn't bother her. Nothing could really bother her right now.

Sure, she wished things were different between her and Sam. She wished Violet Wilde didn't have his sealskin. She also wished things hadn't gotten so out of hand with the sirens, especially Alexander. But even though her heart was grieved at what she'd done—and aching with the hope that he'd pull through and live to be a big scary bastard another day—she wasn't worried about him at this moment.

This moment was peace. Peace she'd never known. Peace with herself, peace with the land she'd come to see as home, peace with the people she now felt she couldn't live without, and yes, even peace with the sea— that terrifying grandness stretching out before her. But most of all, peace because the house on Foley's Point seemed to embrace her, enveloping her like a womb.

She couldn't sell it. No way. She couldn't say if she'd ever be able to get beyond what had happened with Sam and Violet; she didn't know if Alexander would pull through or if the sirens would keep their end of the bargain and let her swim freely; but she did know this: she belonged here. Not Quolobit Harbor, not Maine—but right here, on Foley's Point, close enough to the waves to hear them in her sleep. She was part of the water's wildness. Just as a piece of her mother still lived within her, coursing through her veins, so too did this vast and untamable water. Though she could admit to herself that it frightened her, she knew that she belonged to the sea, and it belonged to her.

THE END

ACKNOWLEDGEMENTS

This book is in your hands thanks to everyone who pledged to my Kick-starter, who saw the value in my dream of bringing this story to life, and gathered to make this happen. You showed me I had a community I didn't even realize was there, and proved to me that sometimes things actually do go right and that dreams can come true.

To my editor and friend, Emma, I am so grateful you came into my life. Working with you has been a pleasure, and your attention to detail and commitment to quality have given me the confidence I've been looking for.

Thank you to my beta readers: Emily, Lizzy, Monique, Elise, Anathea, Kara, Lizz, Morgan, Laurie, and Amanda. Your insight gave me direction, encouragement, and confidence. Some of you read this book more than once, in many different iterations over the years, and I thank you for your dedication and friendship, and for sticking with Kaia and Sam's story as long as I have.

Hannah, thank you for your endless patience in fine-tuning, especially the opening of this book. Your edits and observations have made me a better writer. Also, thank you for feeding me and taking care of me when life got really tough and I couldn't feed or take care of myself. You are, literally, an angel.

I am grateful for the loving support of my parents and my brother, who have seen this story through its many stages and stuck with me on the rollercoaster of being a writer and my life in general. Your humor, compassion, and support are what keeps me going most days. To my husband, Kalin, I give you my deepest gratitude for encouraging me to write, for believing in me when I have doubted myself, and for treating my writing like a priority. Without your support, I would have given up long ago.

Emily, I can honestly say that not one single word would be on these pages if it wasn't for you. There was a time, a long time ago, when I had stories inside my head and wanted to write but was afraid to, and you changed that. Every single word is for you, always. Thank you, soul sister, for reading every one. Like, five times. And then five more times.

To the Kickstarter backers who pulled the heavy weight to make this book happen, I bow down in gratitude:
Abby Jarrett
David Iskowitz
Beth and Brad Batastini
Maureen and Kevin Buzdygon
David Ripley
Breana Felix
Heather and Dale Issler
Meg Evans
Melissa Hooper
Sheila and Gordon Cook
Carl Ohlson
Monique Delorenzo
Michelle Finnerty
Judy Pomeroy
Jason Pomeroy
Adrienne Scott
Christy Belardo
Hannah Ayer
Elizabeth Bowman
Elizabeth Wood

Alison Grech
Richard Pomeroy
Janna Miller and the Calgary Midwives Collective
Jenna Shiappacasse
Abby Murtagh
Carroll Davenport
Trina Borenstein
Trish and Gary Pomeroy
Emily and Nate Pearson
Amanda Sidebottom
Noreen Mulvanerty

ABOUT THE AUTHOR

Sonya Blake lives nomadically with her husband, baby son, and Siberian Husky. She takes great joy in singing, cooking, and sleeping more than two hours in a row.

Stay in Touch!

Instagram: @sonya_blake_author
Twitter: @sonya_b_writes
Website: sonyablake.com

Help an Author Thrive

Indie authors depend upon online reviews for their work to succeed. Leave a review on amazon.com or goodreads.com to let the world know how much you enjoyed *Under the Surface* and follow me online to stay up to date about my next books.